Don't Mention Hi-De-Hi!

FRANK MCGROARTY

DEDICATION

To My Butlins Family

CONTENTS

ACKNOWLEDGMENTS

This book would not be possible without the support of my family and friends. Special mention once again to my daughter, **Rachel McGroarty** for another first class job on the cover design.

And finally, my very good friend, **Valda Warwick** who went above and beyond the call of duty with her valuable help with the proof reading. So much so, she deserves a bigger typeface.

Thank You Valda !!!

Don't Mention Hi-De-Hi!

FRANK MCGROARTY

THE STORY SO FAR...........

For thousands of holidaymakers, young and old, Butlins Holiday Camp was a magic land, full of colour and fun, where the moment you walked through the gates, you forgot about the world outside. For thousands of children it sowed the seeds of many fantastic memories that as they got older would pass on to their own children.

Amongst those happy campers, there were those who would be able to experience the Butlins life from the other side, helping to create that special magic for those guests as members of staff.

Whatever the department, everyone had a part to play in creating that special formula which has served Butlins for decades, making them a British Institution.

Working at Butlins gave you different kinds of memories to that of the campers, but it could also change your life. No more so than the subject of our story. 18 year old Terry McFadden, who previously enjoyed going on holiday to various camps with his family, had now just completed a life changing first season working the summer of 1982 at Butlins Ayr as a Redcoat.

Seven months earlier, **(What Time Does Midnight Cabaret Start)** he had been sitting in his family home in Greenock, with no job prospects, no direction his life until a chance appointment with the job centre, led to a job interview with the Ayr Centre's egomaniac Entertainment Manager Ron De Vere.

He never believed he would get the job, because he remembered Butlins Redcoats as lively personalities who were the life and souls of the party. As someone with insecurity and crippling shyness as a child, he did not even come close.

However, his passion for performing, mainly as a skilful ballroom dancer was enough to convince De Vere to take it him on. Terry looked on this as an opportunity that dreams were made of; he could build on his confidence, get rid of his childhood demons, build on his only passion of performing on stage and become the person that he wanted to be.

What he had not bargained for was falling in love for the first time with kitchen assistant, Angie Bierman from Falkirk. During the second half of the season, their relationship blossomed to the point that returning for a second season was not a priority. They needed to start planning their future.

With the season ending, and not having the luxury of living on the camp, they had to rely on travelling to and staying at each other's family houses, trying to find work and just be together.

We pick up the story shortly after the end of the 1982 season where Angie was set to stay with Terry and his family for the first time..................................

CHAPTER ONE

'Shit! Late for Swanning,' Terry awoke in a dreamlike state after his alarm clock disrupted what had been another restless night.

Ever since he returned from working the season at Butlins, he dreamed the same dream every night, cuddling up to his beloved Angie, only to sleep in for work the next day, even though he had never actually missed any breakfast duties.

As he fully awakened, reality kicked in. He was not in his chalet at the Ayr Camp, but back in his regular bed at, 120 Balloch Street, Greenock; and on his own.

During the previous four months, his life had been transformed, leaving his childhood life behind, working as a Butlins Redcoat, as well as falling in love for the first time. What felt so frightening to begin with, now felt so natural, with him and Angie effectively living together during the second part of the 1982 summer season. Now they were well into Autumn, miles apart. Angie was back at her Grans' at California, near Falkirk, Terry was stuck in Greenock.

They made the most of every spare moment when they were at the camp. It was once interrupted when he was forced to spend half the day in hospital -that was tough. It was then Terry realised how much he missed her. Now they had been apart for a week, it was hurting them both, even though they were on the phone to each other every night.

Sitting up on his bed, Terry slowly came to his senses, and shook off what was left of sleep. This was the day he had been waiting for. Angie was coming to stay with him for a week.

This was their life now, alternate visits to each other's house, trying to get used to living life together, away from camp, and trying to find work. It was under controlled conditions, this week under the watchful eyes of Terry's parents'.

Terry checked out his reflection in the mirror, he was a mess, his room was a mess and he had two hours to fix it. With a renewed sense of urgency, he dived out of the bed, pulling on his old tracksuit, skilfully navigating past the family dog for once, not required for a regular morning wakeup call.

He reached the bathroom and began clinically washing away the sweat pores from the night before. His first real test of the day was to eliminate his early morning stubble, without having to spend five minutes at the end stemming blood loss from his chin or his top lip. He was meeting his girlfriend in a couple of hours. No face blemishes were allowed.

There was no danger of him being allowed a limited time in the bathroom as his Dad, Charlie had left for work a couple of hours earlier and his Mother, Mary was downstairs in the kitchen taking time out for herself with an early morning cuppa and a couple of chapters from her favourite "People's Friend" magazine.

Terry had finished shaving; examining every crevice of his face like a forensic scientist, making sure that there was not the slightest trace of facial hair. When he noticed a bottle of his Dad's *Brut* aftershave underneath the mirror, the temptation was too great. He splashed a small amount on his face to complete the grooming process.

Marching back into the bedroom, he changed out of his tracksuit into more appropriate attire. Whipping off the sheets and blankets off his bed, he clumsily wrapped them around his arms into a ball before dumping them into a nearby wash basket. Those tasks were normally down to his Mother – not today! 'MUM! HAVE I GOT SOME CLEAN SHEETS FOR MY BED?' shouted Terry from the top of the stairs.

After sorting Charlie out for his early morning shift at the shipyards, nothing was going to take his Mother, away from her early morning cuppa. 'AH SO YOU ARE OUT OF YOUR PIT!' she replied. 'LEAVE IT! I'LL SORT THAT!' Mary was pleased that her son was showing some interest in the state of his room, however she still hadn't quite used to the idea that after all these years, he was starting to think for himself. 'IT'S OK! DRINK YOUR TEA! I'LL SORT IT,' shouted Terry.

Terry walked down stairs towards the darkened "Cubby Hole" where there were shelves full of washed towels, sheets and blankets. Mary put down her tea watching Terry's every move as he was about to pick out the clean sheets for his bed, from a pile which collectively was a number of hours washing and ironing. Terry was stopped as he put his hand on the top shelf.

'They are all on the couch," she said.

'Thanking You,' replied Terry.

'Butlins has certainly changed you,' she said. 'Or is it cause Angie is coming to stay?' Terry grabbed the small pile and started to walk back upstairs. Terry smiled. 'It's certainly not Butlins that's for sure.'

'Have your breakfast! Plenty of time!'

'I'll get the bed done first,' said Terry, heading back upstairs. 'DO IT RIGHT,' shouted Mary, going back to the kettle replacing her now cold cup of tea. 'I will be inspecting it later.'

'YOU WONT FIND ANYTHING WRONG!'

'I'LL BE THE JUDGE OF THAT!'

After taking great care shaving earlier, Terry was just as meticulous with the making of his bed. Not a crease was to be seen, no folded hospital corners out of place, pillows perfectly placed. 'I should get a job at the Tontine Hotel,' he said. Finally, he was ready for breakfast, but stopped at the bedroom door. 'Nearly forgot! "The Fonz!"'

Trying to cause minimum damage to his bedroom wallpaper, he removed his once treasured poster of TV's "Happy Days" with "The Fonz" sitting proud on his motorbike. Taking a deep intake of breath, he proceeded to rip it into small shreds before dumping the contents into a black bag with other rubbish. 'Sorry Fonzie. When you've got to go – you've got to go."

Angie was due to get the train into Greenock just after lunch time, which was a couple of hours away. All that Terry could do after breakfast was stand at the living room window watching the many cars and buses trying to navigate their way up the narrow road. Not the most exciting of activities, but it was only way he could try and make the time go quicker. Plus, he was also able to stand guard over the phone.

Bang on 12pm, the phone rang. Terry turned and grabbed the receiver. 'Hello?' There was the sound of continuous pips on other end of the line, so it was safe to assume it was Angie trying to put coins in the payphone.

'Hi Terry? It's me'

'Hi – where are you?'

'I'm at Glasgow Central,' said Angie. 'The next train to Balloch Street has been cancelled, and there isn't another one for an hour.'

'Acch Nuts!' said Terry. 'Are there any other trains going to Gourock?'

'Hang on…. Yeh! There's an express service leaving in about fifteen minutes, but it stops at Port Glasgow then Greenock West.'

'Get the train to Greenock West I'll meet you there.'

'Are you sure?' said Angie, "It is a good bit away from you.'

'I don't care. It gets you here quicker.' replied Terry.

'Get that train and I will meet you there.'

'Will go and get the ticket now. See you soon. I love you!'

'I love you too!'

Terry placed the phone receiver back on phone and turned to see his Mother standing at the living room door, arms folded with a smile on her face.

'That's nice,' she said.

'I am sure you said the same kind of thing at my age.' Mary smirked as Terry quickly put on his coat and headed to the front door. 'Gotta Go! TTFN'

Terry had at least forty five minutes before Angie's train reached Greenock West; plenty of time to catch a bus. Public transport however was hardly reliable, so going on foot was the preferred option. At brisk walking speed, it would at least take him forty minutes. Terry was certainly in no mood for a casual stroll.

After proceeding along the road at a military pace, Terry was soon marching past the location of his former tenement family home at Mearns Street, with the station now very much in his sights. His heart quickened when he saw a train pulling out of Greenock West Station heading towards Gourock'. 'Bugger it! The train's early!'

Oblivious to the dangers of oncoming cars, Terry sprinted across two pedestrian crossings to the station's side entrance. Standing at the top of set of concrete stairs, he inspected the exiting passengers from the last train heading towards him. Right at the back of the small crowd, he caught sight of the mesmerising smile that captured his heart months earlier.

Angie, dressed in a tweed jacket with matching brown cords, carrying a dark brown canvas bag, was the last to head for the exit and was waving furiously the moment she saw Terry standing at the door grinning – but breathing heavily after that sprinting.

Terry dived down the stairs to meeting her half way. She dropped her canvas bag as they wrapped their arms around each other.

'Ohhh I have missed you so much!' said Angie.

Terry placed his hands gently on Angie's face, kissing her gently. 'God, I have missed you. Ever since you got on that train at Glasgow last week, all I could think of was this day.'

Angie smiled. 'So - what have you got planned for this week.'

'Plenty – but first we have got to get you home.'

With his free arm around her waist, Terry picked up Angie's bag. They headed towards the bus terminus half a mile down the road to take the "number 27" back to Balloch Street. Sitting at the back of the bus, for once, Butlins was not on the agenda, just the fabulous week they were going to have.

Thirty minutes later, the bus pulled into the stop two hundred yards from Terry's house. They walked towards the front door smiling. However, as Terry reached out to open the gate, his smile disappeared when he heard a sound from his school days that he desperately wanted to forget.
'HEY IT'S MCFADDEN!'

When Terry was at school, his shy and introverted nature made him an easy target for bullies; they made his life Hell! It was not all that long ago. The person who led these attacks was, Owen Lyndsey. The more Terry suffered, the more he thrived on it, especially as Terry never had the courage to fight back.

It had been a year since he had left school, Lyndsey a year earlier. So, as they never bumped into each other after that, Terry had thought his former Nemesis had grown up, was working in the shipyards and that he had permanently closed that chapter in his life.

However, when he saw the scruffy ginger haired Lyndsey along with four cronies "Cat Calling" from the other side of the street – Terry's heart sank. All he could think about was quickly getting inside the house. 'HEY GUYS WID YE LOOK AT THAT,' laughed Lyndsey. 'HE'S GOT A GIRLFRIEND! COME ON MCFADDEN – WHO'S THE BURD!'

Angie turned to see where the noise was coming from, but when she looked back at Terry, she was concerned to see the tense look on his face. 'Friends of yours?'
'They're no friends of mine,' said Terry. He tried to force a

smile. 'Come on – let's go inside.'

Terry put his key in the lock and opened the front door making sure Angie walked in first. 'HI! WE'RE HERE!' As Terry continued to close the door, he could still see Lyndsey and his gang continuing with the mocking chants and gestures.'

'Hello Hen, welcome back!' said Mary coming out from the living room door, keeping it closed to stop the excited dog jumping on them. 'Lovely to see you again!'

'And you,' said Angie. 'Thanks for putting me up.'

'You are welcome anytime you know that. I'll put the Kettle on. Terry, take Angie's bag and show her to your room.'

Terry was more relaxed now he was back within the sanctuary of his family home. He picked up Angie's bag. 'Let me take you to your sleeping quarters Madam?' Angie smiled. 'That would be lovely Kind Sir!' Terry held open the door to his bedroom. Angie walked in looking around as Terry placed her bag on the bed. 'I hope this meets with Madam's approval?'

Angie smiled as she continued looking around, checking out the various bits of furniture, running her fingers across the candlewick cover on the top of the bed. 'It's lovely, 'she said. 'But this bed has one thing missing.'

'What is that?'

Angie wrapped her arms around Terry's neck, pulling towards him kissing him. 'You of course.'

'Terry looked lovingly into Angie's eyes. 'When I am kipping on the couch, you could always sneak down during the night?'

Angie giggled. 'Now that is tempting. By the way, one thing I need to ask you.'

'What's that.'

'Tell me about those guys out there.'

Terry grimaced. 'Do I have to?'

Angie took Terry's hands sitting him down on the bed beside her. She could see it was bothering him. 'Yes!' she said. 'Tell me.' Terry felt ashamed. But he knew that he could not hide anything from Angie. He took a deep breath.

'At school, I did not like the same things as guys who preferred to hang out with gangs. It was only a matter of time before they turned on me. Ambushes, beatings, humiliation, you know, the usual stuff.' This was not the way he wanted to start his week with Angie.

'How long did this go on for?' she said.

'I was at secondary school till sixth year, so I would say – five years? I always tried to stay out of their way, but they always found me. They loved torturing me.'

Angie squeezed Terry's hand as she listed to him bearing his sole. 'And that is them out there?'

'Yep. I thought that leaving school, they had moved on.' Glancing out the window, he could see them still loitering across the street. 'They obviously don't want to change.'

Angie put her arm around Terry's shoulder pulled him towards her. They held each other in a loving embrace. 'Don't you ever change,' she whispered into his ear.

Terry smiled. He knew he had changed as a person, but this was different. Dealing with physical aggressors was a part of his childhood life; he did not have to address this at Butlins. He always tried to stay clear from it at school. He was easily scared and therefore an easy target.

His Dad tried to toughen him up by getting him into a boxing club. That only lasted a week. 'I know that I have to stand up for myself. I have never been in a fight in my life,' said Terry. ' I am worried about looking like an idiot.'

'Don't think about that,' she said. 'You told me at Butlins when your boss got too much, you took a deep breath and made sure he did not control you. Do the same thing here. You know you are not on your own'

Terry brushed his hand alongside Angie's face. 'I am so lucky to have you. Have I told you that lately?'

'Not since we talked on the phone last night. But feel free to tell me as often as you like, 'she giggled. 'Remember I love you Terry. Whatever challenges we face, we face them together.'

'That has a familiar ring,' he said opening the top drawer of his bedside cabinet pulling out a decorated card. 'Yep it's on the back of a card that this lovely lady gave me last week.'

Any tension in Terry had disappeared. 'I love you,' he said. 'We are going to have a great week. The future starts here.'

'Absolutely'

'TEA's UP!' shouted Mary.

'It starts with a cup of tea,' said Terry. 'COMING!'

Back downstairs, Angie renewed her acquaintance with the family dog. Sitting down at the couch, Mary was determined to find out how Terry and Angie were going to spend the week. She even threw in a few suggestions herself, like taking Angie down to see his Gran.

They chatted well into the afternoon until Mary realised that Charlie was due back from his work and needed to get the tea ready. 'I'll give you a hand,' said Angie.

'Terry, you can make yourself useful, go up to "Gardiner's" for a pint of milk, a plain loaf and some jam.' Terry was now feeling more relaxed since bringing Angie back from the station. He had completely put Lyndsey and his cronies out of his mind. He promptly put on his coat as Mary gave him money for the shopping. He blew Angie a kiss as he closed the door. 'Back Soon!'

"Gardiners" had been the McFadden's local store since the family first moved to Balloch Street. The owner John Gardiner became good friends with the family and even gave Terry his first work experience doing a short paper round when he was 13. The shop was located at the other side of the street where the only convenient route was to walk through a narrow lane that cut between rows of houses, one block down.

Terry casually walked down the street, but as he turned in to the lane, he came to a halt when he saw Lyndsey and his gang congregating at the far end, standing against the fence, smoking and drinking a bottle of cheap wine. He could not turn back as it was the only way to get to the shops. He certainly could not return home empty handed. Terry took a deep breath and continued to walk along the lane, with only one thought running through his head. 'This stops today!'

As Terry headed along toward the other end of the lane, Lyndsey was given a nudge, to make him aware of who was approaching. 'Well Well Well! It's our old school pal, McFadden.' Every muscle in Terry's body was shaking inside as he continued to walk forward but he maintained his concentration, looking directly at Lyndsey. 'Old school pal? You must be pissed, Lyndsey.' 'Oooh!!!' came a collective response from a couple of the gang members.

Lyndsey pulled himself away from the railings, placed his bottle down on the ground and started to walk towards Terry, as the rest of the gang looked on in admiration. 'Suddenly you have become a cheeky bastard McFadden!'
Terry tried to stay calm. He had never faced a confrontation in his life. He was petrified, but was making every effort to control his rate of breathing.

11

'If you don't mind, I am going into the shop.'

Lyndsey took a step to the side, blocking Terry's progress. 'You are going to have a good reason for us to let you past McFadden.' Terry's fear was now turning to anger. 'Why should I give a shit about you?' he replied. 'Move out of my way.'

Lyndsey was taken aback by Terry's newly found bravado. They were anything but convinced. 'You the one going to shift me?' sneered Lyndsey. 'Or do you need your girlfriend to hold your hand?'

Such a comment would have resulted in Terry being on the receiving end of a beating or public humiliation. However, he had discovered some inner strength during his time working at Butlins, something Lyndsey and his gang were not aware of. Taking his hands out of his pocket, Lyndsey revealed a pocket knife which he flicked open to reveal a shiny four inch blade. Terry opened his eyes in shock but was determined to show no other signs of alarm. 'I let you off lightly at school McFadden. Not this time!' Terry took one step backward taking a slow controlled intake of breath. 'Try it!'

Working with Redcoats during the Kids Venture Weeks at Pwhelli teaching fencing, under the watchful eye of Olympic standard coaches, Terry had developed faster than normal reactions. He watched intently fending off the attack as Lyndsey proceeded to swish the blade frantically in his direction. This was far more dangerous than teaching kids how to stage mock sword battles.

After avoiding a number of wild movements, Lyndsey's knife made partial contact with its target, slicing the top of Terry's knuckles. Lyndsey smirked to see that he was starting to inflict damage. The throbbing was intense. Terry briefly stopped to examine the deep gash at the top of his hand. His nerves had gone. He looked at Lyndsey. 'That's it?'

Lyndsey charged forward again, however Terry skilfully side stepped his attacker, grabbing his arm, smashing him against the side railing, forcing him to drop the blade through a fence into a nearby garden. Before Lyndsey had time to recover, Terry stamped on the back of his leg, pinning his face against the railings, prompting the rest of the gang to charge forward to help their leader.

Terry quickly regained his grip of Lyndsey's arm twisting it behind his back, forcing him to scream in pain. 'YOU LOT COME CLOSER AND I'LL BREAK HIS ARM!!' 'Back off!' shouted Lyndsey. This was enough for them to retreat. Keeping him pinned against the fence, Terry told the rest of the gang to keep walking, which they reluctantly agreed to do. 'YOU THINK YOU ARE A HARD MAN NOW MCFADDEN! TRYING TO IMPRESS YOUR GIRLFRIEND!'

Terry lent forward whispering into Lyndsey's ear. 'She's none of your business.' He pushed Lyndsey's arm up his back. 'I'm not a hard man. I'm the school wimp remember? And I have had enough of your shit! I intend to get on with my life. You don't figure in any bit of it.'
'Terry pulled Lyndsey away from the fence, throwing his face to the ground. 'I don't want to see your ugly mug again.'

Five minutes later, Terry's heart was still racing as he came out of Gardiners with his Mother's messages in a carrier bag, still trying to stem the blood flow from his hand. He turned into the lane and was surprised to see Lyndsey standing waiting for him. This time on his own.
'Got some unfinished business with you McFadden!'
Terry was angry. 'What part of "I don't want to see your

13

ugly mug" didn't you understand?'

'That Slapper won't want to go anywhere near you by the time I have finished with you

Having stood up to Lyndsey and his gang minutes earlier, Terry felt no fear. He gently placed his bag on the ground. 'I am not going anywhere Lyndsey!'

Lyndsey charged toward Terry, who once again relied on his instincts, catching Lyndsey square on the jaw. 'You Bastard!' he muttered under his breath, shocked to see blood coming out of his mouth. Terry was just as shocked. He may have spent a week at a boxing club as a kid, but he had never thrown a punch before, where the hell did that one come from? And a perfectly timed punch at that.

Before he had time to recover, Terry hit Lyndsey again, this time with his cut hand – the pain was excruciating. Still stunned and groggy, Lyndsey recklessly charge forward again, only to be floored with a combination of punches which sent him flat on his back. Still conscious, Terry stuck his knee into his chest, grabbing his hair.

'GOT THE MESSAGE NOW?' shouted Terry. 'YOU STAY OUT OF MY LIFE!'

Terry pushed Lyndsey's head on to the ground. Picking up the shopping, he started to walk towards the other end of the lane where he saw his Dad Charlie. Having come back from his work, he had witnessed the whole incident. He was a bit disturbed to see his son fighting, but he knew about Lyndsey, and, he could see that his son was totally in control.

As Terry walked towards his Dad, the adrenalin was starting to subside, he was starting to realise what had just happened. He felt his emotions getting the better of him as Lyndsey slowly started to get back on to his feet, Terry, battled to hold on to his composure.

'Are you OK?' asked Charlie.

'Yeh. Fine.' He briefly glanced behind him. 'Just seen off an unwelcome part of my childhood.'

'I saw that. Henry Cooper would have been proud of that knock down.'

'I don't know where that came from. I certainly don't fancy doing that again.'

Charlie noticed the cut across Terry's hand which was now badly bruised through throwing those punches, and he was starting to shake violently. 'You need to get that seen to. What happened?'

'That was from round one, when he came at me with a knife and was humiliated in front of his pals. What you saw was round two. '

'You should talk to the police'

'I don't want that!' insisted Terry. 'If he wants to get his knife back, the police might want to talk to him. It is in DI Baker's back garden. I told him and his cronies to stay out of our lives. That's all I want.'

'Good for you, 'said Charlie. 'Let's get that hand sorted. Don't want any blood on that bread. It spoils the flavour of the pieces and jam.'

Terry laughed as Charlie opened the door. 'Hi honey! We're home!'

'Is that you,' said Mary.

'Naw, it's a figment of your imagination. '

'That's what I thought. Seen Terry on your travels?'

Terry took a deep breath in an effort to relax himself. 'PRESENT!'

As they walked into the kitchen, Angie noticed Terry's cut hand. She took him to one side. 'You OK? What happened?'

'I ran into some people from school.'

As Mary put the finishing touches to the evening meal, Charlie proceeded to get changed out of his boiler suit and get himself cleaned up. Angie took Terry upstairs to sort out the wound on his hand.

'Was it that crowd?' she asked.

'Yep. They tried to carry on from where they left off.'

Angie continued to inspect the damage to the top of Terry's hand. 'What happened?"

'In that back lane, one of them came at me with a knife.'

'Oh God!' Angie was horrified and immediately led Terry to the sink in to the bathroom, where she pulled off some sheets of toilet tissue, which she dampened, to clean up the cut.

'Don't worry. It is done. They won't bother us again,' he said. 'I just got into a fight for the first time in my life, but I had no choice. Look at me! I'm still shaking.'

Terry was starting to feel more relaxed as Angie continued to clean the cut on his hand. He felt that he had finally exorcized all of his childhood demons.

Now they could now start planning their week. 'Tomorrow, a picnic by the sea. How does that sound?' asked Terry

'Can't wait.'

CHAPTER TWO

It was 8.30 in the morning. Terry slowly walked up the stairs towards his bedroom gently rapping his knuckles on the door, generating a muffled sound from Angie, who was still in bed. 'Yeh?

Terry slowly walked in to see Angie's head slowly emerging from within the covers, opening her eyes and smiling when she saw him standing at the side of the bed carrying a breakfast tray of tea, toast, butter, jam.

'Room Service!'

'Oh My!' said Angie, slowly sitting up in the bed. 'You are spoiling me. What have I done to deserve this.'

'You need to ask?' Terry replied. 'This service is only available to special guests.'

Angie smiled. Sitting up adjusting her pillows, she looked at the selection available on the tray. She leant forward and kissed Terry. 'Thank You,' she said. 'You know I can't eat all of this on my own?'

Terry smiled: 'You will notice that there is more than one cup on that tray.'

'Good! I would have told you to go downstairs and get another one if there wasn't.'

Terry's Mother, Mary was already downstairs tidying up the kitchen, as well as sorting out the early morning washing. He went to close the bedroom door before sitting back on the bed to have his breakfast. 'Bit of privacy.'

'We are not going to get much of that now,' said Angie as she proceeded to tuck into her breakfast. 'I expect that we will have to get used to it.'

Terry smirked. 'We will. Anyway, my folks won't be in the house all of the time.'

They continued to have their breakfast discussing their plans for the day as well as the events of 24 hours earlier. 'How's your hand?' asked Angie.

Terry took a sip of his tea. 'I'm fine. I certainly don't want go through anything like that again,' he smiled, 'unless I am fighting for your honour – of course.'

'Very chivalrous of you sir.'

Terry sniggered, kissing the top of Angie's hand. 'I am but your humble servant Ma'am.

'So how did you manage sleeping on the couch?'

'Very well,' said Terry. 'The fact that it was a double bed certainly helped.'

Angie's eyes opened wide. 'You told me you were kipping on the couch.'

'It's one of those pull down bed settee things.'

'I am definitely coming down to pay you a visit tonight.'

'I warn you now, the bed has noisy springs.'

Angie took another bite of her toast. 'I'll risk it.'

As it was a nice sunny day, Terry explained the plan for the day; a trip to Greenock's Battery Park, a very popular destination for families that fancied a trip at the seaside, without having to travel too far. Terry had already done the preparations, having arranged for his Mother to get some picnic provisions.

'Sounds perfect,' said Angie.

Taking a final bite off her toast and a final slurp of her tea, Angie lifted the tray and placed it on the dresser at the side of the bed. She reached out to take Terry's hand. 'But not yet. Lie down with me for five minutes. I miss my early morning hug.'

Lying together on the bed, holding on to each other, neither of them wanted to move. Everything was peaceful, everything felt perfect. That was until Terry's Mother shouted from the bottom of the stairs.

'TERRY! BRING DOWN ANGIE'S DISHES WHEN YOU ARE FINISHED!'

'RIGHT MUM!' Terry slowly sat up. 'Let's get out of here.' Angie smiled. 'I'll get dressed'

Terry grabbed the tray and proceeded to return downstairs, taking it into the kitchen. 'It doesn't take that long for you to eat breakfast,' said Mary.

'Why rush!' said Terry

'I thought you were going out.'

'We are.' Opening the door of the fridge, he scrutinised the contents on the shelves. 'Got some sandwiches to make.'

'I've seen your efforts at making sandwiches,' said Mary.

'There are some fresh ham and cheese sandwiches in that box along with some caramel wafers.

'Here's some cash. You can get some ice creams and stuff. You will be passing plenty of cafes on your travels.'

'Thanks Mum.'

Terry washed his breakfast dishes, minutes later, Angie appeared. 'Morning!' she said.

'Morning Hen,' said Mary. 'How was your sleep.'

'Smashing thanks.'

'Right – away ye go. Enjoy your day.'

'We certainly will,' said Terry as he and Angie put on their jackets. 'After we have been to the jobshop first.'

'Getting your priorities right – good to hear.'

Terry lifted the shoulder bag containing the food. 'Back whenever,' he said. 'TTFN!'

Terry and Angie jumped on the bus to go into the town centre, the location of the local jobshop, which, in the end turned out to be a very short visit. Angie felt a little despondent as they looked at the many vacancies on the board. She was starting to see the tough challenge facing them in terms of trying to find work. The level of jobs on offer were no better here than in her home town.

A few minutes they turned towards the exit. 'When it comes to getting work, it won't come from here,' said Terry.

'On saying that, it has done me some good in the past.'

'In what way?' asked Angie.

Terry looked at Angie and smiled pointing out a lady dressed in a tweed outfit, sitting at her desk. 'That lady over there, Ms Kilsyth suggested I applied for a job at Butlins. If I hadn't done that, then I would have never have found you.'

Angie hugged Terry. 'We should send them a thank you card.'

Terry laughed. 'That would certainly be a first for them.'

Heading through the main shopping area, they continued to look out for any "situations vacant" notices, there weren't any.

They jumped on to another bus, heading to the West End of the town, getting off at the crossroads on Campbell Street. Directly opposite the bus stop was Greenock's Esplanade, a mile long stretch of road running alongside the water's edge, which went from the Greenock's Ocean Terminal all the way through to the navy buildings which housed the local coast guard.

Next door was the base for the local boat club, a favourite haunt for sailing and kayaking enthusiasts, who were taking advantage of the warm sunny morning, taking their boats out to the water. Walking the first half mile hand in hand, they stopped for a few moments to lean against the Esplanade railings to look out at the sea shimmering by the light of the autumn sunshine.

'This is lovely,' said Angie.

'It certainly is,' said Terry. 'I have some great memories of this area as a kid, especially with the Arts Guild Theatre up the road. I did all my school shows there. I always came here to have my lunch in between rehearsals.'

'Did you not ever want to live here?'

'Nah. It is nice, but the West End is a bit posh for me,' said Terry. 'I saw myself as an East End Boy or living in Port Glasgow. But you can't say where you are going to end up. I mean, I would never have considered working away from Greenock a few months ago. Who knows, this time next year, I could end up working in the Falkirk area.'

Terry winked at Angie. 'I know this gorgeous woman who lives there.'

Angie playfully jabbed Terry in the ribs. 'Right you! I want her name."

Terry put his arm around Angie's waist as they continued to walk along the Esplanade. 'I don't care where we work,' he said 'As long as it's in the same place.

Reaching the end of the Esplanade, they turned on to Eldon Street where four hundred yards along the road,

Angie's eyes opened wide as she came across the vast open green areas of the Battery Park, which was right next to the seaside, cordoned off from the main street by a long craggy wall running the full width of the park, just short of the neighbouring town, Gourock.

'Time for our picnic – Hungry?' said Terry.

'Famished!'

Walking through a set of wrought iron gates, they headed towards the beach at the far edge of the park, which was completely covered with washed up rocks and pebbles. Close by, in front of a bench appeared to be the remains of a paddling pool, this was in total contrast to the long sandy shores they walked along during their days off when working at Ayr.

The view out to sea was just as striking, looking at the land in the distance, as well as watching the ferries and small boats out in the water. They went as close as they could to the shoreline, whilst remaining on the grass where many other families were.

As they sat down to eat, Angie noticed the large building at the far end of the park which had a large platform partially closed off by metal shutters. 'What's that over there? 'She asked.

'It's the band stand,' said Terry. 'They use it for festival type events, open air shows.'

'You have concerts here?'

'I don't know about pop concerts. We tried to get the dance team I was in to perform there at one of their events. It never got off the ground.'

'I loved that Latin dancing outfit you wore at the camp.' said Angie. 'It's a shame I won't get to see you perform with the team.'

'Be careful what you wish for, 'said Terry. 'We got one of those VHS a video of our last TV stint.. Can show you that later'

'I look forward to that.'

Angie paused to take a bite out of her sandwich, still taking in the picturesque Clyde sea view. She turned to Terry. 'So, when are you going to take me out dancing?'

'I would love to,' he said   I need to find out where the discos are around here.'

'I wasn't thinking about discos, I mean proper dancing, ballroom stuff. There must be things like that around here. Did you not do anything like that.'

'I only did competitions,' said Terry. 'The only thing I know around here are the sequence dancing clubs.'

'Is that not the same thing?'

'Oh God no! You use more energy walking. The Cragburn Pavilion's a few miles along the road; that used to be a big dance hall. We could have a look later if you want, see if there is anything on around there?'

Gourock's Cragburn Pavilion, was set up as a premier entertainment venue designed to take advantage of what was a growing holiday trade. Built in the mid 1930's the Art Deco designed building set across the street from the seaside walkway was one of many popular dance halls across the Scottish Central Belt

Like other dance halls around Scotland, the Cragburn benefited from the popularity of the legendary Band leaders like Glenn Miller and Benny Goodman. The venue was regularly packed out during the war years all the way through to the mid-60s with people dancing to home grown "Big Band Sounds" not just to the resident local band, "Henri Morrison and his Swingstars" but also to top British dance bands like "Joe Loss and his Orchestra."

For Terry's Dad Charlie, his regular nights at the dancing would include trips up to Glasgow's "Barrowlands," as well as the number of dance halls throughout Greenock, Port Glasgow as well as Gourock. The Cragburn however held a special place in his heart, for that was where he and Terry's Mother first met, and it played an integral part in their courtship. A point often related to Terry during regular "Father- Son" chats.

Aside from the dance nights, the Cragburn was also a popular venue for variety shows, staging performances from some of the world's top theatrical stars, like American Comic Legend, Jack Benny, along with local revues which was more like Terrys experiences of the popular venue.

Amongst his many childhood Cragburn memories, were going with his family to see Scottish legends like Glen Daly, the Alexander Brothers and Andy Stewart. When he was eight, Terry had the chance to tread the Cragburn "boards" for real as one of the acts performing in a junior showcase event staged by Scottish showbiz impresario Archie McCulloch. Terry had not been inside the place since that night.

There was no rush, as the lure of the coastline was too much to resist. They had finished their lunch and took in the next couple of miles into Gourock, stopping off for some ice creams from one of the cafes along the way where Angie discovered a new, "favourite dessert," a double nougat ice cream with raspberry sauce.

They continued along a street surrounded by sandstone buildings with occasional gaps, showing what was a typical seaside town setting, guest houses, a long promenade with numerous children's rides, Putting and Crazy Golf courses.

Eventually Terry and Angie clapped eyes on the imposing setting of the Cragburn Pavilion.

As they began to check the notices to see if there was anything of interest, Terry was attention was drawn towards a large and colourful poster pinned on the notice board at the side of the main entrance. **'Renfrewshire's Big Band Era – A Celebration."**

When he was growing up, Terry shared his Dad's love of American Big Bands, and often talked about Renfrewshire Dance Halls, as well as the fondly remembered local dance combos that played there.

Even though he only saw them perform once on stage, Terry felt a close connection to local dance legends, *Charlie Harkins and his Kit Kat Band*, a very popular dance band throughout the Renfrewshire area and beyond. They were often in demand for weddings, as well as various private functions at hotel's clubs and dance venues.

One of Terry's Dad's Foremen in the Shipyards, played saxophone with the Kit Kat Band, and many band members were also known throughout the local area working in various businesses, a number of them were school teachers.

Terry's former Geography teacher, Mr Kerr, was a highly rated pianist with the band who would often keep his "after school" musical activities quiet, for during the day, his number one priority was his teaching. Terry was more likely to hear of his teacher's "Kit Kat" connections through his Dad, as opposed to the man himself; however, he did show glimpses of his musical abilities whenever he had to stand in for the school's music teacher, playing the piano during school church services.

The poster at the side of the Cragburn suggested that there was a free exhibition inside so noticing the main theatre door wide open; it was an opportunity to good to resist. 'You asked about proper dancing – fancy a look at a proper dance hall?' Terry took hold of Angie's hand leading her through the Cragburn's main doors into the large theatre foyer. They appeared to be the only people in the building.

There were a number of exhibits and billboards, depicting the history of dance bands throughout Renfrewshire, their rise in popularity, as well as the history of the Cragburn and how it compared to other popular Renfrewshire dance halls. They included archive pictures along with written personal recollections of former patrons and band members.

Perched across the main foyer were examples of sheet music depicting the kind of songs people used to dance to. There were theatrical posters, newspaper advertisements along with musical instruments, band uniforms, and even an evening suit on a mannequin.

Standing pride of place in the far corner was a film screen showing silent home movie footage of a packed Cragburn Dance floor, featuring "Henri Morrison and his Swingstars." On examining one of the billboards, Angie was intrigued when she noticed the section on Charlie Harkins and The Kit Kat Band.

'Harkins? 'said Angie. 'I wonder if he is related to Ted Harkins, the band leader at Butlins?'
'I thought the same thing,' replied Terry. 'One of the first things I asked him when we met for the first time. Ted never heard of him.'

It had been years since he was last in the Cragburn, so Terry could not resist having a look inside the auditorium. Looking through the windows of the double doors, he was fascinated to see an empty stage, with two prominent loudspeakers perched either end. The main floor of the theatre however was empty. If there was a show planned, they obviously hadn't finished putting out the seats.

His curiosity was getting the better of him. He pulled on the door, which surprisingly opened. Holding on to both of Angie's hands, Terry gently lead her into the auditorium on to the large empty floor. 'Is it supposed to be as springy as this,' she said.

'That is a proper dance floor for you. You dance all night and it does not knacker the back of your legs. Come on let's try it out.'

'What now?'

Terry stretched his arm. 'Miss Bierman, would you do me the honour of the next waltz?'

Angie giggled. 'No music.'

Terry took Angie in his arms adopting a classic ballroom pose, smiling, he looked lovingly into Angie's eyes. He then glanced towards the empty platform into the distance. 'That is not an empty stage; there is an orchestra up there playing the most romantic song ever just for us. They are just waiting for our cue. We just think of the most romantic song ever.'

'I don't know how to do a proper waltz,' whispered a bashful Angie.

'Just think of that song in your head,' said Terry. 'Look at me. Trust me. Follow my lead.'

Angie's eyes started to glisten. This day started out as a picnic down by the beach, now here she was being swept off her feet, waltzing in a large empty ballroom. Angie was hypnotised looking at Terry. Together under the guidance of his ballroom dancing skills, they glided around the ballroom floor, perfect timing completely in unison, dancing to a song which was running through their heads. But which one?

They did not care that someone might be watching; they were back in their own special world, covering all areas of the Cragburn floor with their song, running through their heads. Coming to a halt in front of the main door, the song that was running through their minds came out of their mouths at the same time. Singing the final line, they stopped and looked deep into each other's eyes.

'You light up – myyyy life. '

The shock of singing the final line from the same song at the same time, was followed by minutes of hysterical laughter, still in ballroom dancing hold. This faded away as it started to dawn on them that the connection that they had formed at Butlins, was stronger than they first thought.

'You waltz beautifully,' said Terry

Angie smiled. 'I have the perfect dance partner.' Terry leant forward kissing Angie. 'I love you Angie.' Angie placed her hands on Terry's face. 'I love you too Terry. I cannot believe we thought of the same tune.'

Terry smiled. 'I think we have found "our song."'

They were interrupted by some slow hand clapping from the other end of the hall.

'Sorry to interrupt. But you know you shouldn't be in here,' said the speaker in the distance, who was Sandy Watson, the caretaker of the Cragburn.

'Sorry about that,' said Terry feeling slightly embarrassed.

Sandy laughed. 'No worries son. It makes a change to see youngsters still know how to waltz. See if you can do it to music next time.'

'Not much chance of that happening,' said Terry.

'You not read the poster outside?' said Sandy

A puzzled Terry and Angie went back outside the theatre to look again at the poster outside. He then realised he had only read part of it.

Renfrewshire's Big Band Era – A Celebration.
Relive the golden era of the Renfrewshire dance halls.
Next Friday at the Cragburn Pavilion,
Dance the night away!
£1 a pair (Cups of Tea Provided)

'You wanted me to take you out dancing. How does Friday night sound – and with a proper dance band?'
'Brilliant,' she replied. 'Need to get some practise in.'
'I will dig out some of my Dad's old records when we get back,' said Terry.

Their first day out was complete, and it was time to head back up to Balloch Street. After the tensions from the day before, this was the kind of day that Terry had been wanting. They slowly walked along the promenade back to Gourock train station for the next train home, where Mary had the evening meal ready on the table.

As they sat down, Terry told his parents about their planned "Friday Night at the Jiggin.'
'That at the Cragburn?' asked Charlie. 'Oh Aye, we know about that. We're going as well. The club is running a bus there. You can come with us.'
'You better get yourself a new suit,' said Mary.
'Suit is fine,' said Charlie.
'I wasn't talking about yours,' said Mary, 'I was talking to Terry.'
'I need a suit?' asked Terry.
'Of course! You don't go out dancing wearing jeans,' she said.
'Have I got to dress up as well?' asked a concerned Angie. 'I

have only brought casual clothes with me.'

'They don't wear ball gowns or anything like that. Smart evening wear. Keep Thursday afternoon free, we're going shopping.'

Terry was looking around in confusion as it looked as if his Mother was back organising things. Charlie interrupted. 'What all of us?' He had an idea what was coming next.

'Yes. You are off work that day. We will get Angie something nice to wear for Friday, you can take your son shopping.'

'What's wrong with the suit I have,' said Terry.

'You have had that one since fourth year. You are a young man now. Time to act like one.'

'Going shopping.' muttered Terry under his breath.

Charlie put his hands over his mouth trying to curtail his sniggering as it brought back memories of a similar conversation he had with his Mother, when he first hit the dance halls.

'Fine,' said Charlie. 'Won't take us that long.'

'It will take as long as it needs to take,' said Mary.

Charlie gave his son a reassuring gesture. Terry on the other hand was more concerned about his guest. Angie was slightly taken aback, but had no reason to say no. 'Fine by me.'

'You could get some practise in tonight,' said Mary. 'You could come down to the social club with us?'

'Sequence Dancing? I think I will pass on that,' said Terry. 'We can practise here when you are out.'

'You going out tonight? 'asked Angie

'Tonight's one of their numerous Sequence Dancing Nights,' said Terry. 'We have the place to ourselves.'

Angie sitting beside Terry lifted her cup to take another

sip of her tea with her right hand, reached across with her left, and squeezed Terry's hand out of sight of Mary and Charlie. It dawned on her that this was one of the private moments he was referring to and what she had been hoping for.

CHAPTER THREE

When Terry left Butlins, it took him a while to get used to "civi street," trying to get rid of habits that did not belong in the outside world, walking past people smiling, saying hello to passers-by, trying to curtail the urge to pinch people's chips. A normal occurrence when working as a Butlins Redcoat, but, anywhere else would get you arrested.

However, with Angie, this was one part of his Butlins life he did not want to change. When they met at the train station, their feelings were just as strong as when he proclaimed his true feelings for her one night at the Ayr Camp sports field.

Having dealt with the traumatic experience of his schoolboy past 48 hours earlier, and the fantastic day out that followed, it was evident that this was more than a typical holiday romance, in fact they were not even thinking about working at Butlins again. All they wanted to was to build on what Butlins had given them.

Their picnic by the sea had set out the tone for the rest of the week. Their routine began with a morning trip to the Jobshop to check out the latest vacancies, usually ending in disappointment, after that the day was theirs, and it didn't always mean going on picnics or checking out local scenery.

They would be quite happy to just go for long walks, nowhere in particular. It was quality time together, which was the most important thing. Angie never knew much about Greenock, and would often ask about places of interest, especially if they were linked to Terry, or his family.

One day they decided to go swimming at the Hector McNeil swimming baths, one of the town's most popular leisure facilities. Terry was not a great swimmer, in fact, he had only mastered the art of avoiding drowning, during his final years at school PE sessions. Angie however was a natural in the water, being able to do lengths with ease. She regarded it as her personal mission to turn Terry into a swimmer. She had fun trying, and Terry was always a willing pupil.

During their visit, they bumped into Terry's Gran, who was with a group of fellow pensioners. She had never met Angie before but had heard a lot about her, and she liked what she saw, even if she did give her Grandson less than approving looks whenever the two of them got amorous in the pool's shallow end.

At the end of the session, they headed upstairs to the cafeteria for some orange juice, sitting at a table looking out to the pools below, all they could talk about was the highlight of their week, a night out at the dancing, and there was not going to be a DJ in sight.

The whole of the Renfrewshire area had been celebrating the era of local dance bands and dance halls, staging a number of exhibitions, as well as special events throughout the week. And in a few days' time, Gourock's Cragburn Pavilion was going to return to its dance hall roots, with a

33

special big band dance night.

Angie had said that she always wanted to experience a night out doing proper dancing, even more so as her first ever boyfriend had a higher than average level of experience on the ballroom floor, even though it was just at a competitive level.

Terry had often listened to his Dad talking about his nights out at "the jigging" and what he and Angie were going to experience themselves. It was going to be a venture into the unknown for them; for Terry's parents, it would be a trip down memory lane, as that was how they'd first met.

Dance clubs from around the area were heading to the Cragburn. Terry and Angie would be travelling down as part of his parents group. Casual dress was not an option.

Terry's parents, or to put it more accurately, his Mother, had decided that they should go on a shopping spree to make sure that they were suitably attired for the evening. Charlie would take his son to get a new suit, and Mary would treat Angie to a new dress. They had arranged to meet up outside the Arnotts store at Hamilton Way shopping precinct after their swim.

Angie took a sip of juice from her cup. 'I really appreciate your Mother doing this,' she said, 'but she does not really know what suits me.'

'I wouldn't worry about that, 'replied Terry. 'She may have her own ideas, but I know she won't get you something you don't like. Whatever you get, you will look fabulous.'

Angie smiled, reaching across the table and squeezing Terry's hand. 'It is going to be a new experience for me,' he added. 'The only time I ever wore a suit for any occasion was at family weddings. I have not done that for a while. Something tells me that this shopping trip won't take long. I bet that you will find what you are looking for in the first place you go to. I know that I will.'

'I am excited about Friday,' said Angie.

Terry smiled. 'So am I. Forget about the stuff we did at Butlins, we've not had a date as big as this.'

'It's a night out; it's not really a date is it. We will be sitting along with your parents and their dance club.'

Terry took a sip of his juice. 'Trust me - that aint going to happen,' he said. 'We will travel down and back up with them but we will find our own table. They have got their own reasons for going down. I told my Dad this the other night, he said quite right. "I don't want you to cramp my style."'

Angie giggled. 'This is going to be our night,' he said. 'I can't wait to see what you will be wearing.'

'Apart from the clothes you wore on your day off at the camp, I only ever saw you in your Red and Whites,' she replied. 'You wore a suit when you were on duty at "Late Night Cabaret". That was the only time I slept in my own chalet.' Terry smirked as he looked into Angie's eyes. 'We are going to have a brilliant night.' He kissed the top of her hand. 'Time to go shopping I think.'

They put their swimming gear into their bags, heading down to meet Terry's parents outside "Arnotts" which was a twenty minute brisk walk from the swimming baths. Eventually they found them standing outside the main entrance. 'Ah there they are, 'said Mary. 'Have a nice swim?'

'Smashing thanks,' said Angie.

'Yeh great!' said Terry

'Did you actually do any swimming?' asked Mary.

'I did, it helps when you have a great teacher."

'Take your word for it. Come on Angie, we will go in here.

Terry you go with your Dad.'

'This won't take us long,' Charlie whispered in Terry's ear. Terry and Angie blew each other a kiss as they proceed to head in opposite directions.

Fifteen minutes later, Terry and his Dad were sitting in a café just a few yards directly opposite Arnotts waiting for Mary and Angie. At the side of the table was a bag containing Terry's new suit which looked remarkably like his old one, a dark blue pin stripe with matching shirt, tie and a new pair of soft leather shoes – an essential tool for a night dancing. 'See I told you it would not take long,' said Charlie. 'I wonder how Angie is getting on,' said Terry, constantly looking out of the window.

'Stop worrying! She'll be fine. Ladies take their time when it comes to picking outfits. You will learn that as you get older.'

As both men continued to drink their tea, Terry persisted in looking out of the window to see if his Mother and Angie had finished their shopping.

'What you going to be like when she heads back home on Saturday,' said Charlie.

'I am trying not to think about that the now,' said Terry. 'Angie said she wanted me to take her out dancing, I just want tomorrow night to be perfect.'

'It will be. You worry too much.'

Thirty minutes and several cups of tea later, Mary and a relaxed looking Angie emerged from the front door of the department store. Terry knew that Angie was a bit anxious about her shopping trip, but both looked relaxed as they joined them at the café. Angie poured out a cup of tea. She looked at Terry and smiled.

'So how did it go,' he asked.

'It was great! Loved it! Did you get a suit?'

'Yep. Dark blue number along with new shirt, tie and a comfortable pair of shoes.'

Mary glanced to look inside Terry's bag. 'It looks like your old suit.'

'That's cause it is,' said Charlie. 'It fits better and it looks good on him. That's all you need to know.'

'Terry tried to look into Angie's shopping bag to see what she and his Mother had bought. 'So, what did you get?'

Angie beamed. 'I absolutely love it. But you can't see it till tomorrow. Been sworn to secrecy.'

'A café is not the place to show you. We are not going to spoil the moment,' said Mary.

Charlie raised his cup to take a final slurp of his tea and whispered in his son's ear. 'Keep a guy in suspense. You will get used to that as well.'

Charlie and Mary took the bags back to the house, leaving Terry and Angie to spend the rest of the afternoon walking down towards Custom House Quay, checking out evidence of Greenock's maritime past, and to take some pictures of the various tug boats anchored nearby.

Twenty four hours later, the moment had arrived; Terry's parents were already dressed for the evening. Terry, immaculately dressed in his new suit, stood at the bottom of the stairs waiting for Angie, still wondering what outfit his Mother had bought for her.

Minutes later, he got his answer when he caught sight of Angie grinning nervously at the top of the stairs, walking slowly down towards him. She was wearing a three quarter length blue evening dress, the lights caught the subtle design created by the shimmering black sequins, it was beautiful, as was she.

Along with her hand bag, Angie was carrying a light showerproof jacket which blended in with the colour scheme of the rest of the outfit. Charlie and Mary were out of vision, but could see look of pride on their son's face.

'Terry reached out and took both of Angie's hands. 'You look incredible.'

'Thank you kind sir,' said Angie examining Terry's outfit. 'You look so handsome in your suit.'

'You are too kind Madam.

'Ahem! Time to go,' interrupted Charlie.

Terry offered Angie his arm. 'Dear lady, it will be my honour to escort you to the ball.'

'How very gallant of you Sir.'

Arrangements had been made for a minibus to leave Charlie and Mary's social club and take members and their guests to the Cragburn. The club was only ten minutes' walk from the McFadden residence. They all put on their jackets and proceed to walk briskly to the pick-up point, with Angie holding on to Terry's hand, Charlie and Mary locked arms walking slightly in front of them.

'By the way you never said how I looked,' said Mary.

'A million dollars,' said Charlie.

'Good answer.'

Forty minutes later, the minibus pulled up in front of the Cragburn. With the number of lights lit up around the front entrance of the auditorium, it felt like they were special guests of a film premiere. This was a special occasion, as the evening was a celebration of what was a bygone era in local culture.

Angie squeezed Terry's hand as they walked through the main doors. The exhibits from earlier in the week had been rearranged in order to provide a clear path into what was for one night only the main dance hall. Angie had already experienced what it was like to dance in the venue earlier in the week, following her impromptu waltz with Terry. Back then it was just an empty hall, tonight though, it had been totally transformed.

As they walked in, they would see the main stage dressed with a backdrop of shimmering curtains with a colourful floral display across the edge of the platform. To the left of the stage was a large piano and the rest of the area was taken up with a seating arrangement for a small orchestra, that consisted of local session musicians, who would normally be plying their trade as back up for touring variety shows.

The full line up dressed in traditional evening wear, consisted of, a five strong woodwind section, two trombonists, one trumpeter, two double bassists and, a drummer, along with a conductor, very much like the dance bands of old.

With the upper balcony was closed off for the evening, all of the participants would be seated at adjacent sides of the main floor, on slightly raised platforms where a number of tables and seats, were laid out with restaurant style precision, partitioned off by a number of low level barriers running down the side.

'This looks fantastic,' said Angie.

'Doesn't it just' said Terry, who out of the corner of his eye, could see his parents along with the rest of their dance group taking their seats at the right hand side of the stage. Terry guided Angie over to the opposite side of the dance floor. 'We can sit over there,' he said.

Sitting at their table, Terry could see his Dad making the OK sign towards him, he smiled and signalled back. Both he and Angie continued to look around as the rest of the patrons come through the door and take their seats. 'I have been to this place many times but never for anything like this.' He turned to Angie, kissing the top of her hand. 'And being accompanied by a gorgeous woman – it could not get any more perfect.'

Angie blushed and smiled as she squeezed Terry's hands. 'I do love you, you know that.'

'And I love you,' he said.

Before he could say anything else, Terry was interrupted by the "Orchestra's" conductor for the evening who stepped forward towards the microphone.

'Good Evening Ladies and Gentleman and welcome to a special celebration tonight at the Cragburn Pavillion. Please take your partners for the first dance of the evening – a quickstep.

'Shall we?' said Terry.

'Absolutely,' said Angie.

As it was a celebration of a local nostalgia, they kicked off the proceedings in traditional fashion, with the Glenn Miller classic, 'In The Mood.' It took them take couple of minutes to find their feet but under Terry's direction, it was not long before he and Angie were shuffling along with everyone else, with Mary and Charlie looking on in approval.

Despite the reasons for the event, the programme aimed to cater for all tastes as there was a variation in the age group. There were not just traditional dance hall favourites, but there were also arrangements of modern day songs, as well as a brief period of sequence dance numbers. Terry and Angie hardly ever sat down. They were up for almost every dance, but he made sure that they took a break during the sequence dancing part.

The evening had been a resounding success and was

heading towards its conclusion. The Conductor announced, 'Ladies and Gentleman, we are approaching the end of tonight's programme. Please take your partners for a waltz.' The musicians started to play "Moon River."

Terry took Angie in his arms and they proceeded to waltz around the crowded dance floor, but that made no difference to them as they looked into each other's eyes, and proceeded to glide around the floor. Minutes later, a broad smile beamed across their faces when one of the singers got off her chair and stepped up to the microphone, the band changed to a present day number for the final waltz of the evening, the singer began to sing, Debbie Boone's "You Light Up My Life"

Angie whispered in to Terry's ear. 'They are playing "our song".

It was the perfect way to end a perfect evening. Terry and Angie managed to resist the urge to grab on to each other as required for a final slow dance at a disco. They moved effortlessly around the dance floor avoiding the rest of the patrons, only having eyes for each other.

The music stopped and everyone applauded and cheered the band for what was a fabulous night's entertainment. As everyone slowly started to make for the exits, Charlie walked up to Terry to let him know that their minibus would be leaving in around fifteen minutes, allowing time for the rest of crowd to move off first.

'We will be there,' said Terry. 'We are just going to head down to the barrier over the road just now.' Crossing the street, Terry and Angie headed towards the edge of the promenade looking out to sea, it was shimmering like silver, by the light of the moon above.

Angie turned towards Terry, tears were starting to fill up

at the corner of her eyes. After what had been a perfect evening, the reality was that tomorrow they were going to be apart again. Terry looked lovingly into Angie's face as he gently brushed the tears running down the side of her cheek.

'We don't want you to smudge your make up,' he said. Angie was hardly wearing any, but the comment was enough to make her giggle.

'Thank you for this evening,' she said. 'It was a fabulous night.'

'I should be the one thanking you,' replied Terry. 'Remember that first evening we had together in the Stuart Ballroom? You told me that you don't need a building or setting to make it a memorable or romantic evening. I thought that the band were great, I loved all the dancing, but tonight was special as was this whole week, for one reason.' Terry, gently placed his hand under Angie's chin as he leant forward to kiss her tenderly. 'I was with you. '

Angie smiled as she wrapped her arms around Terry. They embraced, holding on tightly, not either of them wanting to let go. This was the biggest test of their relationship after working at Butlins, getting used to the idea that that it would be a week before they would see each other again.

'I wish we could stay like this all night,' she said. 'It is going to hurt so much getting on that train tomorrow.'

'Just being apart for a few hours is bad enough,' said Terry. 'But there will be a time when we won't have to worry about things like that. It is not going to happen overnight, but we will get there as long as you remember one thing.'

'What's that,' said Angie.

'The day you walked into my life Angie was the best thing to happen to me,' he said. 'I love you so much.' Angie looked lovingly at Terry and smiled. 'And I love you Terry.'

'Together, we can achieve anything.'

Terry noticed his Dad signalling from across the street that the minibus was ready to take them back up to Balloch Street. 'I think our transport is ready,' he said.

Terry placed his hand around Angie's waist with her head resting on his shoulder, they slowly walked away from the promenade back towards the main entrance of the Cragburn, where the minibus was waiting. 'Did I mention that you looked fabulous in that dress this evening,' said Terry.

'Several times,' she said. 'But I am not complaining. Thank your parents again for buying it for me?'

'I will. You make sure you phone me when you get back home.'

'Definitely! It will only be a week before you come through to my Grans'.'

'I will phone you every night and I will look at the card you gave me,' replied Terry. 'You just hold onto that St Christopher Medal I gave you. That way a part of me is with you every night.'

'You mean this medal here,' said Angie, lifting the chain that was wrapped around her neck.

After all of this week, this was the first time he had actually seen her wearing it since he gave it to her at the end of the season at Butlins.

Terry smiled. 'That is the one. Speaking of your Gran, is she still Ok about me coming through to stay for the week.'

'She is looking forward to it,' said Angie. 'It is a one bedroom flat, so it is going to be a bit crammed. I hope you don't mind sleeping in the cupboard.'

'The cupboard?'

CHAPTER FOUR

Angie's Gran, Cathy, despite her seventy-five years had the type of energy that would put people 30 years younger to shame. She automatically took to Terry, but like his own Gran, would sometimes look disapprovingly if she caught them doing more than holding hands in her house. Between all of her grandchildren, Angie, being the oldest was the apple of her eye. She could see how much she and Terry were happy together, she could not wish for anything more.

As a former Boy Scout and a veteran of a number of camping trips, Terry was used to having to adapt to unusual sleeping surroundings, but it was nothing compared to whenever he stayed at Cathy's house, just outside Falkirk for the week.

It was a one bedroom flat; Angie would sleep in the same bedroom as her Gran. For Terry, sleeping on the couch was not an option; as there wasn't one. The main seating arrangements consisted of a small settee and a single seat with the structure supported by wooden poles and detachable cushions. And as it was a small living room the only viable option was sleeping on top of an old mattress inside the hall storage cupboard.

It had been two months since Terry first visit to the small village, of California, and this morning would start like any other morning, waking to the light shining through the bathroom window directly opposite, promptly sitting up, bashing his head against the shelf directly above him. 'OWWW! Every time,' he muttered.

Once he acclimatised to the light shining through, he saw a smiling Angie looking down. 'Morning sleepy head,' she said. 'Ready for today?'

'Absolutely! Once I get rid of this headache.'

'Don't tell me. You banged your head again.'

Terry gently rubbed his head. 'I don't do it intentionally – honest.

Angie giggled as she bent over and gently kissed him on the top of his head. 'You will be fine. Bathroom is free. Shall I get some toast on?'

'Smashing! Give me ten minutes. I will get myself cleaned up.'

Terry's sleeping quarters was five and a half feet wide, so there was enough room – just, for Terry to have a decent night's sleep as long he did not try to stretch out fully lying during the night. There was not enough room, so it was imperative that the door remained open to make room for his knees.

Getting up was an art form. He had to carefully place his feet outside the door first before edging out on to the main hallway; he would then sit up and pull on his tracksuit bottoms whilst still under the sheets. Dignity intact, he managed to haul himself up to walk past the kitchen door to the bathroom.

Placing his washing bag at the side of the basin, Terry cleaned himself up before lifting up his shaving brush, applying soap lather to his face, and then placing the razor against the side of his cheek with great care.

Today was going to be another special moment for Angie and himself, more than just a visit to her Grans' He had to make sure he created the right impression; mistakes and face blemishes were still not an option. Today is going to be very interesting,' he thought.

Having finished shaving and changed in to a fresh pair of clothes, Terry walked into the kitchen where Cathy and Angie were sitting at the table having their breakfast. 'Morning,' he said.

'Morning,' said Cathy. 'How was your sleep.'

'Smashing! Thanks!'

'Sit down and have your breakfast,' she said. 'You have a busy day ahead of you.'

Terry enjoyed his visits to California, even though there was not much for Angie and him to do when he got there. During the day, there were the long walks along the nearby park parks and canals. Some evenings they would head into Falkirk itself where Terry helped Angie build on her ballroom experience at Greenock, joining her at local dance classes. This was often difficult for Terry to deal with; watching his girlfriend occasionally dance with the teacher- and doing the steps all wrong.

There were trips to the Cinema, where Terry developed an acquired taste for Angie's love of romantic films like, "An Officer and a Gentleman", which was fast becoming her favourite movie ever. He could not work out whether it was the plot, Richard Gere, the uniform - or all three.

It looked like they were getting used to life away from

Butlins. The biggest challenge remained the alternate visits between Greenock and California. Being apart, even for a few days was horrible, however the enforced absence just made their relationship stronger than ever. They always clung on to the hope that there would be a time where they would be together permanently.

This day was going to be the next big chapter in their relationship where Terry would now be the focus of attention. They would travel to Durham to meet Angie's parents, Dave and Tish Bierman for the very first time. They'd heard plenty of things about their eldest daughter's first boyfriend through her letters whilst she was working at Butlins. Now they would finally get the chance to see how much of that was true.

Breakfast was finished, Terry tidied up his "sleeping quarters" and it was time for them to take the bus into Falkirk for the 11:15am train to Edinburgh, where they would get the 1pm connection to Durham. They arrived in the Scottish Capital in plenty of time, and, as the train pulled out of Waverly Station, Angie was curious to notice a gift wrapped box sticking out of Terry's bag. 'What's in the box,' she asked.

'Chocolates for your Mother, 'he replied.

Angie looked puzzled. 'Why.'

'My Mother's idea. She insisted that I took some with me. She was adamant that I needed to make the right impression.'

'You don't need a box of "Milk Tray" to do that. They know everything about you.'

'Everything?'

Angie giggled. 'Don't worry, you will be fine. They are looking forward to meeting you.'

'I am looking forward to it as well. Anything I need to know about them?'

'My Mother is not the best cook in the world, and Dad likes to think he is funny, as well as being an expert on many things. Stay clear of politics or religion and you will be fine. Just be you. You worried?'

'Nah,' insisted Terry. 'I am going to get know about a major part of your life, I am going to have great week in a place I have never been before and most important of all - I am with you.'

Angie smiled as they both embraced.

'You told me that you were the proudest man when you walked me up your home street to meet your family, but it will be nothing to match the pride I will be feeling when we step off this train.

Terry squeezed Angie's hand. 'I love you, do you know that?'

Angie smiled. 'I love you. You know that. And so do my family.'

'Am I going to get to meet your brother and sister as well?'

'You will get on with my brother Jason; he has just left school and is working with Dad in the Bakery. Alison will be at school. You will get to see them later.'

'Hope we hit it off.'

Angie laughed. 'I remember saying something similar when I met your family for the first time. '

An hour and half later the train rolled into the Durham train station. Terry grabbed both sets of luggage as they disembarked. Walking along the platform Angie smiled and waved frantically as she caught sight of her smiling mum and Dad standing at the exit gate.

Terry thought that Angie's Mother, Tish, was the spitting

image of her. Her father Dave was about the same age as Terry's Dad Charlie. He looked as if he had just come off from a shift from his bakery business, still showing traces of flour on his jacket and trousers. Angie ran towards her parents and threw her arms around them.

She may have chosen to live away from the family home, but they remained close. Dave and Tish hated the idea of their daughter staying hundreds of miles away, but they fully supported her in all of her decisions, regardless whether they were right or wrong -as any parent would.

Terry watched in the distance as Angie continued to talk to her smiling parents. He cautiously walked towards them carrying the cases. Angie then turned and smiled: 'mum, Dad, this is Terry. Terry, mum and Dad.'

'Hi Terry,' pleased to meet you at last,' smiled Tish who gave him a peck on the cheek. 'I have heard so much about you.'

'All good I hope,' said Terry.

'Great to see you Terry,' said Dave smiling firmly shaking his hand. 'Just one question. Are you going to have it done at a registry office or a church? I don't mind, will wear the suit any place.'

'Eh?'

'Shut up Dave,' said Tish. 'Stop winding the boy up. Come on. Let's get you home.'

They all headed towards the station exit. 'Here Terry, give me one of those cases,' said Dave. Your transport home awaits.'

The Bierman household was in a mining village thirty minutes' drive away from the city centre, but there were no taxis, or buses taking them home. Terry's eyes opened wide when he saw that their transport was the Bierman company vehicle, a large transit van, normally used for picking up supplies of flour from the local Mills, as well as delivering produce to their customers. There was only room for Dave and Tish at the front, Angie and Terry had to sit in the vacant space at the back.

Terry looked anxiously at her as Dave unlocked the doors of the van. 'Don't worry, I have cleaned it up,' he said. As he pulled open the doors, they saw an empty back end of a van, except for seats from an old minibus, which he used on special occasions. Having dumped the cases in the van, Terry climbed on board, taking Angie's hand as he helped her up. 'Hold on tight,' said Dave.

'Terry smiled. 'Don't worry we will.'

Dave laughed. 'I meant the seat. It's not fixed to the floor.'

'Oh Kay.'

'We will be fine Dad,' said Angie.

'Right Then! Wagons Roll!'

Dave slammed the back doors and went to the front to join his wife. As the engines of the van started to rattle, Terry and Angie sat cautiously expecting the worst. As the vehicle slowly pulled away, Terry immediately held on to Angie as the temporary back seats shot forward towards the front of the van.

He tried to secure himself by placing his feet firmly on the floor, and the journey had just started.

'Blimey!' he said. 'How long till we get there?'

Angie held on to Terry's arm. 'Not Long. Remember what Dad said "hold on tight."

'That goes without saying.'

'You OK back there?' shouted Dave.

'Yeh smashing,' said Terry, who continued to struggle keeping his feet firmly in position trying to restrict any movement.

As the old transit continued along the road taking tight corners, travelling up and down steep hills, he was wondering how long he could keep in this position. Was the lock in that back door secure? He did not fancy the idea of the two of them along with their luggage ending up in the middle of the street.

Still in the van, they finally arrived at the front door of number 10 Hillside Road, which was actually two buildings combined into one, not the most picturesque of dwellings, but it more than satisfied the Bierman family's needs, especially as one end had an extension that doubled up as their shop.

In the shop window was an enticing selection of cakes, pies along with an arrangement of various shaped loaves. They all stood outside the front door of the house as Tish turned the key ready to let them in. Angie holding on to Terry's hand leant over to one side and waved as she caught sight of her younger brother Jason smiling from behind the shop window. Terry could hear loud barking from the other side of the door. 'Hope you like dogs Terry,'

'I love dogs,' he replied. 'Not too good with cats though.'

'Interesting! We have got two of them downstairs in the workroom.'

'When did you get them?' asked Angie.

'A couple of months ago,' said Tish. 'Your brother stopped someone trying to chuck them in the river. They were kittens when he brought them home. I just fell in love with them. They are like part of the family. The dogs don't have a problem with them as long as they stay in separate rooms.'

As Tish slowly opened the door, they were met by the canine reception committee, two six year old Alsatians, Harry and Lexie, who had been favourite pets since they were pups, and who could not contain their excitement when they saw Angie, barking and wagging their tails vigorously

'Hallo!!!!. Ow I have missed you two, 'said Angie as she bent down stroking their thick coats.

Harry then turned his attention to Terry, ferociously wagging his tail, jumping on to him. He gently placed the dog back on all fours, but Harry was not for backing off as he started to sniff around the lower end of Terry's body. 'Okay pal, don't go there,' said Terry trying discreetly to move Harry's snout away from his crotch.

Angie smiled. 'Harry likes you.'

Terry was determined to create the right impression. He did not reckon having to deal with an over friendly dog. 'He likes me a bit too much. I think he smells my own dog. 'Okay Harry, that's enough! I see you!'

Dave quickly closed the door behind him as they dumped the cases in the kitchen. 'Time to put the kettle on I think,' said Tish. 'You two go into the living room, Angie and I will bring the tea in.'

'Ok,' said Terry. He pulled out the wrapped box of chocolates out his bag. 'I forgot to say- these are for you.'

'Thanks very much,' smiled Tish who turned to Angie mouthing the words 'what am I supposed to do with this?' Angie gave her Mother a dig in the ribs with her elbow as she quickly ushered her into the kitchen and was followed by Lexie. Terry went into the living room with Dave, whilst Angie helped her Mother make some afternoon coffee.

'So what do you think of him?' asked Angie.

''You certainly talked him up in your letters. It is good to see that you were not exaggerating, he is a nice lad. You do look good together.'

Angie smiled. 'It feels so right,' she said. 'Where are the cups?'

'I'll get the cups. You sit down at the table, I want to hear everything. Tell me something about him that you did not mention in your letters.'

'How about I love him,' she said.

'First boyfriend and you are in love? Well, I did ask? '

'I've never been happier,' replied Angie. 'And I know that Terry feels the same. '

Tish picked up the box that Terry had given her a few minutes earlier. 'So what's with the chocolates?'

'He just wants to make a good impression that's all. His Mother suggested that it was the right thing to do. You like those chocolates.'

'Yeh. But…..'

'You are just not used to people buying you any. '

'He does not have to go to those lengths. So what's next for you two.'

'Get jobs, preferably in the same town. It was great when we are at Butlins, but we can't rely on that. '

'Do you see yourself going back to Butlins?'

'Can't rule anything out,' said Angie. 'If we do, then I want to be a Redcoat like Terry. It is a great job and having us working together would be fantastic. But if we get something permanent first, then that would be even better.'

'Well I am sure that your Dad could find a place for him in the bakery. We did talk about that the other day,' replied Tish.

'Thanks for the offer, but we need to find our own place in the world. And beside Terry would not last long in a bakery.'

'He is clumsy then?'

'He has worked in a bakery before and let say it wasn't the best of experiences.' Tish placed a number of cups on a tray, and Angie opened up the jar of coffee and started to spoon it into the cups. Angie was starting to wonder what was happening in the room next door where Terry was sitting with Dave.

'I hope Dad is not carrying out a job interview in there?'

'I wouldn't be surprised,' Tish said, 'amongst other things.' She poured some milk into the jug.

'Some cakes in the tin there.'

'From the shop?'

'But of course.'

In the other room, Terry was feeling nervous as he sat on the couch in the living room with Dave, sitting on his "King of the House Chair'. Not that he felt intimidated talking to Angie's Dad; he was uncomfortable dealing with the unwanted attention of Harry, who continued to sniff around Terry's legs, trying to make sure that he did not sniff anywhere higher.

'I have to be honest with you Terry,' it was tough when Angie decided to leave home. It's great to see her happy, which is all we ever wanted.'

'I can understand that,' answered Terry, but that was not the only thing Dave wanted. Whilst he respected Angie's decisions to stay with her gran, he always had a long term plan of keeping his family together. And this looked like the perfect opportunity.

'So when are you moving down here then?' That was one question that Terry did not expect. Did it mean that he was accepted into the household already? As much as he liked Angie's Parents, he certainly was not in the mood for relocation. It was a nice area, but it was a small village and the employment opportunities appeared to be a lot less compared to Greenock.

'Why would I want to move down south?'

'You could get a job here,' said Dave.

'Doing what? 'Asked Terry.

'Well we could do with extra hands in the bakery.'

Dave's suggestion immediately triggered a flashback to his brief experience working at Aulds in Greenock, and how even though it was a training scheme, he knew that he was one week away from being dumped back on the dole, and he had no desire to go back down that road again.

"Thanks for the offer, but I am not looking to move down south, 'said Terry. 'I want to find work closer to home.'

Dave was not for giving up and tried to lay the 'loving daughter card. 'Have you spoken to Angie about this?'

'Yep, she knows how I feel. It would have to be something major in terms of work for me to move down here. We want to find our place in the world, and at the moment it starts up north.'

Dave realised that it was starting to sound exactly like a conversation he had had with his daughter a year earlier. 'You would love to move down here,' he said, 'you just don't realise it yet.' Terry looked Dave straight in the eye and smiled. 'Trust me, it isn't going to happen.'

Dave had no intention of giving up, but as this was the first meeting, it was important to keep things relaxed. So, his mission would be kept on hold for another day, namely the next time he came down for a visit – assuming he wanted to come down again.

Terry was starting to get annoyed that Dave kept pushing for him to leave Scotland. If Durham was that good why did Angie leave in the first place? But he was certainly not going to get into an argument with Dave, they had only just met. One thing that he learned working for Ron De Vere at

Ayr was to remain respectful, but don't let other people take control.

Whilst the ladies were still in the kitchen sorting out the coffee, Dave took the opportunity to discuss a totally different subject. 'Just to let you know that it is separate rooms I am afraid.' Terry was stunned. He did not expect to be talking about something like this with a person he had only just met. 'Don't deny it,' he said. 'I know that you two were sleeping together at Butlins.'

Terry did not know how to answer that. How much information did Angie give her parents. He had never discussed it with his own folks. He would not dare. Especially with his Mother.

'What's Angie been telling you,' he said.

'Nothing,' said Dave. 'It doesn't take much to figure it out. Doesn't bother me. I totally understand, I am a man of the world, but it's Angie's Mother we have to think about. So, it is best to keep things private. Know what I mean.'

Terry was not going to admit anything, but he was prepared to play along with the game. He felt that they had come to an understanding of sorts.

There was still the matter of fending off the advances of Harry, who continued to get up close and a little bit too personal, still wagging his tail ferociously. 'Right Harry – that is enough!'

Angie poked her head from behind the living room door. 'Coffee is out' She brought in a tray with cups followed by Tish carrying some plates with an assortment of cakes and scones.

Terry tried to stand up from his to seat, to try and give the ladies space to set up the coffee and cakes on the table in the middle of the living room, but Harry and, was not for moving. He was a large Alsatian, so he was not easy to shift.

The top half of Harry's body was now on his lap, so he continued to stroke the top of the dog's head thinking he was just craving attention, as mutts do, but to his horror, Harry was starting to rub himself up and down on his leg vigorously. The more he rubbed the more his panting became erratic. Tish realised what was happening and was as embarrassed as Terry was. 'HARRY !!!!. DAVE! TAKE THE DOG INTO THE BACK ROOM!

Dave grabbed Harry by the collar and promptly dragged Harry off Terry taking him into the room where Lexie was sitting in her own basket, chewing away at one of her toys. Dave threw one of Harry's toys in his direction and finally the dog took the hint and started to flick the objects around the room. 'Right you two stay there!' said Dave.

As Dave sorted out the animals, Terry made the most of his freedom, walking away from the settee to regain his composure and swipe the dog hairs off his tracksuit bottoms before settling down to coffee.

'You Ok?' said Angie.

Terry, having freed as much dog hair from his person as possible, sat back on the couch as Tish started to pour out the coffee. 'Yeh I'm fine,' he said. 'I think I learned something new about dogs.'

Angie smiled 'Like what.'

'That some seem to have an attraction to my right leg.'

'So how you and Dad getting on?'

'Fine. He's been trying to get me to move down here.'

'Did he now,' asked Tish.

Angie sat down beside Terry as he took a sip of his coffee.

'What did he say? Scone?'

'I think we understand each other.   Don't mind if I do.'

Dave came back in the living room resuming his place back in his chair. 'Dog sorted, coffee for me please my love.' 'Certainly sir,' said Tish through gritted teeth.   Dave was more than capable of pouring out his own coffee, but the last thing she wanted was their house guest to see arguments.

'I'll go over to the shop in five minutes and cover for Jason a bit,' said Dave. 'Alison will be back from school in a couple of hours.'

'Great stuff,' said Angie.   'I have missed them both.'

'If you fancy it, you can all go to the disco at the Miner's Institute later tonight, said Tish

Angie looked at Terry. 'What do you think.'

'Sounds great! 'he said.   'I think I may need to change out of these trousers first.'

CHAPTER FIVE

Christmas Day had a new perspective for Terry and Angie, they always believed that this was a special day for families, but as they opened their packages, which turned out to be the exact same present, they both realised that something was missing, each other!

The best they could hope for, for this year at least, was to spend Christmas morning talking on the phone. Not the normal of festive practices, but both sets of parents knew what it was like to be in love. It also gave the opportunity for both sets of parents to connect for the first time. Forget the phone bill for once – it was Christmas.

New Year's Eve was different, Angie had come through to Greenock, so she and Terry would see it in together. He still had to endure the traditional family Hogmanay first footing process, standing outside the house in sub-zero temperatures, waiting for the shipyard horns to go off in the distance, signalling the start of the New Year.

Terry was anything but superstitious, but he played along to keep the peace, as it was a tradition that his parents believed in.   Only this time, he had a reason to enjoy it as he was not standing outside alone.

Waiting for the festive signals from the shipyards, he and Angie stood outside in freezing temperatures. Normally he would be standing outside the front door trying to hurry up the time in his mind, wanting to get back in the warmth of the house.

This time, with Angie by his side, it was an ideal moment to focus on how his life had changed during the last twelve months, and how 1983 was going to be year to remember, hopefully. The horns from shipyards sounded off in unison, Terry squeezed Angie's hand, turned to her and smiled.

'Happy New Year Angie!   You changed my life.' he kissed the top of her hand and lent forward to kiss her. 'I love you! Here is to a wonderful year.'

Angie threw her arms around Terry holding on to him as tightly as she could without damaging the "first foot" contents of shortbread and boxes of chocolates.   She whispered into Terry's ear. 'I love you so much. Happy New Year!'

The noise from the ships horns continued on, but they were oblivious to them as they looked deeply into each other's eyes. They were back in their own special world were nothing else mattered. However, they returned to reality when they heard the sound of the doors opening from the other side of the front door.

Gently resting their heads together, Terry sniggered.   'That sounds like our cue.'

With their shortbread and chocolates still in hand, the house doors opened with Charlie and Mary standing at the door.   'HAPPY NEW YEAR!!!!!!'

After dishing out the usual customary Hogmanay hugs at the

front door, Terry and Angie moved into the front room. In the past this was almost like a routine, but this time he was enthusiastic about the year ahead and everyone could feel that.

There was no party to welcome in the new year in the McFadden Household, just sitting down to a mini buffet of tablet, shortbread and various other party snacks, washed down with plenty of soft drinks and Mary's home-made Ginger Wine, watching the annual Hogmanay Show, on Scottish Television, featuring the great and the good of Scottish Showbiz.

Thirty minutes in, the "excitement " of the start of 1983 had died down, Terry and Angie took advantage of the situation, taking their Ginger Wine to the back room of the house, they opened the back door, sitting at the top of the steps, looking up at the night sky.

'I will certainly not forget 1982, I have got you to thank for that. You are the best thing ever to happen to me,' said Terry, who kissed the top of Angie's hand.

Angie smiled as she leant forward and kissed Terry tenderly. 'Last year was so special. This year is going to even better.' Terry placed his arm around Angie, who rested her head onto his shoulder.

'I keep thinking about what you put on that card you gave me all those months ago. "Together, we can face anything that comes our way." That will be us this year.'

'First challenge is for both of us to get jobs,' said Angie, 'so we can stop all the travelling every two weeks.'

'It has not been for the want of trying,' replied Terry. 'We could not even get any temp jobs at Christmas. All we have work wise is going back to Butlins. We know that for definite. We both have our offers for the summer.'

'I don't want to go back to the kitchens if I can help it. If we go back, I want to become a Redcoat like you,' she said. 'I just don't know where to start. I've not seen any job adverts'

'Just phone De Vere at the camp,' said Terry. 'Ask if he is doing any interviews.'

'I'm not sure.'

Terry could sense how important it was for Angie to get what was now for her, a dream job. He had gone through the same emotions twelve months earlier. Only this time he had a better understanding of the process, and the man behind the interviews. He smiled as he gently brushed his hand down the side of Angie's face raising her head up towards him.

'Don't wait for adverts, just phone De Vere up at the camp. He likes people that are not afraid to push themselves. You have nothing to lose. You can go back to the camp no matter what happens. This is our next chapter.'

Angie raised her glass, clinking it against Terry's. 'Here's to the next chapter.'

She took a sip of Mary's Ginger Wine and grimaced. 'Don't tell your Mother, but I don't like this Ginger Wine'

Terry sniggered, took the half full glass out of Angie's hand and along with his, threw the contents on to the turf at the back garden. 'There you go – it's gone, you will never see it again.'

Two weeks passed, Terry received a phone call from an excited Angie. She had taken his advice and plucked up the courage to phone the Entertainments Office at Butlins Ayr. She had been invited for an interview at the complex with Entertainments Manager Ron De Vere in two days' time for the position of a General Duty Redcoat. 'I am shaking just thinking about it,' she said. 'I don't want to blow it.'

'Don't think about that,' said Terry. 'Don't look it as an interview, just think of it as meeting up for a chat. Just be yourself, I know that you will be fine.'

Terry continued to try and reassure Angie. He knew that given the chance she would be a fabulous Redcoat and this was the moment where he needed to come through for her. 'I want you to do something for me. Close your eyes. Imagine me holding your hand. I am telling you I believe in you, I love you. You will be wonderful I know you will.' Angie voice started to break through emotion. 'I don't deserve you.

Terry was scheduled to come through to stay with Angie after the interview but he made sure that during the two days leading up to it, he was on the phone, reassuring her that she was good enough to pass, what to look out for. He would not physically be beside her during the interview, but he would be with her in spirit.

The day of the interview had finally arrived. Angie had woken up early after a restless night. To allow enough time for her to travel from Falkirk to Ayr, De Vere had schedule the meeting to take place late in the afternoon. Terry made a point of phoning her to wish her luck. He may have been biased, but as far as he was concerned, she had all the requirements to become a brilliant Redcoat.

They agreed that it was best for her to go into Ayr on her own. The last thing Angie needed was distractions. She was going to meet up with Terry the following day anyway when he came through to stay at her Grans', so he would get a full report then.

The train rolled into the station where Terry saw a smiling Angie, waiting at the platform. Apart from the usual excitement when either of them came to visit, Angie seemed relaxed as she wrapped her arms around Terry as he stepped off the train. He was anxious to find out how the interview went, so they decided to delay their bus journey for a while so they could nip into a nearby café. As they queued up for a coffee, Angie refused to say anything until they sat down at their table at the far corner of the café away from the other customers.

'Don't keep me in suspense,' said Terry. 'How did it go?' 'I think it went OK,' she replied. 'My nerves disappeared the moment I walked into the camp. It immediately brought back happy memories, even though the place was deserted. It felt weird.'

'What about the interview with De Vere?'

Angie went on to explain that he was in the Entertainments Office and that the whole interview felt relaxed to begin with. He asked about her background, what she was interested in, was particularly interested when she said that she used to do trampolining at school. 'Then he asked me why I wanted to become a Redcoat?' she said.

'What did you tell him.'

'I said that I enjoyed working in the kitchens last year, but I love being around people, and I felt that this would be a job that would suit me and my personality.'

Terry smiled. 'Good answer,' he said.

'He then asked if I got to know any of the Redcoats last season. I did not know where he was going with this, but I said yes anyway. I mentioned that if you worked there during the season, it would only be natural to know people from different departments. It was only then he said that he recognised me from the Stuart.'

Even though Terry wanted more than anything to see Angie get the Redcoat job, his only concern was that she got the job in her own right and not through any Redcoat connections from last year – namely him.

'Did my name come into the conversation at all?' he asked. 'When he said that he recognised me from the Stuart, he remembered the dance off duel you two had towards the end of last season. Remember? You got me involved.'

Terry laughed. 'Yes, I remember.'

'It didn't take him long to work it out about us. He asked me what it was I saw in you? I said your personality. He said "He has one?"'

'Yeh, that sounds like him - cheeky bugger,' said Terry.

Angie continued to say that De Vere concluded as she was going out with Terry, an accomplished ballroom dancer, she must know some herself. Without thinking she immediately said yes, which promoted De Vere to get out of his chair to adopt a ballroom hold when he asked her to demonstrate a Foxtrot.

'So, you danced a Foxtrot with De Vere in his office?' said Terry. 'I certainly did not expect that.'

Neither did I,' replied Angie.

'But you managed it OK.'

Angie smiled. 'Of course! He said that you had trained me well.'

Angie explained that when the interview ended, De Vere said that he would let her know if she was successful or not in a couple of days. Terry would still be staying at her Gran's house, so at least he would there when she would got an official "Yes" or "No".

Two days past and after spending all day waiting for a call from De Vere, there was no response. Three days later there was still no contact from the Butlins Camp. Angie was starting to worry that the whole interview had been a charade and that he had no intention of employing her. Terry was due to go back to Greenock the following day and as far as he was concerned, she had waited long enough.

'De Vere may be many things, but I would never have put him down as someone who is unprofessional and not return a call to a prospective employee.' Terry handed Angie her phone book. 'Call him now.'

'What do I say?'

'Just say that you said that you thought he was going to call back but hadn't heard anything as yet.'

Angie nervously picked up the phone. 'OK! Wish me luck.' Before she started to dial the number, Terry gently placed both hands on either side of Angie's leaning forward and kissing her gently on the lips. 'You don't need any luck.'

Angie carefully dialled the number of the main number at the camp which seemed to ring forever. Eventually she got through to the main switchboard. Taking a deep breath, she was put through to De Vere's office where his abrupt response caught Angie off guard.

'I am in a meeting. This better be important!' he said.

'Mr De Vere, this is Angie Bierman, I had an interview with you the other day for a GD Redcoat….'

'God! Yes Miss Bierman. I was supposed to phone you the other day.'

'Yes,' replied Angie. 'As I had not heard from you I was wondering if you had come to a decision.

As Angie continued to talk on the phone, Terry moved as close as he could to the receiver so he could listen in on the conversation. 'Please accept my apologies for not contacting you when I said I would. Very unprofessional – not like me at all.'

Terry smirked whilst nodding his head. Angie responded by

giving him a dig in the ribs. 'That's OK. 'I just needed to know if you had come to a decision yet?'

De Vere paused. His abrupt behaviour had vanished. 'I was very impressed with you,' said De Vere. 'You wanted to use your own personality to get the position as opposed to relying on other connections to get you the job.'

A broad hopeful grin started to appear on Angie's face as it indicated that De Vere was about to give her the news that she had been hoping for. 'But I am afraid that it is not up to me,' he said. 'I am no longer the Entertainments Manager at Ayr. I am moving to another camp.'

Angie's heart sank. Did she travel all of that distance for nothing? Would she have to go through another interview?'

'So what happens? Do I need to apply again to the person taking over?'

'Can you hold on a minute?' said De Vere.

'Eh sure,' said Angie, who was now convinced that her opportunity had now gone, but she became curious when she could hear De Vere having what appeared to be a conversation in the distance. She could hear him say, "I would, if I were you."

Both Angie and Terry, continued to listen intently as the background noise faded away. Suddenly there was a loud noise as De Vere picked up the phone. 'Hello – are you still there.'

'Yes we're, erm I'm still here,' said Angie, who was by this time was a bag of nerves wondering what was going to happen next. 'My successor is here with me and he has accepted my recommendation that you are offered a contract as a General Duty Redcoat at the Butlins Ayr for the 1983 season. Is that OK with you?'

Angie was struggling to contain her emotions. 'That's

wonderful. Thank you so very much!'

'My pleasure. I will hand the paperwork to my secretary and you can expect a contract in the next few days – I promise.'

'That's wonderful.' Terry walked away from the phone as Angie completed her conversation. He could not contain his delight as he punched his hand in the air 'YES !!!!' he said.

'Do I hear Terry's voice in the distance?' asked De Vere.

'Yes that's him,' she said.

'AFTERNOON TERRY!' shouted De Vere down the phone.

Despite standing well away from the phone, Terry could hear him loud and clear.

'AFTERNOON BOSS!!!'

De Vere started to snigger but soon returned to the matter in hand. 'Congratulations on your appointment and I hope you have an enjoyable season.'

'Thanks again,' said Angie, now shaking with excitement.

'My successor has asked me would you be available for the Venture Weeks at Pwhelli before the start of the season.'

Terry was now back listening to the conversation down the phone. The moment he heard him say that, his eyes opened wide and promptly nodded his head vigorously. 'Of course,' she replied.

'We will add that contract to the main one for the season,' added De Vere It will be a great opportunity for you to get to know some of your colleagues that will also be working at Ayr.'

'Looking forward to it,' said Angie.

'Your boyfriend can come along as well - as long as he behaves himself.'

CHAPTER SIX

As Terry disembarked on to the platform at Penychain train station he had an instant flashback of what had gone through his mind twelve months earlier, the feelings of nerves, anxiousness, not knowing what was around the corner. What he did not know back then, was that, this was the beginning of a journey where his life would begin to change.

This time, the emotions had moved to feelings of great excitement, especially as he was not making this journey on his own. Was his life going to change again? He wasn't going to look that far ahead.

He loved his spell working in Wales last year, and having gone through months of trying to find regular work, he was back to where his new life had started. For a few seconds he reacquainted himself with the surroundings, before turning to help a smiling Angie and her case off the train.

Apart from a day visit to the Filey camp, near Scarborough, during a touring holiday with her family, (she was only nine at the time; not long enough to make a lasting impression) Ayr was the only Butlins camp Angie had ever been to.

This was also Angie's first ever visit to Wales, so when she got off the train she was not in the mood for moving off the platform right away. She just stood there wanting to take in some of the picturesque Welsh scenery, and the colourful setting of the camp in the distance, before actually making any further move. 'It is absolutely beautiful,' she said.

'Isn't it just,' replied Terry. 'And this is going to be our home and workplace for the next month.'

Terry picked up his bag and Angie hers; he then stretched out his free hand. 'Shall we check in?'

'Absolutely!' replied a very excited Angie. Holding onto Angie's hand, he led her through the pathway leading from the station platform on to the road that connected both sections of the Pwhelli Camp. As there was no one else around, they took their time heading downhill to the main Reception; as Terry remembered, the check in place for arriving members of Venture Week staff.

Terry held open the door as Angie walked into the building. He closed the door behind him and was delighted to see a familiar face standing behind the desk in the shape of Bill Drummond; back for his second season as an assistant entertainments manager at Pwhelli.

'God! Not you again,' laughed Bill.

Terry smiled: 'Funny, I was thinking the same thing.' Terry warmly shook Bill's hand. 'Good to see you again sir.'

'And you mate.' Bill turned his attention to Angie, checking the list on his desk. 'Are you Miss Angie Bierman?'

Angie smiled. 'I am indeed'

'Welcome to Pwhelli Venture Weeks,' said Bill, shaking Angie's hand and proceeded to head to the back of the desk to retrieve two sets of keys and paperwork. 'I hope you will enjoy your time down here.'

'I'm sure I will. I have heard so much about it.'

'Oh yes. Who from?'

'From Terry.'

It did not take Bill long to work it out. 'Right. Are you two an item?'

'Admit it. You guessed!' said Terry.

Bill grinned. 'You know I thought there was something different about you Terry. That is one thing you'll find about me Angie, as a manager I am always on the money.'

Terry sniggered. 'Stop laughing you!' said Bill, he handed both of them sets of chalet keys, security passes, name badges along with copies of their contract for 1983 venture weeks. 'There will be no snogging or slow dances during working hours OK?'

'Terry smiled nodding his head. 'Understood Boss!'

'Right you two, sign here to confirm that you have received your documents and keys. Terry, you will be joining the team teaching fencing during your stay with us. Same place as last time.'

Terry grinned, as it was his most enjoyable part of his venture weeks. 'Excellent!'

'I thought you would like that, and Angie, looking at your details, the Boss has decided to put you on Badminton.'

'Right!' said Angie, looking slightly puzzled. She whispered to Terry. 'Where about is that?'

'Same building as the fencing?' said Terry. Bill nodded. 'Even better.'

'Meeting in the Empire tomorrow morning, 9.00am. Don't be late. I will let you settle in to your chalets. No doubt I will see you two later this evening in the bar along with the rest of your colleagues.'

Terry and Angie picked up their cases and headed towards the exit. 'Great! Thanks Bill. Will see you later.'

There was no rush for them walking back to their chalets as they headed along the road of what was a deserted camp. It was a lot bigger than Ayr that was for sure.

'I wonder what the staff chalets will be like, 'said Angie.

'Probably no different from ours,' said Terry.

'Did you not stay there last year?'

'We don't stay in staff chalets during Venture Weeks,' said Terry. 'Look at your chalet key.'

'G64. Coloured key hob. We are in one of the Guest Chalets?'

'Yep. One of the "Full Board" ones at the end of the road.'

It then dawned on Terry to check his own chalet key which resulted in a broad grin appeared on his face. 'G65. I am next door.'

Angie smiled and had a glint her eye. 'We shall see about that?'

Arriving at their accommodation, they simultaneously opened the doors and Terry simply dumped his case in to his chalet. He was more interested in seeing Angie's reaction as she looked inside hers. It was the total opposite of the chalet she lived in at Ayr twelve months earlier.

She took one step inside checking out the bathroom, the various bits of furniture, eventually pushing her hands down on the mattress, of what appeared to be a comfortable double bed – compared to the Ayr staff chalets, this was pure unadulterated luxury. She turned to see Terry standing grinning at the front door.

'What do you think,' he asked.

'Brilliant! And I love this double bed.'

'My chalet is exactly the same.'

Since the end of the 1982 season they had been alternating their "living arrangements" under supervised conditions between Falkirk and Greenock, they were now excited about the prospect of actually getting the chance to "live together" again, in a more comfortable private setting. Angie had checked her chalet, placing some of her clothes away before checking out Terry's room, which was as he said, exactly the same.

'There are a couple of hours before the bar opens, so we've got some time to kill,' he said. 'Any suggestions?'

Angie grinned as she locked the door of her chalet, giving Terry a long and lingering kiss. She pushed open the door to his.

'Just one. Get in!'

Two hours later, they emerged from Terry's chalet, making the most of the quiet before the impending madhouse the following day when the school children arrive. They walked along the chalet lines with their arms around each other, instead of heading along the main road to the Neptune Bar, they took a slight diversion across the sports fields toward a low tunnel which ran under the train track.

'That's the way to the staff canteen,' he said

Angie giggled. 'You are winding me up.'

'No honest! Go under that tunnel, out the other side and you are there. Takes minutes. The only other way is crossing that bridge we came over which is a lot longer. You come out of the sports centre straight across this field, under the tunnel and there you are. Just make sure you keep your head down, and there are no trains coming.'

Angie started to look towards the Sport Centre, a familiar venue for Terry from last year. He led her back across the pitch towards the main entrance. 'There you are,' he said.

'That is where I will be working? It's certainly big enough.'

'They have the Badminton, Trampolining and Sword Fencing. There are concrete walls that separate them. So, I will only be able to see you from a distance.'

'I won't get to see you doing your "D'Artagnan" bit, that's a shame.'

Terry laughed. 'We still have four weeks, you never know.'

Terry looked at Angie as she continued to visualise what it would be like during the next few weeks. He could see it in her eyes that she was going through similar emotions to what he had gone through twelve months earlier.

'You nervous about starting?' asked Terry.

'I am a bit,' she replied. 'I don't want to mess it up.'

Terry put his arms around her giving a loving hug. 'You will be brilliant. You will be working with school children who want to have a great time, and the people here will be great as well.'

'Do you know who is going to be working here?' she asked.

'No idea. There might be some people from last season, but everyone gels together really quick, which is a perfect way to get ready for the season at Ayr. I found that out last year.'

Angie smiled. 'There is one problem. I don't play Badminton.'

'You won't be the first person to say that,' replied Terry. 'There will be someone that knows how to do it. You just learn from them, and make sure the kids enjoy themselves. So, you don't have to coach them too much. Just help them have fun.'

'I was hoping to get on trampolining. I did that a lot at school,' she added.

'Well you might still get to do it. Last year I started on

Archery, but I finished my time here doing fencing. I learned that in school.'

They continued their walk in the direction of the indoor swimming pool, which was above the bar and the TV lounge where most of the staff would be gathering. They stopped briefly at the boating pond, watching the ducks as they swam near the island in the centre.

Apart from the early meeting, there would be no work the next day for most of them, as the kids would be arriving; however, there would be a chance to meet up with the young guests at a "getting to know each other disco in the Princess Ballroom.

Finally, they arrived at the quiet lounge entrance, which was directly below the swimming pool and next to the Neptune Bar. Terry opened the door for Angie as they went into the building.

It appeared to exactly as it was last year, an eerie silence as they stood in the lounge, but as they walked toward the open door of the bar located at the back, the sound of chatter and laughter became louder. When they walked into the venue there was an immediate cheer from one table in the centre, where both Terry and Angie grinned having recognised some of the faces.

'TERRY!!!!!, said a number of voices, coming from the centre of the bar. Right in the centre was thirty two year old Deke Campbell, a familiar larger than life figure from Stirling. Standing at six foot two and 20 stone, he worked as a barman in the Stuart Ballroom during the 1982 season at Ayr. He was friends with many staff members from the various departments, including Terry and Angie.

Along with an extrovert personality, Deke, loved to sing. Away from the camp, he earned money performing in pubs and clubs displaying his vocal talents across the country. Throughout the 1982 season, he was a favourite in the staff bar, especially during talent nights.

On a visit to Ayr on his day off, he caught the attention of the then entertainment boss, Ron De Vere, who heard him sing in a pub alongside other Redcoats also on their day off, he was more than an equal. On hearing him, De Vere took him to one side and insisted that the moment a job became available, he would join his department as a Redcoat.

However, when De Vere moved on to his new post, Deke had thought that the opportunity had passed him by, but it emerged that Angie was not the only recommendation he had made to his successor who should be part of the 1983 Entertainments Team.

'Ladies and Gentlemen, the dancer is amongst us once again. And he has not come alone. Angie!!!!!. What is a lovely lady like you still doing with an ugly sod like him, when you could have a fine figure of a man like me.' This automatically triggered laughter from around the table, which generated a puzzled expression on Dekes face, 'what's so funny?' Cue even more laughter.

'Nice of you to say so,' said Angie, but I don't go for men with a fuller figure.' Deke gave out a slight cough, leant back slightly. 'Are you Miss Beirman trying to tell me I am portly?'

Angie was in the company of mostly strangers, but with Deke, she was starting to feel more relaxed. 'Would I ever say such a thing,' she replied.

The laughter continued, but Deke could take it as much as he gave it out and by then end he was laughing along with the rest of them. He pulled out a couple of spare seats. 'Sit yourself down you two. What are you drinking?' Terry

looked Angie. 'Coke for me,' she said. 'Make that two.'
Deke looked puzzled. 'When you going to start living it up and have a real drink.'

'Do they sell Irn Bru down here, said Terry.

'You know what I mean. Right, Coke it is this time. I bet you will be drinking something else by the end of the season.' Deke got off from his seat and returned minutes later with two full glasses of coke with ice.

Following a series of introductions around the table, Terry and Angie soon started to feel part of the team. Once everything had settled, Terry was wanting to find out what his old pal had been doing since last season and what exactly was he doing in Venture Weeks.

'So, you back at Ayr again,' asked Terry.

'Better than that my friend. No more working behind the bar for me. I am in Reds this year.'

Terry leant back and started to eye Deke up and down. 'What are you looking at.'

'I am just wondering if they have uniforms in your size.'

'Of course they have them in "Real Man" size.' Cue more laughter from around the table. 'See they are bloody laughing again.'

Deke decided to break from the joviality as he picked up his glass and smiled. 'Well I think that this is a good time to say. We are going to have a great few weeks here. And here's to a great season. Cheers everybody!'

Everyone around the group of tables simultaneously picked up their glasses and responded to the toast in unison. 'A great season!'

Amongst the other newcomers sitting around the table was 28 year old, Jonty O'Hara, a former nightclub bouncer, who'd had more than regular run-ins with the law. When he appeared in Court two years earlier on another assault charge, he sat in an empty police cell staring at damp concrete walls, and decided there and then that he did not want this life anymore.

He became more involved in sports, rediscovering his school boy love of Rugby, and with his powerful frame, standing at 6 foot, made an immediate impression as a Full Back for his local club. However, it was a bronze medallion lifeguard qualification that was set to change his life when it landed him the post as a lifeguard at Ayr.

He was amongst the new faces at Pwhelli, revelling in his new life, developing a strong connection with Deke. Sitting amongst the rest of the occupants, they were the gentle, jovial, giants of the group. They shared the same sense of humour, something that Jonty had forgotten about during his teenage years.

Terry knew from previous experience that they did not always match people's skills to the appropriate tasks during the venture weeks, and he was intrigued to see what the management had in store for Deke and Jonty. 'So, you guys got your work detail sorted for this weekend,' he said. Deke almost choked on his beer.

'Go on! Let's see if you can work it out.'

Angie looked Deke up and down. 'I would say a Keep-Fit Instructor,' she said.

'Thank You Miss Beirman,' he sarcastically replied. 'Jonty plays Rugby and is doing Arts and Crafts, and the numpty has me down for Trampoline.'

Angie tried her best not to laugh, but the rest of the table were not has restrained, as it was the first time they'd heard him talk about it. 'I will be doing Badminton,' said Angie. 'I will be looking forward to seeing you in action'. The sniggers continued. 'That's right laugh you buggers,' and laugh they did. By then the volume continued to rise. 'The man's an idiot. Who the hell is he anyway.'

One of the ladies in the group put down her drink and smiled. 'He is my husband.'

Deke for a brief second was lost for words. 'And a fine figure of a man he his too. A fine taste in clothes for a manager.'

When Bill walked into the bar, Deke was the first to stand up and give him a round of applause. He knew that there was a time and place for being a crawler. This was as good a time as any. It made great viewing for everyone else.

The first evening at the bar was a success. They still had not started work, but the team bonding was already there. Terry and Angie left the others to have one more drink before closing time, and they headed back towards their chalet alone. There was an eerie silence as they walked along the main road of the camp, and Angie held on tightly to Terry. They would not be able to do that when the children arrived.

'I am more than happy to be back, 'she said. 'but I hoped that we would have found steady jobs by now.'

'I thought the same, but let's be positive,' insisted Terry. We are working now, in a great job and working together. Even better, we don't have to worry about travelling back and forwards to each other every couple of weeks. We should focus on that'

'Yeh. I suppose you are right. So, what happens tomorrow?'

'Well the kids arrive and there is the disco at night. So, if you fancy it, we can go into Pwhelli, after breakfast, oh and there is the meeting first, I forgot about that.'

Minutes later, they were back standing outside the door

of Terry's chalet. 'That is tomorrow, but we still have the night ahead of us,' said Angie, who placed her hands on Terry's face pulling her towards him, kissing him long and tenderly.

Terry smiled. 'Well what do you think. Your place or mine.' Angie took Terry's key out of his hands and opened the door. 'Does that answer your question?'

CHAPTER SEVEN

It was the first Saturday of the 1983 Venture Weeks; the Weather Gods were smiling. The actual programme did not officially start till the next day; however, the staff could not totally relax. Their presence was required at the first team meeting after breakfast; after that, the rest of the day was theirs. For some, it was a trip to the *Slate Mines*, or enjoying the hospitality offered by the *Ffestiniog Railway*.

For the rest, it was a trip to Pwllheli, in particular the *Black Lion* Pub, located at the start of the main road into town. It was a favorite haunt for many Butlins employees during their days off, even for Terry last year, despite not being a drinker.

The staff meeting was held at the camp's Empire Theatre where they were given clear instructions by the management on what was expected during their stay, and delivering the professional standards expected of Butlins staff. This applied to not just on site, but whenever they were away from the camp. So, no one could say that they had not been warned.

Despite having the day off, they were "encouraged" to make an appearance in the Princess Ballroom later that evening with the kids at a "get to know" you disco. There was also an opportunity for the teachers to get to know the staff in the more "adult" setting of the Neptune Bar later that night.

With the meeting finished, Terry and Angie decided to make their own way into town, meeting up with the rest of their colleagues at the pub later in the day.

Waiting for the bus outside the main entrance, they passed the time watching the numerous coaches of excited children arrive; some of them pressing their faces at the window waving to them as they passed through the gate.

After ten minutes of constantly waving back at the arriving coaches, the bus to <u>Pwllheli</u> finally arrived. It was a short journey, which ended with them getting off at the Black Lion. As they disembarked, Angie squeezed Terry's hand. 'Well you know this place better than I do. Where do we go now?'

Terry did not know Pwllheli all that well, but past experience prompted him to direct her down a curved road cutting in between two sets of houses, which lead all the way to the main square, with its outdoor and indoor markets as well as the numerous souvenir shops and cafes. Plenty to keep a self-confessed shopaholic like Angie satisfied for the next few hours. But not before grabbing some ice creams and head down to the beach, to sample the delights of the town's coastline.

As they sat on a rock, basking in the sunshine, all they could think off was the upcoming weeks and the summer season. Angie never thought for one minute she would get to work alongside Terry as a Redcoat, but was determined to make the most of it, starting with a four weeks preseason in Wales.

Terry could relate to Angie's feelings of doubt as he went through the same emotions the previous year. They finished their ice creams but remained seated, watching the hive of activity around the shoreline and harbour area acknowledging some familiar faces from camp, who, like them were using the day off to become acquainted with the town. 'So, what do you think of Pwllheli,' asked Terry.

'It's lovely,' said Angie. 'I wouldn't mind coming back here as a holidaymaker.'

'I see no reason why not. We can make this our first holiday once we get permanent jobs.'

'We might have to wait a long time for that happening then,' she replied. 'We didn't come close during the last few months.'

Terry smiled and put his arm around her. 'It will happen,' he said. 'We just need to think about what is happening now. I didn't think that I was going to come back to Butlins either, but now I am here, I am so glad I did. Especially as I am here with you.'

Angie smiled as she leant forward and kissed Terry. 'You know how to say the right things,' she said. 'I couldn't do it with anyone else.'

They had spent enough time on the beach for today. It was time to head back up towards the square where they started and into what was a busy market. Terry found out during the visit to Angie's parents in Durham, how much she liked to shop even though she hardly spent money.

If there was a down side to the visit, that was it.

His Dad would often remind him, going round the shops with your "other half" was a test for any relationship; the trick was to just smile and look interested now and again. However, with the various market stalls, this was nothing like the conventional shopping experience. There was no need for pretence on this occasion. Terry was actually enjoying himself. After a couple of hours checking out all the stalls and neighbouring shops, they were starting to think about lunch.

Angie fancied lunch in an old-fashioned teahouse, in a side road just up from the square. The scones and cakes on display were just too good to resist. Sitting down to have afternoon tea, they realised that they were not just the youngest of the customers there, but they were the only ones speaking English. There were a couple of occupied tables where the other diners were conversing in Welsh, occasionally glancing in Terry and Angie's direction. They did not understand a word being said; but listened intently.

'I could listen to them all day,' said Angie. Terry took a sip of his tea. 'So could I,' he smiled. 'I love the sound of the Welsh Language. I wonder if they are talking about us.' Angie sniggered. 'I wouldn't mind learning some of it, while we are here.'

On finishing their lunch, they were now starting to think about joining the others at the Black Lion. Instead of retracing their steps, Terry and Angie headed towards a road at the top of the square that would take them full circle back to where they first started.

As it was the High Street, they would be passing more shops on route. Having enjoyed the markets, Terry had enough retail therapy for one day. Surprisingly so did Angie. However, she was making mental notes for the next time they went into town.

But they could not resist the urge to nip into a souvenir

shop on one of the street corners. Like any tourist business, this retail outlet promoted all that was good about their town, the Welsh Culture, a selection of souvenirs from their holiday camp neighbours plus their own special "Butlins" souvenirs located near the main entrance.

Like a number of the Butlins camps, the Pwllheli base was once a training ground for military personnel during the second world war, and when converted into holiday camps, the company was tagged with a POW camp image, linking it with a popular TV Drama from the 1970's, a label that the shop picked up with some special badges.

'Butlitz Holiday Camp Escape Committee.' Terry grinned. 'I have got to get me a few of them. I never noticed them before.' Terry continued to inspect the rest of the shop display. 'There is also a "Teach Yourself Welsh Phrase Book" here.'

'I am definitely having that,' said Angie.

Leaving the shop, they continued along the road walking 500 yards practising basic Welsh phrases, stopping at the main door of the Black Lion. 'Let's not stay here too long,' said Terry. 'We can get some time back at the camp before the disco tonight.'

'Sounds good,' replied Angie. 'It's a shame I can't get any slow dances off you tonight.'

Terry smiled and winked at Angie. 'You can have many as you want back at the chalet later.'

A wide smile beamed across Angie's face. 'I'll hold you to that.'

Terry held the door open for Angie as they both walked into the bar, where there were already many Butlins staff enjoying the hospitality. Some were drinking at the bar, a few of them were hanging around the pool table, and there were sounds of raucous laughter coming from a group at the far corner, which was occasionally interrupted by burst of community singing, with Deke and Jonty's voice heard above the rest of them. The punters didn't seem to mind, as a lot of them were joining in too.

Their appearance was met with a welcome cheer by the group, who beckoned them over to join them. Terry suggested that Angie grabbed a couple of spare seats and he would get the drinks in.

Team work was vital when it came to working at Butlins, so Terry looked on this as an ideal opportunity for Angie to get to know some of her co-workers on her own. Minutes later, he came back with the drinks, sitting down beside her and across from Deke.

'So where have you been all day,' said Deke.

'Seeing what the shops of Pwllheli have to offer,' replied Terry.

'What did you buy me.'

'Nowt. What did you have in mind.'

'I quite like the look of that badge you are wearing. Butlitz Escape Committee. That is definitely me and Jonty. Where did you get it from?

'There is a souvenir shop at start of the High Street, just on the corner, you can't miss it.'

'Look it is only four o clock, is the place still open?' asked Jonty.

'Should be,' said Terry. 'About five minutes' from here. Go past the street that cuts between those houses and it is the first shop on the corner. There were some badges on the display at the front door when we were there about half an hour ago.'

Jonty took a swig of what remained of his pint of lager. 'I'll get us some badges, Brother?'

'That sounds an excellent idea Brother,' replied Deke.

'I will be back in five minutes. Keep an eye on my seat for me.'

'I don't know about eye,' said Deke. Will my right leg do?'

Jonty pulled on his jacket and returned twenty minutes later with a Butlitz badge on his lapel, as well as carrying a small bag containing another ten. He opened the bag and handed it over to Deke. 'Pick one,' he said.

'I only wanted one,' replied Deke.

'Terry and Angie already have theirs, so I persuaded him to sell me a dozen with a discount. I said that we would bring him regular business.' Jonty promptly gave out the others to remaining occupants around the table, who graciously accepted his gift.'

'So you have a talent for buying stuff at bargain prices?' said Deke

'I love to haggle,' said Jonty. 'I used to help my Uncle out with his stall on the markets when I was a kid. '

'There's a Fiver, see how many pints you can get out of that.'

When Angie decided that this was a convenient time to visit the Ladies, this was a perfect moment for Deke to have a more serious discussion with Terry. As he got to know them both whilst working in the Stuart Ballroom Bar last season, he could see their romance blossom. And having met up again this year, he was delighted to see that they were still together.

'So how has it been with you two since the end of the season,' he said.

'We have had our challenges,' said Terry, 'travelling to see each other every couple of weeks, but we are determined to make this work, and I am still the luckiest guy in the world.'

'Excellent! I could see the change in you when you started going out together. You definitely hit the jackpot with her. You must tell me your secret.'

Terry smirked. 'I am trying to work that one out myself.'

Deke raised his glass. 'Whatever you two have, long may it continue.'

'I will drink to that,' said Terry.

'Well you would if you had a decent drink,' replied Deke. 'We are going to have to educate you this year.

'I am happy as I am thank you very much.'

'Well we still have the full season ahead of us, you never know.'

Angie was back from the Ladies and resumed her seat beside Terry and Deke. 'Ah the lady has returned. Just per chance did you hear us when you were in the Ladies.'

'No I didn't,' said Angie.

'Well we heard you.'

'I have not heard that line in a while,' said Terry.

'The old ones are the best eh,' said Angie.

Deke huffed and puffed. 'I resemble that remark,' he said. 'I am not old. I am only twenty-seven.' This response generated laughter from around the table. 'I think you are about five years out,' said Terry.

'I know on my birth certificate it says thirty-two, but in my head, I am always twenty seven.'

'Well it's the thought that counts,' said Angie.

'Thank you Miss Beirman.'

Angie smiled. 'My pleasure.'

Terry and Angie stayed with the group for another two hours before deciding to head back to camp. There was a still a while before the evening disco and they wanted to freshen up before heading over.

Deke giggled. 'Is that all you are going back early for.'

Terry laughed. 'Wash your mind out you.'

'WE KNOW WHAT YOU'RE DOING, WE KNOW WHAT YOUR DOING!' sang Deke, prompting other members of the group to join in.

Terry laughed as he and Angie put on their coats heading for the exit. 'We shall see you lot back at base.'

'See you later guys,' shouted the various members of the group. 'Missing you already,' said Deke.

Now they were back outside, their timing could not be better as they ran across the street to catch the approaching bus back to the camp.

'Are you ready for work now?' asked Terry.

'I think so, 'said Angie. 'The people here are great. I have just got to figure out how to teach children a sport that I have never done before.'

'Get there about half an hour early, have a few practise swings before the little angels arrive. You will be surprised how quickly you pick things up. I had to, doing the trampoline last year.'

'You doing the trampoline,' said Angie, 'now that I would like to have seen.'

'Not this time. Really looking forward to doing the sword fencing again. I hope it's the same guys as last year. I got on well with them. Whenever you have a lunchbreak free I will give you some private lessons.'

The bus stopped just outside the main gate of the camp. After showing their passes to the security guard, they walked down towards the main reception where there was a lot more activity compared to the day before.

The children who arrived early were already walking around the venues with their programmes and maps, familiarising themselves with their new surroundings. As they continued to check out the facilities, they were oblivious to the sight of Terry and Angie heading in the opposite direction back towards their own chalets.

Angie opened the door of her chalet, to pick up a change of clothes and toiletries. She still left her luggage in there, just in case of spot checks by the security guards. However, she placed her items into a spare drawer in Terry's chalet, which was now their unofficial accommodation during their stay in Pwllheli.

It was not unusual for staff members to make their own sleeping arrangements as long as they remained discreet about it. It was something that Terry and Angie had learned during the latter stages of their stay at Ayr last year.

For the next hour, all they wanted to do was draw the curtains and crash out on the bed, before heading over to the staff canteen for the evening meal, not forgetting to put their name badges on. With all the staff and first guests now arrived, they were officially on duty and would have been in trouble if they didn't.

As they sat down to eat, they were soon joined by Deke, Jonty and a few other members of staff who arrived straight from the Black Lion. When they finished, it was now time for their first official duty as resident staff, the first disco of the week at the Princess Ballroom.

In charge of the record decks was first year Redcoat, 23 year old Jason from Swansea, who prior to working for Butlins, was presenting a weekend show on local radio. He was the complete opposite of Si, the Redcoat DJ from Ayr last year in terms of personality, but he did possess a similar record collection, packed with all of the chart hits and party dances.

As far as his radio bosses were concerned, there was more than happy with the level of work in the studio. However, they thought that it would be good for his future development to take a break from broadcasting and gain valuable people skills working the season at Pwllheli.

When it came to playing music, Jason certainly knew his stuff, as the disco was in full swing when Terry and Angie walked in. The floor was packed with children dancing away on the floor with a number of staff joining in, as well as a number of them watching the action from the side of the stage. They went across to join the others; however their progress was halted by a couple of young lads.

'Hey Mister, did we see you at the gate this morning?' asked one.

'You probably did,' he replied.

'What's your name.'

'I'm Terry and this is Angie'

'Are you his girlfriend? 'Asked his friend

'Go to the top of the class, 'said Angie

Terry smiled. 'Yeh! So hands off!' He made a series of joke eye pointing gestures to the young men who responded in kind. They had connected with some of the young guests and this was only the first evening.

They were about to sit down at the side of the stage when the music changed to 'Papa's Got a Brand New Pig Bag.' A favourite amongst the party dance records with the Ayr Reds last year. 'Recognise this one Angie?'

'This is where we show them how to do a Slosh?' she asked. 'Definitely!'

Terry and Angie immediately moved to a free space in the centre of the ballroom doing the fast paced version of the Slosh and were immediately joined by other members of staff and children.

The 1983 Butlins Pwllheli Venture Weeks was up and running.

CHAPTER EIGHT

They had only been days in to the start of Kids Venture weeks, and it felt like Terry had never left. He was working in the sports centre alongside sword fencing coaches, Freddie Jones, Geoff Wilson and Dave Bryant, teaching the little angels the basic rudiments of sword fencing.

Across the other side of the building, Terry could easily see Angie enjoying herself with other staff members, taking the badminton sessions despite admitting earlier she had never played it. In way, it was like being back at Ayr; both of them doing their respective tasks and making the most of what time they had together.

The only difference was, Terry and Angie were working as part of the same team now. Their real quality time together, would be just before closing time with a quiet romantic stroll back to the chalet lines, via the boating pond.

It was Friday night and they had completed their first working week together. As usual, they took their walk alongside the boating pond, stopping half way, sitting down on a small wall at the water's edge.

Angie held on to Terry's arm, looking around at the parts of the camp lighting up the night sky, with her eyes eventually drawn towards the moon rays shimmering on the water of the boating pond. 'It's a beautiful camp isn't it?' said Terry.

'It certainly is,' she said, 'but Ayr is still my favourite. I love working there, plus ending the night looking out of the window of the Stuart Ballroom, and seeing the sunset over Arran, I would miss that. You certainly look glad to be here.'

Terry smirked. 'It is very easy to fall in love with a place like this.' he said 'I keep remembering what it was like before, I was so nervous, not knowing what to expect, but not this year. It's much better.'

'Why's that,' replied Angie.

Terry gazed lovingly into Angie's eyes, 'It's simple" he said, 'I'm more confident and like I said to you before, I'm with you."

Angie smiled, she leant forward and kissed Terry. They could not do it during the day, but there was no one around now, the kids were in their beds and the teachers were still in the bar. They were sitting there enjoying the summer night air, there was no rush to go back to the chalet just yet.

'You look as if you have settled in quickly yourself,' said Terry.

'It has been great working with Natalie and Tracey. Tracey was here last year. You came up in conversation a few times.'

Terry looked puzzled, trying to remember the name: 'Eh really?'

'You worked together at the trampolining. She asked me if you can teach her how to Jive again as she has forgotten.'

Soon as Angie mentioned Jive, Terry immediately

remembered Tracey, who along with Kim played a major part in him settling into the job the previous year, especially coaching children on something that he had little knowledge of himself.

Terry laughed: 'I am sure that can be arranged.'

Angie smiled: 'You just save the Waltzes for me.'

'That goes without saying,' insisted Terry. 'So, can you play badminton properly now.'

'I can hit, what do you call that thing, the shuttlecock?

'Terry sniggered. 'That is good enough for me,' she said.

'It has been great fun. Today we had those kids that we met in the Ballroom on the first night.'

'Ah the ones that were chatting you up,' replied Terry.

'They kept asking me if I still had a boyfriend. I said that he was at the other side of the hall with a sword in his hand, and not afraid to use it.'

Terry laughed. 'I wondered why they were so well behaved when they came over to us.'

It was nearly closing time at the bar, so they decided to get up and continue their walk towards the chalet. 'What do you fancy doing after the meeting tomorrow,' asked Angie

'Eh, let's go back to Pwhelli, maybe go to the pictures.'

'I wonder if there is anything decent on?'

Terry smiled: 'If that is your way of asking if they are screening "An Officer and a Gentleman," then I am afraid not.'

Angie sighed: 'Oh what a shame. Beside why would I want Richard Gere when I have you.'

Terry smiled: 'Excellent answer.'

Minutes later they had reached their chalet line, well away from the main road of the camp, out of the view of prying eyes. Terry grabbed hold of Angie's hand as he walked down towards the front door of his chalet.

'Well tomorrow is sorted, but we still have the rest of the night.' There was as sparkle in Angie's eyes. She grinned as she took Terry's chalet keys and opened the door. 'I was thinking the same thing. Get in!'

The light of a new day crept through the letter box, shining on to the double bed, where Angie and Terry, lying under the covers were slowly waking up. They had come through the first seven days of Venture Weeks and this was another official rest day; neither of them were in the mood for shifting. However, they did not have the full day to themselves as there was a Saturday meeting to deal with first. Terry and Angie had one last embrace. 'Ok come on then, ladies first for the bathroom.'

Angie smiled. 'Forever the gentleman.'

She slowly got out of bed and headed towards the bathroom. Terry could not take his eyes off her as she walked towards the bathroom door. After all of the travelling back and forward the previous months they were starting to live like a proper couple, living under their own rules.

Ten minutes later, Angie was finished. 'All yours,' she said. Terry dived out of the bed giving Angie a quick peck on the cheek as he went into to get washed and shaved. As usual, his enthusiasm to get ready meant he rushed shaving, resulting in him spending the next couple of minutes stemming the blood flow on his chin.

The tried and tested wet pieces of toilet paper on the face were not working, so as he was keen to get into town, he had to resort to more painful methods, slapping on the *Hai Karate* aftershave on to his open cuts.

'OWW.'

'What's the matter,' said Angie from behind the bathroom

door.

'I really need a decent razor blade, 'said Terry.

'Or a less potent bottle of aftershave.'

'Thank you my love.'

My pleasure sweetheart.'

They waited until the chalet lines were clear of children before heading towards the back end of the camp, dealing with the low level tunnel link to the canteen. Both stuck to a light breakfast and after negotiating the tunnel for a second time, they headed towards the Empire Theatre.

All of the entertainment staff had assembled inside the theatre's auditorium for their meeting, where the agenda would focus on feedback from the bosses on the past seven days; for the first one, the report was impressive

One of the major surprises was Deke and how he came through the first week coaching trampolining. When he got the Venture Weeks job, the bosses looked upon the appointment as a bit of a gamble. His extrovert personality and his ability to connect with people was his strength, that part was never an issue. However, they had to place him somewhere, and trampoline was deemed the best option, as long as he stayed clear of giving a demonstration; there was uncertainty as to whether the trampoline could cope with his 20 stone bulk.

So there was no need for them try him on anything else. They could see that he was enjoying himself, and the children enjoyed being taught by him. He was not always a natural coach but he was a natural comic talent.

Also with someone like Jonty, who had originally come from a background of ejecting trouble makers from clubs and discos, here he was discovering a new discipline of arts and crafts, as well as new people skills in teaching the children. He had a big and powerful physique, but to the young guests, he was a gentle giant, and a very popular character with both children and staff. When in Deke's company, they were a comic "tour de force", especially during the evening discos when they tried to join in with the various party dances; and usually failing spectacularly.

'A perfect start. Well done everyone, said AEM Bill Drummond. 'Now we would not want to disrupt a set up that appears to be working, we will however make some changes for this coming week just to freshen things up.' This was no surprise to Terry as he had been swapped about during the opening week last year before spending the rest of his time doing sword fencing. He was not going anywhere, but Angie was. Thankfully not too far.

Angie loved trampolining at school, and could not resist the urge to have a few practise sessions during some of the tea breaks. Those who had been coaching trampoline, as well as Terry, often watched in admiration, as it became apparent she had not lost any of her old skills. It appeared that the news had reached the management, and so she was set to join the trampoline team on the other side of the wall for the rest of her time in Pwhelli, this was what she had been hoping for. Terry was delighted as well.

The group bonding amongst staff was evident at the meeting. So Bill decided this would also be a good time to set them a new challenge, with the re-introduction of a scheme that was familiar to returning Pwhelli Redcoats. He pulled out of his pocket a long piece of string where hanging at the end was a squeaky pink elephant, resulting in a groan from some staff members.

The idea was that you nominated a member of staff that did an embarrassing and idiotic thing the week before, which meant they had to wear this elephant around their neck all week. If another member of staff saw them not wearing it during that time, they then had to buy that person a drink.

For children it would be a subject of curiosity, but other members of staff were not allowed to divulge the reason why they had to wear the pink elephant. Teachers could try and guess why they were wearing the object around their necks, but if they got it wrong then they would have to buy that member of staff a drink. The fact that the embarrassing incident happened during the week that they were not at the camp, the idea was that they would never get the right answer.

When Bill officially opened the nominations for who would be the first recipient, Deke was the first to stand up by mentioning Julie Meadan, a first year Redcoat who had been working with Angie on the badminton, and was a friend of Clacton Redcoat, Debbie who was coaching the trampoline.

If Deke had demonstrated his trampolining exploits, then he would have been a sure fire candidate for the first "Pink Elephant" accolade. However Julie was the clear favourite.

One day, during a tea break, she had decided, to take a short cut to meet her friend, jumping over the concrete partition, landing on one of the fire extinguishers and setting it off, resulting in suds spewing out from the back of the seated area.

As there were no other nominations, Bill walked towards Julie hanging the pink elephant around her neck resulting in laughter and rounds of applause from her colleagues. She smiled through gritted teeth, thanking Deke for his nomination in her "acceptance" speech.

She was awarded special dispensation not to wear it away from the camp, but whenever she was on site, she had to stick to the rules. The bonus was that even though she was the going to be the victim of gentle ribbing from the children, she would at least come away with some free drinks from the teachers.

The meeting was brought to a close and whilst Julie returned to her chalet to deposit her "prize," many of the staff headed to the train station, others jumped into taxis whereas in the previous week, Terry and Angie headed to the main gate to take the bus into town, acknowledging the arriving punters for the new week.

Their bus finally arrived; first stop was lunch at their now favourite tea shop, and hopefully pick up some Welsh phrases along the way. Following that was a trip to the Cinema, along with a short stay at the Black Lion before returning to camp for the first evening disco of the week.

At the end of the night, Terry and Angie, took their usual walk alongside the boating pond sitting at the water's edge. Angie had really enjoyed her first week teaching badminton but was now thrilled at the idea of being paid to teach something that she loved doing.

'Can't wait to get started,' she said.

'I knew that you liked the trampoline, but I didn't know you were that good. You are going to be brilliant,' said Terry. 'It makes a big difference teaching someone and you know what you are talking about. Just don't let Deke influence you in any way.'

Angie smiled: 'I'll be out of his target range, don't you worry.'

Working at Pwhelli was everything they expected and more. They were together, working alongside some fabulous people, and in an environment that they had both felt was becoming a second home. And, ever since they arrived at the camp, they had not had a single drop of rain. It was perfect summer weather.

They both knew that working at the Venture Weeks was a short-term arrangement, and they were determined to enjoy every second of it, working, as well as spending quality time together.

It was not long ago they were trying to exist in the real world and build their relationship from outside the holiday camp. It was anything but easy. There were some special moments, but testing times as well. They had come through a lot in such a short time, still smiling, feeling stronger as a couple, which showed how determined they were to build on their relationship.

They had never entertained the idea of returning to work at a Butlins camp, but they were here, and, during the coming months they had a chance to focus on themselves again, while having fun.   Despite loving their new surroundings, the new summer season was only a few weeks away, and Terry was starting to recognise the signs of self-doubt going through Angie's mind.

He had expected it to happen, and did his very best to reassure her.   Angie knew that he would be there for her, and, she was excited about them working together.   She had come through a very nerve wracking interview, but she knew that she still had to deliver.

'Don't think about Ayr just now,' said Terry. 'Just think about enjoying these next few weeks. When we get to the final week, you will be chomping at the bit to get started.

'It is a big step up from doing the dishes,' she said. 'In fact, it's a big step up from anything I have ever done.'

'There is nothing wrong in thinking that,' Terry replied. 'I am sure all first years Redcoat thought that. I certainly did last year.'

Angie smiled and grabbed hold of Terry's arm. 'So Mr Redcoat, can I take advantage of your experience.'

Terry gently ran his fingers down the side of her face. 'Well Miss Redcoat, feel free to take advantage of me as much as you want. When you get there, you'll be surprised at how quickly you'll settle in. You just be yourself. They're going to love you. '

'I am very excited about it, but I'm also very nervous,' said Angie. 'It would have been nice if we shared a chalet at Ayr.'

'We will, even though it is unofficially. We just need to hope that we have understanding Chalet Mates.'

Angie sighed: 'I suppose will need to spend some time getting to know them first.'

'Absolutely. How long shall we give them to get used to the idea? End of the week?'

Angie laughed. 'I don't know if I can wait that long. But, you're right..'

'It is going to be hard work, but we are both going to have a brilliant time,' said Terry. 'You are going to experience some amazing things. It is such a brilliant feeling when you get into your Reds the first time.' Terry kissed the top of Angie's hand. 'But the most important thing this season, will be us.'

'And that starts with the next three weeks here,' added Angie. 'Our lives changed for the better last season. I wonder what will happen this time.'

'Let's think of this as our next chapter,' said Terry.

Angie squeezed Terry's arm as she turned, smiled and looked deep into Terry's eyes. 'Here's to the next chapter.'

'I said to you last year, that this is a great job, but it means nothing without you.'

Angie's eyes started to glisten and she smiled. 'I love you Terry.'

'I love you so much Angie, never forget that.'

They continued their walk back to the chalet, taking in the summer night air. They were taking a different route alongside the boating pond, away from the other guests and staff members, heading back to their accommodation, making the most of their privacy being together laughing, joking and just being together. They never felt happier

As they continued along the water's edge, Terry felt inspired to test his balance walking across a narrow wall running alongside part of the pond, Angie did not look too impressed. However, in his desire to show off his balance and coordination skills, he was oblivious to a loose stone which gave way the moment he stepped on to it, resulting in him partly stumbling into the water.

Thankfully for Terry, he stumbled into a shallow end where only his pride was hurt along with drenched shoes. Angie whilst laughing reached out and helped him back on to dry land. 'Are you OK.'

Terry smiled as he saw the funny side as well. Thankfully there was no other witnesses to his late night paddling. 'Well that's good preparation in case they use me for 'Hunt The Pirate', this season.'

'I don't think so,' said Angie. 'You can't swim. But I would say that you are a contender for next week's Pink Elephant. Terry laughed. 'Don't you dare.'

CHAPTER NINE

A special team had come together in the space of four weeks at Pwhelli and now this team was going to be split up. Nevertheless, despite the sadness of parting company from new found friends, excitement was in the air.

The summer season was days away and for the majority of the staff, the time had come to head to their respective camps and officially take up the positions that they had originally applied for – Butlins Redcoats.

For some, it meant just moving to the other side of the Pwhelli Camp, out of the guest chalets into the official staff accommodation. For the twelve Ayr Reds, a long train journey awaited them. They were the only ones on the platform.

After saying their goodbyes, the Ayr contingent were standing on the platform of Pennychain Station waiting for the first leg of their journey north to start. Terry and Angie holding on to each other's hand, partially broke away from the group, walking towards the back fence to take one last look at the place before their train arrived.

They were sad to leave, but they knew that an exciting chapter was ahead for them. As there was no sign of the train, they were quite happy to just hold on to each other's hands and take in the scenery for as long as possible

'Ahh! Look at those two lovebirds,' said Deke.
'Do you think it was something we said?' replied Jonty
Terry smirked. It wasn't a very big platform, so it was easy to eavesdrop on other people's conversations. He knew that could not stray too much away from the group. 'OK we can take a hint.'
Jonty put on a false shocked expression. 'Us? As if we would do such a thing.'
'Please feel free to join us any time,' added Deke.
Terry and Angie smiled as they picked up the case, still holding hands. They re-joined the others.
You are going to have to let go of her hand sometime you know,' pointed out Deke.
'Train isn't here yet,' said Angie.

Right on cue the train rattled along the track stopping at the platform. Opening the train doors, they boarded the carriage, scrambling in-between the narrow pathway putting their cases on the overhead shelves, determined to get the best possible window seat so they could take in the picturesque welsh scenery.

It was a short first leg of their journey before they changed train carriages at Chester for the final run home. After sitting in small compartments in the beginning, the Ayr group were now amongst passengers from all walks of life; so to pass the time, there was a desire to provide some extra entertainment in the form of community singing and some games at no cost to British Rail.

That was two thirds of the journey taken care of. The

group had run out of material and were now starting to focus on what was waiting for them at Ayr. Deke and Jonty, sitting with Terry and Angie started to discuss how the season would go for them.

'You going to be the dancer again, Terry,' asked Deke.

'I would assume so,' he replied. 'I would like to do more stuff with the mic. I enjoyed doing the discos' in the Stuart and the compering.'

'Don't forget it is a new guy in charge this time. You might have to prove yourself again. '

'Do you know anything about this new manager,' asked Terry.

'Nowt. Except that he is called Simon Barker and is nicknamed the Squadron Leader.'

'Ex RAF then.'

'Probably. But If he says "Chocks Away," then I am out of there.'

Angie and Jonty listened intently as Terry and Deke continued planning the next few months. 'Well you are a second year Redcoat this year, so you won't be working at the Amusement Park for a start,' added Deke. 'So you are going to have to think about doing different things this year.'

Terry had not really given something like that a lot of thought. 'Like What?'

'What else can you do?' asked Deke.

'Nothing springs to mind.' This was not quite true.

Terry had acquired various skills through his performances on local stage as well as being a dancer with the Scotland Latin American Formation Team. The dancing got him the job initially and was happy to build on that, but thought that it might be a step too far in trying to move in a different direction.

Deke had worked under a different manager to Terry last season but was more that familiar with the style and demands of De Vere. Like Angie, Deke had worked in a different department, so it was a brand new challenge waiting for them as well. 'So what you are going to do this season Deke,' asked Angie.

'Have a bloody great time for a start,' he announced, which met with a resounding cheer from the rest of the group.

Deke was an extrovert who possessed a fabulous singing voice and it was that which caught De Vere's attention the previous year, entertaining punters in the town's Isle of Skye Bar singing along to the pub's latest attraction, the "Singing Machine". He loved the idea of being a Redcoat and having fun with the campers, but getting to sing in front of an audience was what he was really hoping for. That was his true passion.

'And why not,' insisted Angie. 'You have a great voice.'

Jonty had never heard his pal sing. 'Is it anything like when he is pissed.'

Deke sat back looking at Jonty in mocked astonishment. Terry then intervened. 'This man has a cracking voice. He won the Staff Talent Contest last year.' Jonty was quietly impressed.

Terry continued. 'Because of his joining Butlins, he signed a new 2-year TV contract with Granada TV.'

'Really,' said Jonty. Deke smirked as he knew what was coming next.

'And if he does not keep up the payments, then they will take the set away.' All four immediately laughed. 'There you have got yourself sorted for what you are going to do this season.' said Deke.

'What's that?' enquired Terry.

107

'A bloody comedian.'

Terry grinned. He knew that when it came to making people laugh, he was not in Deke's league. But he did like performing, but with a new guy in charge, he had to see what opportunities would be available. He could only hope. If he could get more than three minutes as a backup Rock and Roll dancer in the Redcoat show, he would happily take that. Anything else would be a bonus.

Angie had no real performing aspirations, but if the opportunity came her way during the season then she would happy to join in the fun. 'I bet you will be doing stuff with the Beavers and the 913 Club,' said Deke.

The Beaver Club was an entertain club for children aged 3-8 years old. When it was set up in the early 1950's it became an iconic part of the organisation, looking after and entertaining hundreds and thousands of children which evolved into a similar set up for older children aged 9-13 years, the 913 club. The club badges were much prized possessions as well as the birthday cards that would drop through member's letterboxes throughout the year.

For any Redcoats detailed on any of those club's activities or any Junior competitions, they are known as Uncle and Aunties amongst the eager Beavers. 'You have to admit that Auntie Angie has a nice ring to it,' said Terry.
Angie smiled. 'I have never been an Auntie before,' she said.

As the train finally crossed the border; tiredness was starting to kick in. This had been more of a train journey; it was a test of endurance. However, the energy levels did pick up when the train finally rolled into Ayr station.

Everyone was quick to grab their cases and set foot on what was a familiar platform. Once passed the Station Guards, they walked through the main entrance to see a yellow and blue Butlins Minibus waiting to transport them to their new home for the next seventeen weeks.

'Now that is a welcoming site,' said Deke.

The driver pulled open the doors of the vehicle as the group climbed on board. The bus had enough seats to cater for all of the group, but having to squeeze in all of their cases, this short journey was anything but comfortable. But having been on train for several hours, what was 15 more minutes on a cramped mini bus.

Pwhelli was starting to become a distant but happy memory. Terry put his arm around Angie's shoulder. 'How are you feeling,' he said.

'Tired, excited, a bit sad though,' she replied.

'Sad?'

Angie, rested her head on to Terry's shoulder. 'We had been sleeping under the same roof for the last few weeks. When I wake up tomorrow I won't have you beside me.'

Terry understood what Angie was meaning; but he needed to be a voice of reassurance. He kissed her on the top of her head and whispered gently in her ear

'I cannot think of anything more wonderful than waking up with you in my arms,' he said. 'But we knew that we would be in different chalets after Venture Weeks.' Angie slowly nodded.

Terry smiled: 'But it won't be for long. We have to break in new Chalet Mates first.'

Angie sniggered. It was enough for her to focus back on the positives.

They were going to be working together in a job that would be with the ultimate in employment satisfaction. For the next seventeen weeks, it would also give them a chance to build on their relationship and help them plan for the future.

They may not get to live in comfort like the last four weeks at Phwelli, but there was nothing stopping them being together unofficially. They managed to do it last season. They just have to hope that their Chalet Mates would be as understanding as last years

'I wonder who we will get,' she said.

'It is certainly going to be interesting,' he replied. 'It is certainly won't be boring.'

The bus was now well clear of the town and a mile away from the entrance to Butlins Ayr. As they reached the top of the final incline, they soon noticed a number of flag poles and a sign just behind it saying "Welcome to Butlins Ayr", which met with a resounding cheer from all of the passengers.

'WE ARE HERE LADS AND LASSIES,' said Deke

'You think that they would have the Flags Flying now that we are here,' said Jonty. 'Do you think Pwhelli have warned them already.'

The bus reached the opening of the camp turning right, past the go-kart track, heading down the hill towards the main entrance passing between the two main pillar. For returning members of staff, there was an extra cheer as they started to reacquaint themselves with some of the camp's favourite venues like rediscovering old friends.

The Continental Bar was still there. Travelling along the main road, they could see the outdoor swimming pool with the heated indoor pool in the distance. On the opposite side was the guest dining hall, with the games room still on the floor above.

The bus eventually pulled up in the main car park just outside the main door of the reception. The place was deserted, but as they disembarked, Deke noticed the main door was open, he deduced that this should be the first line of enquiry.

The group went into what was a deserted reception except for a lone figure sitting at the small enquiry desk located against wall in-between a series of main door facing the guest check in desks directly opposite.

'Welcome to Butlins Ayr. About time you lot got here,' said the man at the desk, who turned out to be Roderick Jackson, dressed in casual shirt and trousers with the exception of the Black Blazer with the Butlins Badge on the breast pocket, which was the main uniform of the assistant entertainments manager.

'Sorry there was a delay due to a Streaker on the line,' said Deke.

'As long as it wasn't you,' said Jackson.

Deke paused to gently run his fingers down the side of his bulky frame. 'My body is my temple,' he replied. Only a selected few would have the pleasure of viewing this fine physique.' This automatically resulted in spontaneous laughter from the group, including the new AEM. 'Let me guess, you are Deke Campbell,' he said

You have physic powers then.'

'All the managers have the gift. It goes with the job,' said Jackson.

'That's me buggered for the rest of the season.'

Jackson was one of the new members of the Butlins Ayr management team. He knew all about working in Reds having spent three summer seasons in Barry Island as well as providing cover in the various hotels during the off season.

During his time in Reds he had made a name for himself as a hardworking popular Redcoat who was not lacking in talent as a singer and compere. He loved working for Butlins and did not hesitate to pick up the new challenge when he was offered his first management post north of the border.

'I am sure that we are going to be fine Mr Campbell,' said Jackson. 'As long as you get the first pints in at the Staff Bar tonight.'

'Bribery – and the season has not even started yet.'

'You are learning fast.'

Having introduced himself to the rest of the group, Jackson proceeded to hand out the staff passes for the season. 'You will need this if you want to get paid, get access to the staff canteen and the staff bar which is where you will be gathering to meet the rest of the team later on this evening. '

Jackson continued: 'There will be our first official meeting tomorrow morning at the Empire 9am sharp. The Accommodation Office has left your chalet keys in order for you to settle in. Staff canteen opens at 5pm, Staff Bar opens at 7pm.'

'Or we could kill birds with one stone and eat at the Staff Bar,' said Jonty.

'I like the sound of that. Well said Brother!' replied Deke.

Jackson smiled. 'You are still getting the first round in Mr Campbell.' Deke had given him a mock grimace, but he realised that this was a boss that he could work with.

Grabbing their cases, the group headed down to the staff chalet lines where the only changes to last season was a fresh splash of cheap paint outside the walls. Terry was allocated in staff chalet ZL116, Angie was in the accommodation directly above. Reluctantly they headed up to their respective billets where they would no doubt meet up with their official Chalet Mates.

Terry watched briefly as she took her case up the metal stairs of the staff chalet lines. 'Cheer up son, you will be seeing her again in the next thirty minutes,' said Deke. Terry responded with a mocking laugh, however he knew that he had to get himself settled in, maybe use the opportunity meet his new Chalet Mate.

He slowly opened the door. He was not surprised to see that inside the staff accommodation was exactly as he remembered, the two rusty beds on adjacent sides of the wall, the solitary wash hand basin the corner, in the middle was the wooden frame with a flowery curtain that was supposed to resemble a wardrobe. On the opposite side was a chest of drawers where there was someone already in the process of loading clothes into one of the drawers. The occupant immediately turned when he heard the door opening.

Remembering the mix up he had with accommodation at the start of last season, Terry approached the man with caution. He was about the same age and height as Terry, with short wavy hair and what looked like a first attempt at growing a moustache above his top lip. 'I hope am in the right place,' he said.

'You are if your name is Terry McFadden,' replied the stranger in a thick scouse accent.

'I am indeed, so I take it we are going to have the pleasure of each other's company during the next seventeen weeks.'

'We certainly are. I'm Nick Nesbitt,' said.

'Pleased to meet you Nick,' said Terry shaking his hand. He had only met Nick for a few seconds, but he was already getting a good vibe that they were going to get on fine.

Nick was a first year Redcoat from Birkenhead who like Terry, was someone who used to enjoy going to Butlins in

Filey as a kid, but was now about to experience holiday camp life from another side in what would be his first season in Red and Whites.

'So, what got you the Redcoats job,' asked Terry.

Nick smiled: 'Apart from my good looks and charming personality? I have no idea. I did tell them that I could play musical instruments and sing. I brought me guitar, just in case they were interested in using it, which they were happy about, but they were more interested in me bringing this with me as well.'

Terry's eyes opened wide as Nick opened up a small suitcase to reveal a full set of bagpipes. Judging by the pristine condition they were in, they were looked after by someone who cared about playing them. 'I have been told that they want me to play them at the main gate on a Saturday.'

'Well you certainly have a good reason for not doing the Amusement Park. How did a guy from Birkenhead end up playing the Pipes.'

'Me Dad was a Pipe Major in the Scots Guards and I think his enthusiasm passed on to me. These are his pipes. He taught me to play them. I did play in a Pipe Band up until a few months ago.'

'Birkenhead is certainly not a place I would expect to find a Pipe Band,' Terry

'I am not with them now,' he replied. 'I am just keeping a family tradition going. Plus, I like playing them.'

He gently placed the Pipes back in his suitcase and picked up his acoustic guitar. 'This is more me.' He then proceeded to run his fingers up and down the fretboard of his guitar giving a brief but impressive guitar rift. Terry responded by giving his Chalet Mate a deserved round of applause.

'Very impressive,' he said. 'An accomplished bagpipe player who is deep down a rock and roll man at heart.'

Nick was just as keen to find out about Terry as he was of him. He knew that he was a returning Red and was keen to benefit from his first year experience. 'So what is it going to be like' he asked.

'Hard work but a lot of fun,' replied Terry. 'It can be the best job in the world or the worst job. You only get out of it what you are prepared to put into it.'

'So how did you get the job?'

''Cause I could do ballroom dancing, get people to do waltzes and quicksteps and not crush their toes.'

'Can you do anything else?'

'Did some Compering last year, but we will just has to see what happens. At the moment I am GD Redcoat like everyone else.'

As both men continued to unpack their case, the conversation continued about the season ahead. I wonder what the rest of the team are going to be like,' said Nick. I have not seen any of them yet.'

'You will soon enough,' replied Terry. 'My Girlfriend, Angie is coming down to meet us with her Chalet Mate and we will be heading up to the staff bar.'

'She a second year Red as well?'

'Nah. We met last year when she was working in the kitchens. It was decided that if we came back for another season, it would both in Reds.'

'A Butlins Romance that has lasted more than a fortnight. When is the wedding.'

Terry sniggered. 'There is a while before we think about things like that.'

'So you are attached and the season has not even started yet,

I take it you want me to make myself scarce from time to time.'

'Let's just settle in first,' said Terry. 'We can work something out later that everyone is happy with.'

'Doesn't bother me mate,' insisted Nick. 'Just keep your moments of passion under control when I am trying to kip.'

Terry smiled. 'No worries, we will sort something out.'

At that moment, Angie peered into the window of the chalet. Terry immediately got up and opened the door. 'Angie, meet Nick my Chalet Mate, Nick – Angie.'

'Good to meet you Angie,' said Nick. 'Terry has told me about you.'

'Oh Yes?'

'Don't worry your secrets safe with me.' Angie gave Terry an inquisitive look but Terry remained the picture of innocence. But she gave him a playful dig in the ribs just same.

'Good to meet you Nick. Guys, this is my Chalet Mate, Gwendoline.'

From behind the door emerged a petite young lady with peroxide blonde hair, tied up in a bun. She had over indulged on the mascara and was dressed in cream coloured trousers and a nylon zipper top to match.

'WELL HELLOOO! IT IS WONDERFUL TO MEET YOUSSS !!!

CHAPTER TEN

Terry had only been back at the Butlins Ayr Camp for a few hours, but the signs were there that this was going to be a totally different experience compared to twelve months before. He was a second year Redcoat and was now classified as a bit of a veteran. At the age of 19, he certainly did not feel like one.

But this was a job, where you did not have much time to learn and once you had got the first season under your belt, you were classified as a seasoned worker, whether you wanted that label or not. Returning Reds would not be overawed by what was ahead of them and that was a key factor in helping the new recruits. They certainly played a part in helping Terry during his first season.

Even though they knew what it was like to work a season at Butlins, they still had plenty of stuff to learn like being adapt to new situations or programmes on the camp as well as changes behind the scenes, like proving themselves again with new managers.

Sitting in the crowded Staff Bar, Terry's first test of the

season was trying understand Gwendoline, Angie's new Chalet Mate's questionable accent. She said she was Scottish, but what part in Scotland did people speak like that. Somehow, he found a way to tune into what she was saying. It was a start.

As a group, they were starting to bond as all they could do was talk about the plans for the next day and for the season ahead. During that time, Angie and Terry occasionally gave each other knowing glances, eventually holding hands under the table.

They knew that they would be working sixteen hour days, sometimes even more, so they would need to make the most of the time they had together, they just had to hope that they at least got the same day off

The table space gradually got bigger as the contingent from Pwhelli appeared where Terry enjoyed watching Deke and Jonty trying to get to grips with Gwendoline's accent. Some familiar faces from last season were now starting to appear, which made Terry feel relaxed even though he was not really close to them socially.

With a new man in charge, he expected to see retuning Redcoats joining from other camps, but as the evening progressed, there was a point when he wondered how many of the team from last season at Ayr would actually be returning. There were stories that a number of last year's team were teaming up with De Vere at Clacton.

'Why am I not surprised to see you here.' Terry immediately got out of his chair turning around to face the speaker. It was a voice that he immediately recognised. 'Bill! Ya Bugger!'

Bill Watson, Terry's Chalet Mate from last season became a firm friend with Terry and Angie during the 1982 season and became a source of strength for him during some of his lowest points of the season, which included run ins with the then Manager, Ron De Vere. Terry threw his arms around his pal. 'Great to see you again mate! Did not expect to see you here.'

Bill grinned. 'I got myself a new Agent. She thought it would be a good idea if I did another season. I think she needed some time to work out what to do with me.'

'What would you like her to do with you,' replied Terry

'Not what you are thinking,' laughed Bill. 'She is old enough to be me Gran. So, what about that lovely girlfriend of yours?'

'Evening Bill,' said Angie, appearing from behind Terry.

'Hello Gorgeous!' said Bill. 'Don't tell me you are one of us this year?'

'I certainly am,' she replied.

Bill stepped over to give Angie a hug. 'I expected to see you two married by now.' Both Terry and Angie laughed. They did not really know how to respond to that.

Bill looked around the rest of the group sitting around the tables. 'So, are these members of our new team?'

'They are indeed, Guys, this is my Chalet Mate from last year, Bill. Bill, you may recognise some of the faces here.'

'I certainly do. Deke don't tell me you are a Redcoat as well. Do they stock uniforms in your size.'

Deke laughed. 'I resemble that remark Mr Watson. They got them in specially. Real man size. You ready for some competition for your cabaret spot?'

Bill smiled. 'I look forward to it mate. Great to see you again.' Bill shook Deke warmly by the hand and promptly went on to introduce himself with the rest of the group, eventually sitting down alongside Terry and Angie. 'Right the season starts here.'

The team bonding continued during the next hour, but thoughts soon started to turn towards the next morning, the start of the first working day of the new season at Ayr, starting with the first official meeting of the new Redcoat Team where they would get the chance to lock horns with the new bosses.

The evening was drawing to a close. Slowly they came out the doors of the Staff Bar, heading en masse towards the chalet lines. There was nowhere else to go. The only venue opened was closing and the only option was get some sleep. Terry and Angie tipped off their Chalet Mates that they were not ready to return to their accommodation just yet. They asked them to make sure that they left the door latches up.

They did not intend to be too long, but after living under the same chalet roof in Wales for the last four weeks, they felt that they needed some privacy before retiring to their separate billets. As the group walked along the main road passing the doors of the main reception, Terry and Angie turned down through what was a deserted "Blue Camp" taking the long route "home".

They walked down the partially lit chalet lines hand in hand, revelling in the quiet of the night air, on their own and away from the crowds. During Venture weeks, they were part of a team, but were working on different tasks. When they were in the ballroom, with the children at night, it did not feel like they were on duty, but they were just joining in on the fun. This time they will be working closer together, and Terry hinted that he would have to have to control himself if they are ever detailed together

Angie smiled. 'You are just going to have to behave yourself.'

'Just a little bit,' replied Terry. 'Redcoats are not meant to behave themselves totally. You can still do the job and still have fun. We will be professional. Promise. You will have to get used to the possibility of me being in charge if we are detailed together.'

'I think I can cope with that,' Angie replied. 'If you step out of line, I can deal with you later.'

Terry grinned. 'I will hold you to that.'

Even though they were back on familiar surroundings, this was a new learning curve for Terry and Angie. They knew what ever happened during the next seventeen weeks their relationship was the most important thing. But they could not forget that they still had a job to do.

However, that night they had come to an opening in the middle of the chalet lines; they knew that after four weeks together they would be sleeping in different chalets. They could see their accommodation in the distance, but Terry stopped, grabbed hold of both of Angie's hands, looking deep into her eyes. Before they parted, there was something he needed to say first.

'I remember standing just over at those doors last year saying the day you walked into my life was the best thing that ever happened to me. Here we are back at where it all started and I am still the luckiest guy in the world.'

'I treasure every moment we are together. It will be so tough watching you walk upstairs to your chalet and I will not be there with you. I know it won't be for long. But as you go upstairs tonight, just remember, I love you so much.'

Angie smiled. 'I never forget,' she replied. Tears were build up in the corner of her eyes. They were tears of happiness 'I fell in love with you the first time I saw you. The St Christopher medal you gave me on that final day of last season, I always wear it close to my heart. It's a part of you. I am so looking forward to having you waking up beside me again. But until that moment comes, then hold on to this thought. '

Angie placed her hands on to Terry's face. She pulled her towards her kissing him long and gently, locking themselves in a passionate embrace. 'Time to retire I think,' she said.

Holding on to Terry's hand she led him across to the bottom of the stairs which was directly outside his own chalet. Terry kissed the top of Angie's hand, eventually letting go of his grip and she slowly walked up the stairs, maintaining eye contact as she walks across the top ledge.

As she reached the door of her chalet, Terry mouthed the words "Goodnight". Angie responded by blowing him a kiss before opening her door. Terry then opened the door of his chalet to see Nick just about to get into his bed. Terry flopped on to his bed slowly unbuttoning his shirt. 'How are you doing?'

'I am good mate,' said Nick. 'I take it you were away saying goodnight to your good lady.

'I was indeed.'

'Well anytime you need me to make myself scarce, then just let me know.'

'I appreciate that pal,' said Terry. 'I am more than happy to return the favour if you ever have romantic plans any evening.'

'Appreciate that,' he replied. 'But I did not come here looking for love. I am here to have a great time.' Terry smirked as his Chalet Mate's statement did have a familiar ring to it.

Hours later, the light of the new day shone through the curtains directly on to Terry's head slowly waking him up from what was a deep sleep caused by all that travelling from the day before. Terry strangely felt refreshed as he raised his head to see that Nick was not in his bed.

He spent five minutes trying to tune his brain into his surroundings, suddenly the chalet door burst open as Nick entered carrying a toilet bag with a bath towel wrapped over his arm. 'Morning Boss! Sleep Well?'

'Surprisingly enough, yes. Sleeping off yesterday's travel I think. You had a bath this morning.'

'Yep. And all the better for it.'

'So you have commandeered one of the bath plugs. That is worth remembering.'

The new season was 24 hours away, but there was still work to do, starting with their first team meeting after breakfast in the Staff Canteen. Reds Uniforms were not required. If fact they were yet to be kitted out yet. Today it was casual working clothes. Nick proceed to pack away his toiletries and started to change. Terry slowly got out of his bed opting for a less than extreme waking up routine, settling for an all over wash.

Terry was now starting to think about breakfast, regarded by those in the know as the most important meal of the day. He only used the Staff Canteen during the first two weeks of last season and blamed the experience working whilst being ill. He could not go anywhere else for his breakfast so he made sure that he stuck to cornflakes as it was one thing they could not mess up. Lunchtime would be nothing more than chips or a sandwich. Having a history of digestive problems, he thought that light eating would keep things safe for now.

It did not take long for both of them to get ready, Terry wanted to wait for Angie before heading up to the Staff Canteen. She eventually came downstairs with Gwendoline, laughing and joking looking forward to the day that awaited them. Their conversation immediately stopped when she noticed Terry and Nick waiting at the bottom of the stairs.

'Morning Ladies! Sleep Well?' enquired Nick

Gwendoline smiled. 'Verrrry Well. Thank You.'

Terry motioned over to Angie whispering in her ear. 'How about you?'

'All things considering, very well,' she replied. 'How about you.'

Terry squeezed her hand. 'I managed.' He then turned to towards Nick and Gwendoline. 'Well guys, shall we head up for Brekky.'

'Ohh Absolutely!' replied Gwendoline. 'One is fair starving.' All four proceed to head up to the Staff Canteen located above the guest dining hall. Most of the Entertainment Staff were already in the queue, waiting to be served. It would not take too long as they were due at the Empire Theatre for the important first meeting.

The main doors of the theatre were already wide open, so there was no need for them to squeeze their way through the narrow corridors of the Entertainment Office located directly above. Nick Terry, Angie and Gwendoline along with Bill stayed close as they walked up to the stairs and in to a large and dimly lit auditorium, with the only real source of light coming through the windows of an open and deserted stage. 'Welcome home mate,' said Bill.

Terry gave his former Chalet Mate a knowing smirk as they took their place on one of the seats located on the second row. One thing he learned from last year was never sit right at the front during a team meeting as you did not want to be in the Manager's direct line of vision.

The rest of the team took their places waiting for their

appearances. 'Do you know anything about these new people,' said Terry. Bill shrugged his shoulders.

'All I know that he was a Redcoat at Skegness years ago and worked as a manager one of the hotels.   I would imagine that he we would totally different to De Vere.'

Terry giggled as he got flashbacks of his first boss, who originally turned him into a nervous wreck but in the end, played a major part in what was a successful first season. 'I could not imagine anyone else like De Vere.'

Their conversation stopped as Angie gestured to both of them that there was signs of activity at the back of the theatre where there was a set of stairs leading to the Entertainments Office and the Projection Room. The door was flung open as four figures appeared at the top of the stairs.

They proceeded to march down the side aisle towards the front of the stage. This appeared to be the moment that they had been waiting for. The only thing was that if this was the new Ents Manager and his assistants, who was the other guy?

CHAPTER ELEVEN

'Welcome to a new season at Ayr,' said Simon Barker, the new Entertainments Manager at Butlinland Ayr, also known as "The Squadron Leader." 'This will be a new experience for many of you and I will include myself and members of the Management team as well. We will be learning together so will be looking to you returning Redcoats to lead the way.'

Despite his formal appearance, Terry could see that this was a totally different Boss to the one that he had worked for before. Having just heard him say a few sentences, he could see that he had better people skills than his predecessor did. He was less threating for start.

Despite being new to the Ayr Camp, Barker had a lot more hands on experience working at Butlins as well. He had come through the ranks as a Redcoat in the mid 1970's at Skegness, an assistant Entertainments Manager at the Minehead Camp, before being in charge of the Entertainments Department at the Metropole in Blackpool and the Grand Hotel at Scarborough.

Barker had no desire to always be at the front of the stage, compering shows like De Vere. He was more at home working behind the scenes, and throughout his short managerial career, he was regarded as someone who could identify real talent, where a number of his former charges had gone on to successful careers in the Entertainment industry.

'I like to think of myself as firm but fair,' he said. 'We are here to provide the best holiday possible for the thousands of holidaymakers that are going to pass through those gates.'

'It is important that everyone remembers that it is why we are here and that we maintain a professional approach. You do that and you will get everything you want out of this job; plus have a bloody good time into the bargain.' Barker's opening statement was met with murmurs of approval by the majority of the assembled gathering, especially the last bit.

Barker announced that everyone would be on Office duties for most of the day. Not the most popular of details for Redcoats as it would normally involve cleaning, manual tasks, helping the regular office staff; but with no campers around, there was nothing else for them to do. Plus, this would be the first time they would be working together as a unit.

They would collect their Red and White uniforms later in the day and would assemble for a final meeting and inspection in the evening at the Junior Theatre. There would also be an unofficial team picture for the local newspaper, who were publishing a special Butlins Edition at the weekend to mark the start of the 1983 season.

'The Entertainments Section is part of a new structure within the company,' said Barker. 'Will be part of the Leisure and Amenities Department, which will include other areas from within the company. So, I would like to introduce the Gentleman, who will run this new section. He is not just your boss, but is also my boss, Mr Chappell, who wants to say a few words.'

Hugh Chappell, a former Entertainments Manager at the Minehead camp, issued his own personal welcome to the new team. He went on to explain that whilst he would be coordinating different departments within the centre, Barker would remain in full control of the Ents Office. He reinforced Barker's insistence of professionalism and ended by wishing every member of the team an enjoyable and successful season.

That was his sole contribution to the meeting. The feeling amongst the assemble group was that this would be the only time they would deal with him. Chappell took his leave of the group, returning to his Office along with Barker, leaving the two Assistant Managers to finish off the meeting. Starting with a little bit more team bonding.

Most of the Reds knew about, Roderick Jackson, however it was down to his fellow AEM, 30-year-old, Jim Hutton to take the lead in the next item of the agenda.

Hutton, a former Scottish Footballer, was once billed as a notable prospect coming through the ranks of Ayr United Youth side before being transferred to Cardiff City.

Whilst on the brink of breaking in to the first team, his playing career at Cardiff was cut short through an injury on the training field. Despite regaining his mobility, he moved into coaching with the youth team, picking up some preseason work at Butlins in Minehead as a football coach for ten years. And when the opportunity came for him to work in his old home town, it was too good an opportunity to pass up.

As a Coach, Hutton was more than capable of dealing with large groups. He walked across the front row pointing at everyone. 'Now I expect the first thing you are going to say, "who are they?" Well we are going to go around you one at a time. Introduce yourself, where you are from, your previous experience with the company. Starting with you.' Hutton pointed directly at Bill, who immediately stood up and smiled. He loved nothing more than an audience.'

'Hi there, my name is Bill Watson, second year GD Redcoat from Dundee and a singer for my sins.'

'That is true, I have heard you sing,' replied Deke, which resulted in laughter from the group.   Bill was quick in his reply.   'Deke Campbell, a man who is good to his wife, he never goes home.'

The laughter continued.   Hutton smiled as he could see the interaction starting to build from around the group.   However, he calmed things down and decided Deke should be the next one to introduce himself.

'Deke Campbell, first year, GD Redcoat, part time stud and showbiz personality.'   Terry and Angie immediately burst in to laughter along with the other members of staff.   'That is enough from the "love birds" over there.'   That statement automatically directed everyone's attention towards Terry and Angie, prompting Jackson to point over to Terry as the next one to introduce himself.

Terry took a deep breath and smiled.   'Terry McFadden, aged 19 and three months from Greenock, second year Red, one-time dancer – avoiding standing on women's toes a speciality.'   Angie was then the next to stand up.   For the next ten minutes, the introductions continued with both Assistant Managers keeping their eye on the clock.

For Terry the moment he had been waiting for came when Gwendoline introduced herself to the group. Terry was not able to find out much about Angie's Chalet Mate the night before in the Staff Bar. Now here she would fill in some of the blanks.

'Helloo, my name is Gwendoline, first year Redcoat fae Porrrt Glasssgow. Lovely to meet yous all.'   There was a stunned silence amongst the smiling group. They had never come across anything like her before.   Hutton broke the silence by thanking her. Gwendoline smiled in appreciation and sat down.

Terry did not know anyone from Port Glasgow that talked like that.   Gwendoline came from the same place as his Dad. Port Glasgow, like Greenock is a working class Scottish town, with a proud industrial past. Something did not ring true with her. However, she must have something that made the bosses want to hire her.

'Right! Now we have gotten to know each other. We certainly have the makings of a strong team here,' said Jackson. 'We have around 4000 guests arriving tomorrow, but there is a lot of work to do today. You will be divided into groups and will go with the people sitting behind you.'

"When your name is called, go into your sub teams and make sure you are at the clothes store at 3:30 to pick up your Reds, 'continued Hutton. 'You then make sure you are at the Junior Theatre in your uniforms for 7pm. Don't be late! If you don't know where it is, then the returning Reds will show you.'

Everyone was dispersed into their small groups, with Terry stationed at the sports field, painting benches and chairs around the Games Issue hut whereas Angie would be working with others at the back stage of the Gaiety Theatre, cleaning and sorting out the props.

These tasks were not their normal duties, but it gave the staff, particularly the first year Redcoats an early reminder that working as a Redcoat, was not always a glamourous job.

He always stayed clear of the DIY tasks at home, but Terry was acting like an expert, painting all the fences and benches and even had to deal with the challenge of painting the lines on the football pitch. Normally not the most taxing of activities, except that the machine to mark the pitch was missing a wheel and he had to paint the lines by hand. At least it didn't rain.

Later in the afternoon, Terry was back at the chalet cleaning himself up before heading to the clothes store to pick up his uniform. It wasn't going to take long.

He just had to make sure that they had a pair of trousers and jacket that fitted, a blue and gold coloured tie and a name badge.

So, he was good to go. Only difference this year, he was also issued with a Red Butlins tracksuit; an indication that as a second year Redcoat, he was going to be a lot more active with his duties this season.

Like last year, he had had to supply the remaining parts of the uniform himself, the bow tie, shirt, shoes etc. There was no panicking buy shopping spree this year. Angie was just as organised, when it came to getting the obligatory items of uniform, except for the evening shoes.

She could not find a pair that fitted properly and finally had to settle for a pair that she purchased during her four weeks in Wales. They at least looked the part.

Angie would often test them at nights in the ballroom dance floor with the children and did everything she could to break them in to make sure that they were reasonable comfort ahead of the trip back to Scotland

Before the evening meeting, there was the matter of another assault on the staff canteen. There was nothing risky on the evening's menu that would make Terry want to go for the starvation option. The canteen had just opened and as Terry sat down to eat, he caught sight of Angie, Gwendoline and Nick queuing up to get served. They had just come back from the clothes store themselves so Terry decide to take his time finishing off his meal as the rest came to join him.

He did not want to get changed too early, so they all went back to their quarters, with Terry, Angie, Gwendoline and Nick sitting and talking in Terry and Nick's chalet. An hour later it was time for them to head back to their rooms to get ready for their evening meeting; their first in their Red and Whites

Terry placed his uniform meticulously on the bed as he started to change into his uniform for the first time this season. He knew that as a second year Redcoat, he had to set the right example.

Even though he had done this many times, Terry took greater care than usual getting into his uniform. Minutes later, he was standing front of the small mirror secured above the wash hand basin fastening his tie, before the finishing touch of pulling on his Red Blazer.

The transformation was complete. He had stopped being Terry McFadden and resumed his previous identity of Terry the Redcoat. He looked at this revamped version of himself in the mirror. 'I did not think I would be back in this gear again.' He took a deep sigh and smiled. 'But I admit it does feel good.'

He was conscious of Nick watching what he was doing and replicating his every move. Twenty minutes later both men were ready. Terry turned to his Chalet Mate who was brushing some fluff away from the shoulders of his jacket. 'How are you doing.' 'I keep thinking of coming here on holiday as a kid looking at Redcoats, wanting to be one,' said Nick. 'Now I am one myself. It feels great.'

'You will remember this moment, it never leaves you. Shall we make a move?'

'Absolutely!'

Terry opened the door and both men stepped on to the pathway noticing a number of other Reds emerging from their accommodation. Standing at the bottom of the stairs, Terry looked upwards towards the upper level of the staff chalet lines and beamed as he saw Angie and Gwendoline coming out of their chalet wearing their uniform, walking cautiously down the stairs.

'Evening ladies,' said Terry.

Evening Terry, Nick,' said Gwendoline. 'Looking incredibly smart.'

Her accent still brought a smile to Terry's face as it was the strangest thing he had ever come across. It looked as she was trying too hard. But he did like her. She was Angie's Chalet Mate, so despite her obvious eccentricities he was determined to make her feel part of the team.

'Thank you good lady,' he said. Terry quietly moved over towards Angie.

'Well do I pass,' she enquired.

Terry grinned. 'You look stunning,' he whispered.'

All of the Redcoats headed en masse ready for the meeting at the Junior Theatre, located at the other end of the camp. They were not sure exactly where. So it was down to the returning Redcoats to lead the way. Angie was the only first year Red who knew the camp well and joined the front of the group as they walked along the main pathway of the camp.

The camp's Stuart Ballroom was just a few hundred yards into the distance as the leading group turned right down a path leading to the children's playground. Right at the back was the First Aid department and Nursery building. Directly above was the Junior Theatre.

The Redcoats slowly climbed the stairs into a room lined with rows of wooden benches. At the end, was a small wooden stage. On the other side of the wall was the Quiet Lounge; a major attraction for holidaymakers during their stay where they could escape the day to day madness and also the ideal venue to hold the Whist Drives; a very popular card game for the more mature guests and often a short straw for the Redcoats

Standing on the stage was both assistant entertainment managers as well as Barker. 'Welcome everybody,' he said. 'Please take a seat.' The Group quickly obliged; with Deke, it was very carefully as because of this size, they were not the most comfortable of trousers and he did not want to damage them. He had doubts that these trousers were going to last him seventeen weeks. 'I am taking these back tomorrow,' he whispered to Terry.

Barker continued to address his team. 'You all look very smart,' he said. 'This is how I expect you to look every day. Every department on the site has a part to play this season; you guys will be on the front line so standards must be at the highest level in the way you look and in the way you behave.'

'You were issued with instructions on what your job as a Redcoat requires. Make sure you read them and have a programme with you at all times. They will be changing every week, so make sure you get an up to date one at the Ents Office. There is no excuse not to carry one about you.'

Before the main business of the evening, there was the matter of an unofficial team photograph for the newspaper to deal with first. There was a Press Photographer on site, but the newspaper Editors insisted on sending one of their own snappers, who arrived right on cue, much to the delight of the management.

This was a small stage, so this was not going to take long to arrange this photoshoot. The photographer was determined to make sure that was the case as after what had been a hard long day at the office. There was pint of the finest ale at a high street drinking establishment with his name on it. So he was in no mood for hanging about.

The two assistant managers immediately pulled in two long benches from the side of the stage. Terry along with a number of male Reds were instructed to clamber on to one of them with the rest of the group assembling in front of them. Deke, in his uncomfortable fitting trousers had difficulty in joining his colleagues on to the long narrow platform at the back.

'I need some assistance gentleman.' Terry and Jonty, reached down to pull their colleague up alongside them. However, their combined strength brought him alongside them a bit too quickly and Deke's trousers could not take the extra pressure.

RIPPPPP !!!!!!

'Bugger!' exclaimed Deke.

Jonty casually glanced over his shoulder to inspect the damage. 'You not supposed to wear white underwear with your white trousers,' asked Jonty.

'That is a technicality,' replied Deke, desperately trying to make light of his embarrassing predicament, which thankfully was hidden from the camera lense. 'I suppose it could have been a lot worse, it could have ripped at the front.'

'That would have been a bit too naughty for the Courier,' giggled Terry. 'Well look at it this way, it is a warm night. You will have the added advantage of that extra bit of ventilation.'

When the picture was finished, Deke stepped off the bench very carefully, not to inflict any more damage on his trousers; making sure that he was between Jonty and Terry as he went his way back to his seat.   There were after all, ladies present.

They now had to go through an induction process, which was mandatory for all staff before the start of the new season. This consisted of basic first aid, whom to contact in case things became too complicated, as well as briefings on how to deal with small fires, what signals to listen out for from Radio Butlins in case there was a big one and how not to panic.

Thirty minutes later, both Hutton and Jackson returned to stage to talk about the first day's work details which would see a number on duty, catering for the day visitors as well as the first batch of holidaymakers arriving.

Duties would include the Amusement Park; a requirement for first year Redcoats. Angie was surprised not to hear her name being mentioned for that. Some were scheduled for Reception with a few other Redcoats based throughout the other sections of the camp.

In the end Angie could not have asked for a better start to her first day in Reds. She would be working with Terry at the Ayr train station. This was a new detail for Terry as there was nothing like that last year. On the plus side, it looked as if he and Angie were going to get the same day off. He could not have planned this any better.

At the end of the meeting, both Hutton and Jackson made a final rousing speech to the troops. Before the evening was brought to a close, Hutton issued a final instruction to the staff regarding a very popular television programme based on the Holiday Camp Life in the 1950s which was very popular amongst guests. A connection that company was keen to distance themselves from.

'Please don't mention "Hi De Hi,"' he said. 'You might think it is lovely but will drive you nuts after seventeen weeks.'

Deke smiled: 'We shall see about that.'

CHAPTER TWELVE

Saturday morning; the 1983 summer season had finally arrived. Terry from force of habit had made sure that he had positioned his window curtain to allow the morning light shine directly on his face. He preferred to rely on Mother nature's alarm clock as opposed to his wind up clock which had been prone to the occasional mechanical breakdown.

He slowly opened his eyes and thought that he was still in a dream, in fact a nightmare looking at what appeared to be a large menacing "Yeti" figure. But his brain quickly brought him back to realty to see he was looking at his Chalet Mate in full Highland Regalia, red kilt, with matching sash draped over a thick dark embroidered jacket and what looked like a large feathered animal on his head

To complete the picture, he was wearing Highland Brogues, with thick knitted socks and a small plastic dagger placed down the side. 'Hell Fire! That is some sight to see first thing in the morning!' exclaimed Terry.

'And good morning to you too mate,' smiled Nick.

'It's the first day, why are you not in your Reds?'

'I am not in Reds,' he replied. 'I am on bagpipe duty, remember?' It was then Terry remembered Nick talking about how he got the job. 'Of course, you are playing the bagpipes at the main gate. It is going to be roasting hot today. You are going to be cooked in that gear.'

'Well they do say that this job is challenging. I have been told that I do get breaks.'

'You are going to need them.'

During the early days of the Butlins Ayr Camp, it was not unusual to have kilted Pipers on site as they would sometime march around the camp slowly waking the campers before breakfast. Even the early Redcoats were prone to wear kilts instead of the customary white flannels. And with the new management in charge, having a Piper playing at the gates was bringing a flavour of the old Butlins Ayr back.

Terry was glad that they were not going to turn the clock back too much, cause the idea of wearing a kilt filled him with dread. Nick continued to check over his uniform

'Are you not getting breakfast first?' asked Terry.

'It takes me ages to get into this gear. And I am certainly not going to up to the Staff Canteen dressed like this. I've got a few bars to keep me going. I will have at least an hour after I finish before I need to be in Reds this evening.' Nick opened up his small case and picked up his bagpipes. Right that is me ready? I will see you later.'

Terry sat up on his bed, reaching across to open the door for Nick who had his hands full. 'Good luck mate? Have fun'

'I certainly will.'

Terry's first detail was going to be at the Ayr train station, another example of the new management bringing back a taste of old style Butlins. A train station was once situated between the camp and the former "Heads of Ayr Hotel" at the top of the hill, where Redcoats would welcome the guests as they came off the train.

This time there would be two Redcoats in the town welcoming the holidaymakers as they arrived, getting them in the holiday mood, directing them to the specially arranged transport to the camp.

Terry was in no mood for breakfast. As he got out of his bed, the adrenalin was starting to kick in. He was back doing what he described as his dream job, a job that changed his life. He was not the nervous and shy individual from the year before. He was more confident, had more job responsibility and with Angie alongside him, this year was going to be even more special.

Angie may have worked at the camp before, but this was her first year as a Redcoat, so he wanted to make sure that her first year was as memorable for her as it was for him

The plan was to jump on one of the buses to town early and make sure they were there for the first load of arriving campers. They did not need to check into the Entertainments Office first. If they did not reach the station by 9am, the Bosses would know about it. That was one thing a Redcoat could never be for any detail – late. Terry was designated in charge (I/C) so if anything went wrong, it would be down to him

He still had an hour before heading to the car park to take the bus into town. He had no worries about Angie being late on her first day. Terry got out of bed, went over to the sink and started to shave, get the painful part over with first. He then refilled the sink with cold water as he started to wash himself. Not the most comfortable way to wake up, but it certainly got the circulation going.

Terry laid out his uniform on the bed and carefully got himself dressed, finally putting on his Red Jacket, 'Well Terry boy, I think you are good to go.'
'Yes very handsome looking,' said Angie, standing admiring from what was an opened doorway. Terry grinned as he turned round to face Angie standing there looking immaculate in her Redcoat uniform. 'Now that is a beautiful sight first thing in the morning.' Terry walked forward towards her as they were locked

in a brief embrace. He guided her towards the mirror as they looked at this reflection.

'I think we look the part,' smiled Terry.

'But we don't want to be late,' said Angie. 'Time to go!'

'Absolutely!'

Terry closed the door behind them as they started to walk up the chalet lines toward the side door of the reception. Only a small number of Redcoats were on duty this early, there was a lot of activity not just at reception, but throughout the different parts of the camp. There would be a few hours before the regular campers start to arrive, and they were also expecting a healthy turnout of day visitors.

Angie and Terry were the only ones to board the double decker bus as it began its first shuttle run of the day. As the bus passed through the gates, Terry and Angie gave a wave to Nick, standing at the security hut talking to the guards. There was no point in playing his bagpipes just yet as there was no campers.

As they were the only passengers on the bus, Angie briefly grabbing on to Terry's arm, rested her head on his shoulder as they headed into town. However, with the housing schemes started to appear in the distance, it was the sign they needed that they had a job to do. They can get all loved up during their day off.

'How you feeling about today,' asked Terry.

'Excited,' she replied. 'Don't know what to do. But excited.'

Terry grinned. 'Just be you,' he said. 'We are basically there to welcome the punters off the train, point them in the direction of the bus to take them to the camp. We may help them with the cases if we have got time.'

'And that is it?' asked Angie.

'Yup. Remember down in Wales, we liked the idea of connecting with the kids as they arrived at the camp for Venture weeks. Here we get to meet some of the guests before they get to camp. Make a first impression with the punters as it were.'

'Sounds good.'

It was not long before the bus pulled into the back car park of the Ayr Train Station, parking just up from the rear entrance.

Waiting for the bus to stop, both Angie and Terry stood up, brushing down their uniforms before disembarking. As they walked towards the entrance, Angie, stopped Terry for a brief moment. 'Hold on a second,' she said. 'Let's sort out that tie.' Terry smirked as he looked at Angie sorting out his attire 'Thank You. Do I pass?'

'You look gorgeous,' she said.

'Funny I was going to say the same thing to you.'

'What, that you look gorgeous?'

Terry laughed. 'There is only one gorgeous person. And I am looking at her.'

'We can talk about how gorgeous we are tomorrow during our day off.'

'I look forward to that,' replied Terry. 'But for now. Work calls!' Terry held out his hand gesturing to Angie towards the Station Entrance. 'Ladies First!'

Angie smiled. 'Forever the Gentleman.'

Walking through the entrance, they both found themselves at the bottom of a flight of stairs of a metal bridge that appeared to have been part of the station since it was first built. On the other side were two adjacent platforms with one end cordoned off by a metal barrier.

Fixed against the wall on the other side was numerous left luggage compartments. With another entrance leading to the town centre and the ticket office running alongside, it seemed only natural to conclude that they should be on that side of the bridge.

The only instruction they received from the regular staff was to stay at least five feet away from the exit gate, giving the staff the room to do their job and allow sufficient room to move clear. If they were able to direct the passengers over the bridge to the waiting bus on the other side, away from the exit into town, then it would be very much welcome by British Rail Staff.

The first official train was due to arrive in the next ten minutes. Tempted as they were, they avoided sitting down on the benches, just in case habits were broken and it arrived earlier than scheduled. They certainly did not want to appear bored standing there. Plus, they had only started their first day, they did not want to get their whites dirty.

'So, what do we do then?' enquired Angie.

'May I have the next dance?' Angie laughed as Terry led her into a traditional ballroom hold and started to waltz on the spot whilst humming the Blue Danube waltz, only to stop thirty seconds later. 'Right that's us warmed up,' said Terry.

Angie looked around and there was still no sign of any activity. 'No trains yet.' But Terry then pointed in the distance to see a rail locomotive rolling along the tracks towards to the Rail Buffers at the end of the platform. 'I would say we are in business.'

With precision the train stopped a few feet away from the clearing. The doors of the carriages swung open as passengers of all shapes and sizes with cases to match stepped on to the platform walking towards the guards standing at the gate, ready to check the tickets. Terry and Angie moved further back than originally agreed allowing the passengers to pass through the obligatory checks.

Once clear, the mood of travellers picked up when they caught site of a smiling Terry and Angie in their line of vision.

'Hey Mammy – Are they Redcoats?' asked one excited

toddler.

'They certainly are,' said the Mother, which was the cue for Terry to get back into what he used to refer to as Redcoat Mode. 'MORNING ! Who's here for Butlins.'

They certainly did not expect to see any Redcoats, until they arrived at the camp at least. It certainly got them in the holiday mood. If they get them in the bus all happy and smiling before they even reached the camp then their work was done. Terry became the focal point for all of the parents with the children latching on to Angie.

Once through the barrier, Terry and Angie led the group over the bridge to the waiting bus and waved the passengers away before darting back over the bridge to welcome the next arrivals. 'And that is how we do that,' said Terry.

'I enjoyed that.' Added Angie.

'Plenty more where that came from.'

The moment that they reached the other side of the bridge, the next train started to arrive, full of more enthusiastic campers, who loved the idea seeing Redcoats ready to welcome them.

Terry knew that they there would be more than one bus travelling back and forward from the camps, so there was no pressure on them to keep them occupied till their transport arrives. They set a precedent and now they needed to maintain that high level of energy with the rest of the passengers and keep that enthusiasm going when they did eventually reach the camp. So lunch breaks were brief, but vital.

The number of arriving trains started to increase, and as the station clock reached 4.30, it was time for them to return to the camp as the last bus was about to leave. Terry and Angie joined the remaining passengers as they boarded the bus and when it pulled into the car park for the last trip of the day, they stayed behind for a few minutes as the travellers headed towards the reception.

As they walked past the side door, the reception door was packed with arriving campers with scores of people dragging their cases towards their chalet lines, mingling along with the hundreds of day visitors along the main roads of the complex. As their next detail was at the dining hall for their first evening's "swanning", they moved away from all of the activity going on back toward the staff chalet lines.

As Angie went back to her chalet, Gwendoline was already there having just finished her first duty at the Amusement Park. Both of them made use of the spare time they had, freshening up before heading to the dining hall. Terry was back at his own quarters relaxing with Nick, who finished his Piping duty and changed out of his tartan regalia in to his Reds. Both men were sitting chatting as Angie and Gwendoline came down the stairs and joined them.

'Evening ladies,' said Nick. Angie noticed that both men were sitting on their beds, with their shirts opened at the collar with their jackets still hanging up in their wardrobe. 'Are you not getting ready?' asked Angie.

'Just need to put the bow tie on,' said Terry. 'That will take two minutes.'

'You both look very relaxed,' said Gwendoline.

'Of course. It has been a fun day, 'said Terry. 'And so will be the night. How was your day.'

'It was sooo much FUNNN working at the Amusement Park,' she replied. 'The children were great, but I think the Mums and Dads had trouble understanding me.'

Nick smiled as it took him a while to get used to her accent as well, but he tried to remain diplomatic as he had not quite used to being in her company, she was part of a team, and more important was part of what was their own personal small sub group.

Amongst the four of them, only Terry knew what it was like on his first evening in Reds and what "swanning" was all about. This was where the Redcoats welcome the guests as they entered the Dining hall and even getting to eat with them.

'I am looking forward to seeing who we get,' said Angie.

'I always enjoyed sitting with them, 'said Terry. 'Plus I know that I am going to get something decent to eat. I can only take so much of the staff canteen.'

'Well do you not think it is time we made a move?' said Angie. 'Come on you two, we are ready. Get your ties and jackets on.'

Terry smirked. 'Yes Boss.'

Terry, Nick, Gwendoline and Angie, walked up the chalet lines past the now near empty reception building. As they almost reached the top of the stairs leading down to the dining hall, Terry knowingly smiled at Angie, for out of the four of them they had an idea what was going to happen next. With Nick and Gwendoline, their eyes opened wide as they were faced with hundreds of hungry campers waiting to go into the camp for their first meal.

The new management never talked in great detail about what to do whilst on Dining hall duty, so it was down to the experienced Reds to lead the way, including those who had never actually worked at the Ayr complex before. Terry immediately went back on "Redcoat Mode." It was if he had never been away. As he sprang into action, the others immediately followed suit.

'EVENING!!!!' shouted Terry, which met with a response from a small section of the other holidaymakers assembled outside the other main doors of the dining hall. There was other Redcoats walking down the stairs behind him but Angie, Nick, Gwen followed Terry's lead, getting amongst the smiling campers, talking to the waiting campers. 'All hungry I hope!' said Terry.

'Starving!' exclaimed one holidaymaker. 'What's on the menu tonight?'

'It will be the finest holiday camp cuisine.'

'So chips are on the menu?'

Terry smiled. 'Probably. Will soon find out.'

Whilst talking to the campers, Terry was looking around for an open door for them to get into the Dining hall first, but soon clocked his former Chalet Mate, Bill peering from behind an open Fire Door 'Hey Mr Travolta! In here!'

Angie, Nick and Gwendoline followed Terry in through the door into the main pathway running alongside the main doors of the dining hall, broken up with partitions. On the opposite side were waiters and waitresses putting the finishing touches to the hundreds of immaculately set up tables with every one of them numbered.

The guest started to get restless, looking through the windows of the dining hall, waiting to see when they would finally open the doors. The Redcoats could not do anything without a signal from the manager or the I/C to let the guests in. There was no sign of either of them, so the Reds gathered around a pinned note on one of the walls at the far end, checking their allocated guest tales throughout the rest of the week.

Bill was dining hall I/C for the night. He had finally been given the go ahead to finally open the doors. Returning to disperse the group and positioned them along the different parts of the dining hall. Terry, Angie, Gwendoline and Nick made sure that they stayed close together. 'Right Guys. Let em in!' announced Bill.

Right on cue, the Redcoats simultaneously pushed open the fire doors, where the crowd of grateful holidaymakers pushed their way through looking for their tables. "Finally! We are wasting away,' exclaimed one of the guests. 'EVENING !' shouted Terry. 'LAST ONE IN DOES THE DISHES!' A line that seemed to go down well. Terry knew that as he tried that last year. Which only proved one thing. Holidaymakers have short memories when it came to gags.

The campers continued to pile in through the doors as all of the smiling Redcoats endeavoured to take their minds off the long and uncomfortable wait. As the guests made their way to the tables, Terry noticed that amongst the line-up of Reds standing at the Dining Room doors, there was one of them not dressed in his Redcoat Uniform but looked more like an oversized school boy.

'HI DE HI!' shouted Deke, who walked through the crowd of campers into the dining hall. A small section of the crowd responded in kind. That might not have gone down well with certain members of the management, but judging by Deke's manner, he did not care; and the punters loved him for it.

He was wearing an old style Redcoat Jacket, unlike the others, it was lined around the edge of the cuffs and collars, his white shirt was open at the neck with his tie half done around his neck below there was dark blue trouser which was previously long trousers cut off at knees. On his head was soft peaked cap half perched on his head.

'Nice to see you dressed for dinner,' sniggered Terry.
'They did not have any white trousers left,' said Deke. 'Our beloved assistant entertainments manager, Mr Hutton produced a tatty pair of trousers and this old Redcoat Jacket, so it was deemed that I should spend the week as a wee school boy. If I do it right, I might get some proper trousers. So, I have been selling beaver badges all day, looking like "Dennis The Menace.'
'What did the Squadron Leader have to say about that?' enquired

Terry.

'It was his idea,' he grimaced.

Bill focusing on his duties as I/C had been moving along different parts of the dining hall but was stopped in his tracks as he saw Deke in his revamped schoolboy outfit, trying to curtail is laughter. 'Hello Sonny have you lost your mummy?'

'Aye Mr Redcoat. And what a card game that was. Must dash, there is a guest's table with my name on it.' Deke continued to walk along the narrow area of the Dining hall. 'Hi-De-Hi !!!!'

'Ho-De-Ho,' shouted back the crowd. Deke was dressed as a little rebel, and enjoyed behaving like one. 'Not so fast Dennis,' we have some birthdays to do first.'

'Anything you, say Dad.'

By then the guest had already taken their seats at their table waiting to be served their first course. However, the waiters and waitress were gathered at the front of the serving areas leading to the kitchens, but could not move until the Redcoats carried out the birthday parades.

As in previous years, the guests had warned the dining hall manager of a family member's birthday and arranged for a cake to be presented by the Redcoats who in true Butlins fashion would parade around the hall, cake in hand, getting the "victim" to stand on the chair in order for the 1000 strong guests to sing "Happy Birthday.'

Bill led the Redcoats towards the manager's office located at the back end of the hall next to the serving bay. Angie was one of the few first year Redcoats who knew what the Birthday Parades entailed having watching Terry from her spot whilst working in the Kitchens.

There were two cakes with names and table numbers lying on the table of the manager's office. Bill arranged the Redcoats in to two groups taking charge of one with Terry to lead the other.

'You guys follow Terry, we can follow after you have finished. Ok Terry.'

'No worries,' said Terry, carefully picking up the cake for the first cake which also had a bottle of bubbly. 'Angie you grab the cake, I will get the bottle. Ready? EVERYBODY CLAP !!!!'

CHAPTER THIRTEEN

Evening meal passed without a hitch, no calamities in the birthday parades. The Redcoats had dispersed to get ready for the opening night's entertainment. Terry wasn't sure what he was doing yet, but he knew that it was going to in for a long and busy night.

Last year, he was in charge of the opening night's festivities at the Stuart Ballroom. However, after a conversation with Deke the other day, he was coming to terms with, rather reluctantly, that he would be doing something different this time.

When he realised he was coming back, he wanted to build on what he did last year, maybe test himself even more. With a change in the managerial line up, Terry was going to have to just take whatever opportunities that came his way. He may have to create them himself, but he had no idea where to start.

If he was not the DJ at the Stuart, getting to work the dance floor would certainly be an acceptable second choice for now. He would get to get to know the campers as well as lead the main dances on the floor; after all, it was the dancing that got him the job in the first place.

He had not checked his evening detail; he was actually reluctant to find out, in case he was placed well away from his "other home." It was too early for the bingo, thankfully there were no Whist Drives on the opening night.

He would have been happy being in the Gaiety Theatre during

the Resident Review Shows; however, Angie was already on her way over there. Then again, there was always a chance he would get the preferred option of working the Ballroom floor all night.

Regardless of his feelings of disappointment at not getting the Saturday night DJ duties, Terry knew that he needed to put self-interests to one side. He had not even met the new I/C of the Stuart.

He was an experienced second year Redcoat, so he needed to act like one. Prima donnas never lasted long in this job. If he was detailed in the ballroom, he knew that he would probably enjoy it. The atmosphere at night was always buzzing.

He could not leave it any longer. Terry headed over to the "Reds Room" at the Ents Office to check his evening detail. Walking through the fire doors at the side of the Empire Theatre, he bounced up the stairs two at a time past the entrance to the Snooker Hall stopping at the main door.

He was back in the long narrow corridor of the Entertainments Department. On one side was windows all the way to the end where there was the door of what was Ron De Vere's Office, however this time it belonged to the new Director of Leisure Amenities Department Hugh Chappell. Such was the level of responsibility; it was only fair that he had the only office with a door.

The new Ents Manager, Simon Barker's office was one of numerous open planned partitioned areas that ran along the rest of the corridor. His office was formerly the secretary's work area, who now had to share her workspace with the operators of Radio Butlins.

There were over thirty Redcoats on staff, so there was not enough space to cram them all in the Reds Room, a small cordoned off section at the other end of the corridor away from the main offices. It was not a social spot, but it was just a place to check what the orders were, pick up any packages and check the daily detail.

Terry scrutinised the document on the noticeboard and it was as he hoped. He was going to be working at the Stuart from seven pm, all the way to midnight. Five hours in the one place; he could not have asked for a better way to finish his first day back in Red and Whites.

He looked at the evening detail again and could see that the I/C was 24 year old Roddy McKenzie, from Pitlochry who previously had worked all kinds of jobs selling menswear to working as a labourer.

Apart from paying his bills, any extra money he had would fund his real passion of music and performing, working as a part time Disc Jockey doing gigs around the local area, where he built his own following. When the job at the building site ended unexpectedly, the offer of working as a Redcoat DJ/Compere was too good an opportunity to pass up.

Terry did not get to talk to Roddy during the early meetings, so he thought it might be a good idea to get across to the ballroom now and help him set up. As he came out of the Reds Room, there was no one around. However, he could hear some noise coming from the Radio Butlins room which also doubled up as a storage space for the microphones and other accessories for the various venues. His decided to investigate.

As he peered around the door frame, he could see Roddy picking up his microphone and leads from the cupboard. Terry smiled: 'Evening! How are you doing.'
'Ah it's Terry, I am doing fine. I am glad I bumped into you.'
'You are?'
'I saw that you are on with me at the Stuart, I was told that you were always I/C on the Saturday night last season.'
'Yeh. But that was last season. It's a whole new ball game this

time,' replied Terry.

'I just wanted to make sure that you were OK about me doing it this time. I was a bit concerned that you might be ticked off that you did not get it.'

Terry immediately put his colleague's mind at ease. 'Why should there be? There is a new team in charge, of course there would be changes. I am happy being in the Stuart, the floor is my other home. But if you need any back up on the mic now and again, then you know I'm your man.' Terry was starting to sound like an experienced second year Redcoat.

Roddy smirked: 'I will remember that. I just need to nip back to the chalet to pick up my records and I am ready. What is it like in the Stuart?'

'You will love it,' insisted Terry. 'The place is buzzing every night.' Both men continued to walk down the stairs back on to the main road of the camp. Roddy, turned back towards the staff chalet lines. 'I am heading over there the now,' said Terry, 'so I will see you up there.'

'Absolutely.'

Terry was now marching along the main road, remembering the first Redcoat rule of always smiling and say hello to passers-by, some of them that he remembered from being on duty at the station. He could see the Stuart Ballroom entrance in the distance, with the usual notice for the Beachcomber Bar, hanging at the top with the customary stationary totem poles at the side of the short staircase.

When he came through the doors, standing at the bottom of the stairs, there appeared to be no sign of life at the Beachcomber, even though the doors were open. There was a billboard just inside, facing the opposite way, but Terry had no time to check out who was appearing that night.

Terry stood for a second, looking up directly towards the top of the steep staircase leading into the ballroom. He was not bothered that the escalator running alongside wasn't working. As Redcoats were supposed to be full of energy he started the way he meant to continue, sprinting up the stairs towards the Stage Door which appeared to be closed. As he walked round on to the main floor, he could see the campers starting to come in looking for the best seats, some close to the floor, but for others it was the closest to the bar, which had only just opened.

At the far corner of the Stuart, the Café Bar area was busy as it had been all day, catering for day visitors. At the opposite end of the ballroom, the slot machines could be heard banging away in the distance. It seemed that he was the first of the staff to arrive as the stage was completely empty.

The only sign of life on the ballroom floor was small groups of children running about chasing each other. There was nothing else to do, as the only music coming out of the venue speakers was a play list courtesy of Radio Butlin. Terry stood in the front of the stage, looking around the venue. He did not expect to be back here, but he was delighted.

As the kids started to see Redcoats appearing, they took that as their signal for them to join in their games, but when first year Redcoat's Chrissie and Alison appeared, they took over keeping the children occupied. Terry knew his services would be needed soon to help Roddy to set up his unit as well as assist the Resident Band with their stuff, whoever they were going to be. 'You are late.' Terry immediately turned around to see what was a familiar face from last year.

Chic Wilson, the leader of last year's band, "Caledonia" was back for his second season at Butlins Ayr. Unknown to Terry, he had been working back stage and did not hear him creeping up behind and making him jump. He smiled and reached out to shake his hand. 'Ah Mr Wilson! And how are we this fine evening.'

'Ahm daeing fine son. Good to see a familiar face. So as you are in charge, you should have been here to help us sort out the stage.'

'Well I am here. Let's do this.'

After a successful first season, "Caledonia" had obtained regular work playing at various clubs around the central belt of Scotland as well as backing visiting artists at his own local venue. The money was good, but it did not match the experience of playing in front of around three and half thousand people every night. So when the job offer came from the place that effectively launched his band, he did not take much persuading.

It felt like the opening night of last season, when Terry headed to the room at the back of the stage to help set up the band's speakers. As he carried the first one on stage, he saw that Roddy had finally arrived, having come though the other entrance, sorting out his leads and records for this evening.

Terry carefully carried the speaker towards the far corner of the platform where Chic and other band members who had also appeared, were starting to sort out their own microphones and instruments.

He continued to assist the band in setting up their equipment as Roddy went back stage to get his disco unit. 'Just to let you know that I am not I/C tonight,' said Terry.

'Oh really? Who is?' enquired Chic whilst still connecting the cables to one of the speakers

'That would be me,' said Roddy, appearing from the behind the curtain carrying his large DJ turntables.

'Chic, meet Roddy, Roddy, meet Chic, the leader of our Resident Band, "Caledonia."

Chic temporarily stepped away from his setting up duties and reached out to shake Roddy's hand. 'Pleased to meet you son,' he

said. 'Hope you are better than last year's guy,' he was rubbish.'
'Thank you for that Mr Wilson, I have always been a big fan of
yours too.'

Everyone laughed, but they could not relax for too long as
they still had a stage to set up. With the main speakers for the
band sorted, Terry went over to help Roddy finish up with the
setting up of his DJ gear. The band disappeared to get changed
into their stage gear, the Disco was now ready and it was down to
Roddy to get the evening up and running for the first thirty
minutes. 'Right! I will leave you to it,' said Terry.
'Muchos Gracias Bud. Go Get Em!'
Terry smiled: 'Right Boss!'

Roddy kicked off the evening with a couple of favourite songs
from last year, "Baby Jane,' by Rod Stewart, followed by ABC'S
"Look of Love. He had realised that party dances was a
requirement for holidaymakers in a ballroom, but as he only
needed to play music for the next thirty minutes, he wanted to
see what kind of music the band played first. He thought it
would be a good starting point for working relations if he stayed
clear of the official party dances to begin with and make sure his
running order did not conflict with theirs.

Roddy's DJ skills became obvious, in his microphone, his use
of the mixing desk as well as the way he worked his audience.
His professionalism shone through. Terry was very impressed.

Losing the I/C job did not seem so bad as he could see that
he was lot more skilful in the mic than he was. However, when it
came to being on the floor, he knew that he was the man in
charge

When Roddy put on Hot Chocolate's "Girl Crazy" it
prompted, Terry to lead from the front demonstrating to
holidaymakers along with his colleagues a dance that was not on
Caledonian's Party Dance List. Known amongst the Reds as the

"Redcoat Hustle," it was a party dance that looked complicated but it was actually straightforward and it would give everyone that attempted it a sense of achievement when they got the steps right.

Last season, Terry had picked up on the dance that was started by other Redcoats, he did not know if it started by his former colleagues, but it remained at hit with the campers. Terry was determined to keep it going. Redcoats liked to encourage people to get involved and what a better opportunity than now.

As the evening went on, the venue became more packed, with campers and Redcoats coming in from the different venues. Backed with the best party music around, it was the perfect atmosphere for an opening night.

CHAPTER FOURTEEN

When he had been a holidaymaker at Butlins, watching the Redcoat Show from his seat in the theatre was always a highlight for Terry, imagining himself as part of a much-loved production. However, he would usually come back to earth, reminding himself that it was nothing more than a far-fetched dream. When he actually did get to take part in one last year, he was thrilled, even though his contribution was less than he hoped.

Now he was a returning Redcoat, he hoped that he would have a greater input in this season's show, probably not singing, maybe doing sketches or routines for which the Redcoat shows were famous.

He loved anything to do with comedy, but never had a chance to perform any. His problem was that, although he was a likeable character amongst the staff and campers last year, he was not deemed to have a comic persona. Nevertheless, if he could get to do more in the Redcoat show than last season, it would be something.

They were all gathered in the theatre for the first late night rehearsals, and Jackie Cooper and Simon Barker were handing out the respective parts in the show. However, thirty minutes in, Terry had not been allocated anything to do. It looked as if he was not going to contribute at all. That was until Deke intervened.

'Excuse me can I say something?' he said. 'Terry over there is an experienced dancer, but he has not been selected to do anything. Sorry but that's just not right. 'The compere, Jackie Cooper, and Entertainment manager, Simon Barker, were taken aback by Deke going all serious. Terry too, was shocked, but he sat there and said nothing.

'Everyone is going to play a part Deke, we are not finished yet,' said Barker.

'That is good to hear Boss. Carry on!' he replied.

'That is very nice of you, 'answered Barker.

Terry smiled at Deke, acknowledging his interruption, but he still did not say anything. He was not sure if Deke's support was going to make any difference. As Cooper continued his delegating, Terry did not have too long to wait.

"We are going to do a routine that was done at my last camp, which always goes down well, our own special version of "Swan Lake". Terry started to get heart palpitations. During his brief time with the Scotland Latin American Formation Team, they used to entertain audiences during public appearances with many party dances and comic routines, as well as the Latin American Dance routines that they performed on the TV.

Such routines included a mock ballet number, in which he was shanghaied along with the rest of the team's male members; not one of Terry's finest experiences on the dance floor. As he listened to Jackie, he feared for the worst.

'This "Cod Ballet" will feature two Prima Ballerinas with a Supporting Cast. Gavin and Alan will be the lead dancers. We will have three apprentice swans, Nick, Terry and Mike.'

Terry's face was expressionless, but Angie, sitting beside him, broke into a broad grin, because she had worked out what they had in mind, which involved Terry, dressing as a Lady Ballerina. 'Ohhh God!' Terry muttered under his breath.

However, even he was starting to laugh when it was

announced that Deke would occupy the last Ballerina slot. They would have to wait to find out what the actual routine involved. There was the matter of the finale to sort out first, a medley of songs from the hit musical, Oliver, based on the Charles Dickens classic novel Oliver Twist.

The Compere and Entertainments Manager allocated the lead roles to first year Redcoats, Gavin and Maddie; not the strongest singers amongst the group, but they appeared to fit in to their idea of the characters. Gavin was taking on the role of Oliver and the Artful Dodger rolled into one, despite looking like neither of them. Alongside him was Redcoat Maddie, recreating the leading female character, Nancy. However, there was the matter of the films other iconic role, the scoundrel, "Fagin".

Barker smirked, twisting the edges of his prominent moustache pointing his finger across the assembled group before directly settling at Terry, who sat there open mouthed. Having watched the film many times on television, he was more than familiar with the character, but could not for the life of him figure out why he was deemed the most suited to the part.

There was no indication as to whether he could actually replicate the character with his performance. He had never had to do anything like this before.

What was even more worrying, the costumes for the Ballet would require them to wear handmade Tu Tu's, the material would be provided by the Theatre Wardrobe Department. The costumes would be made by a group of female Reds. Angie was one of the eager volunteers to carry out the task, especially as she wanted to have the pleasure of fitting Terry out herself.

However, it was down to Terry to get the matching pink tights, not for the first show, but by the following week at the latest. Angie offered her moral support as well as the benefit of her experience when it came to ladies lingerie. 'Appreciate that,' said Terry. 'But I will need something else from you.'

'And what's that,' she asked.

'On our next day off; we go shopping. I am sure as hell not doing this on my own.'

Angie laughed. 'OK. Agreed my sweet.'

It was time for everyone to be divided into respective groups for rehearsing their respective routines. Angie joined a group of female Reds who were to perform a backing dance, dressed as clowns, supporting Redcoat Maddie singing "Puppet on a String." They just had to act like puppets behind her back. It did not take long to work out how to do that.

Terry on the other hand, joined five of his male Redcoats, including Deke to learn their ballet number, which was anything but complicated either. The routine consisted of two Prima Ballerina's doing a serious performance of Swan Lake, which would be difficult, as one of them would be dressed in a Tu Tu. Their efforts to play it straight would be hampered by a number of interruptions, mainly by Deke, dressed in his own pink ballet outfit.

Terry's contribution would consist of no more of than a 30-second appearance, dancing on and off the stage with the other two guys as "Apprentice Swans", wearing L Plates, as well as joining the full group chasing the main comic foil, namely Deke, around the theatre, in Tu Tu and pink tights as well. This was Terry's debut to comic performing; he had to start somewhere.

The first rehearsal concentrated on the sketches and routines, where Angie would also be making a contribution. The shows' opening number and finale rehearsals were for another day. Therefore, Terry had a couple of days to work out how to do the character of "Fagin". As far as he could see, these would be his performing exploits for this season. However, when he checked his "Daily Detail" the following morning, it appeared the Boss had other plans for him.

Having taken charge of the table tennis tournament, Terry had returned to the Ents Department to drop off the results for the secretary. Before heading back to his chalet, he briefly nipped into the Reds Room to refresh his mind about the rest of the detail. Apart from his swanning duties, he was due at the Conti Bar for afternoon Bingo. That was not for another two hours.

His eyes were drawn to towards a notice that had escaped him earlier in the day; his presence was required at the Beachcomber Bar after lunch for additional rehearsals. 'Thought they had done enough last night,' thought Terry. However, he could not think about that just now, as his growing hunger pains, suggested that there were more important things to think about – namely his lunch.

Terry walked downstairs towards the dining hall where the pathway was filling up with waiting guests, along with a small gathering of Reds, which included Angie, who had just finished the first of leg of a double helping of shifts at the Amusement Park.

'AFTERNOON PEOPLE!' shouted Terry. Nearby guests, responded in kind, as he walked over towards Angie. 'HALLOOO. And how was your first session of AP?' he whispered.

'It was fun, of course,' she replied through a forced smile 'Operating the Lady Birds ride, would you believe.' Having spent most of her spare time with Terry operating the Lady Birds ride at the Amusement Park in between her shifts last year at the kitchen, she had known exactly what to expect.

In the event of inclement weather, the boredom would be broken; as Redcoats would be taken away from their machines to go on the adrenalin, filled "white knuckle" rides with the children. However, as the summer sun was shining in all of its glory, Angie, along with a number of other Reds were on operational duty at the Kiddies rides. Thankfully, Angie had more than her fair share of customers, and it led to more than an interesting morning's work.

'Any sign of getting in for the food,' asked Terry.

'Funny we were thinking the same thing,' interrupted one the campers. Terry noticed Redcoat Andy poking his head from behind a partially opened door. 'Over here Guys,' he said.

Terry smiled at the camper, 'We will try and chase them up for you.'

'Good Lad! We are wasting away here.'

'Shall we Angie?' Terry reached out his hand the direction of the opened door. 'After You!'

'Thank you kind Sir, always the Gentleman.'

'You'd make a lovely couple,' said the camper.

'Why thank you.' whispered Terry. 'We already are.'

Some of the campers heard Terry's comments as he and Angie walked towards the door at the far side of the dining hall. 'AWWWWWWW! 'Angie was blushing as they headed into the dining room. They were now standing in the main passage of the dining room waiting for the doors to be opened. 'Is my face red,' said Angie fanning her face.

Terry smirked. 'You are going to be fine,' he said. 'Just tell them it is your natural rosy complexion.'

'You're such a funny guy,' she replied.

'You will get used to it. More AP this afternoon?'

'Yep, what are you on?'

'I have got Bingo at the Conti, but I have to go to the Beachcomber for some rehearsals for another show.'

'Doing what?'

'I have absolutely no idea my love.'

Lunchtime had passed, and Terry walked enthusiastically along the road towards the entrance of the Stuart Ballroom, of course never forgetting the first Redcoat rule, of always smiling and saying hello to passers-by.

Arriving at the main entrance, he walked up the short flight of stairs through the set of doors, which led through to the Stuart, which also doubled up as the way through to the Beachcomber Cabaret Venue. Standing at the foot of the double set of stairs leading up to the Ballroom, he veered left in the direction of the much-loved Cabaret Bar.

It was as exactly as he remembered it from the previous year, the dark cave like décor at the entrance, the wooden bridge that crossed the narrow stream that ran all of the way down to the main pond at the other side of the venue, when it was turned on, but not today.

Walking across the bridge, Terry navigated through the bamboo style furniture before walking down stairs, towards the main performing area. On the far side was iconic Beachcomber "Volcano" directly above the main pond, which was undergoing an emergency repair by members of the stage crew.

The stage was still in the exact same place with the pillar, and the totem pole style carving right in the middle of the small dance floor. As he approached the stage, Terry could see the Ents Manager, Simon Barker and Compere, Jackie Cooper, sitting at one of the tables chatting and they appeared to be comparing notes.

Their conversation stopped when they noticed Terry arriving, closely followed by seven of his colleagues, including Deke. 'Nice of you all to turn up,' said Barker. 'We don't have much time, so take a seat and I will hand over to Jackie to take it from here.'

'Right Guys!' said Jackie. 'I know that you are feeling it after the rehearsals the other night and we are all happy with how things are coming together. But we have another show to go out tomorrow evening and you are the cast.'

Everyone started to look around at the venue, puzzled as to what kind of show that could be done by them, in a venue like this, it would normally be set for Midnight Cabaret stars, or night shows from the main theatre revue company. 'We are going to do an Old Time Music Hall.' The announcement met with smiles of approval from the cast.

Terry's family were fans of the Old Time TV Variety Show, "The Good Old Days," a show with modern day performers done in a style of an old style Music Hall. Terry never stopped trying to do some singing in the Redcoat Show; it looked as if he might actually get his chance. With the short notice, he assumed that this was going to be an all-singing production.

'It is going to be similar to "The Good Old Days,"' said Jackie. 'I am going to be Mr Chairman introducing an assortment of characters, singing traditional songs. Songs you should all know. If not, you have 24 hours to learn, which I am sure that you can do, as it is one song.'

Terry was thrilled, but nervous at the same time. He was going to get to sing on a professional stage, albeit as another character. It would be just like in the days when he was in a concert party that performed at Old Folks Homes around the town. This should be easy. The only thing is though, that everyone has to be a character, but what kind of character?

Jackie explained the format of the show; everyone would come on, and take a seat on the stage. They would then be introduced by "Mr Chairman." Jackie continued to explain the format of the show, and who would take on the weird and wonderful characters. The characters consisted of a washer woman called Florrie Ford, a lady in the lurch, Eileen Dover, known affectionately as a lady of the night, and Charlie, a drunken waiter (obviously not much thought power to come up with that name).

That character list continued: a Scotsman in full highland regalia by the name of Jock Strapp, a strong man who is basically a wimp called Billy The Bouncer, with Deke being made up to look like an over amorous Military Man by the Name of "Colonel Crumpet Hunter." There was still no mention as to what Terry was going to do yet.

Jackie continued: 'I introduce each of the characters, and when they each get up to sing, they will be interrupted by Rigger Mortice who is desperate to sing…'

'Rigger Mortice?' asked Terry.

'Played by you Terry,' replied Jackie. 'You will be standing at the side of the stage, in front of your coffin.'

'Coffin?' Terry was flabbergasted, he wracked his brain, but no memory of a coffin featuring in the Good Old Days came to his mind. "I am playing a Zombie, desperate to sing?' he asked.

'The idea is that none of the cast wants you to sing, and when you come forward, they always tell you to get back in your box,' replied Jackie. "By the end of the show, the audience will be totally on your side. Then, when you do get to sing, you will sing completely out of tune. You play the cards right you will have them shouting for more.'

'And how exactly do I do that?' asked Terry rather worriedly.

'That's simple! Just keep your facial expression like this for the whole show.' and Jackie proceeded to demonstrate his best deadpan impression of a "Zombie". 'You have to stay like that for the whole show and for it to work, you must not smile, and, you must not react to anything that happens on the stage.'

It was the simplest of instructions, but this was more than a simple singing show. They were obviously going for laughs and plenty of interaction that you would expect from an adult audience. Start laughing and the whole concept of the character does not work - no pressure. In addition, when he did get to sing? He had to turn in the worst vocal performance ever to be witnessed on a Butlins stage.

Terry always enjoyed singing, this was the first time he had ever taken on a role where singing out of tune was obligatory. It was not the kind of singing role he was hoping for, and it was the first time he had been asked to attempt a comic character. He would have to be dressed in a shroud with white greasepaint on his face as well as dark zombie eyes and straggly white hair, standing motionless in front of a custom-made coffin. Oh, what joy!

Terry's eyes opened wide when a member of the stage crew brought on the coffin that had been hurriedly put together. It would never be strong enough to carry a corpse in a funeral service, but in an upright position, it certainly looked the part, and Terry was in no rush to try it out.

'Apart from keeping a straight face throughout the show,' said Jackie, 'there will be a section where the cast members will be given a half pint of Lager, so you will have to drink yours in one. '

'But I have never drunk Lager,' said Terry. The strongest thing he ever had, was a glass of his Mother's home made Ginger Wine at New Year.

Jackie smiled, 'Well you are going have to get used to it.'

'Talk about suffering for your Art,' thought Terry

Having featured briefly in the Redcoat Show last season, this year he had more than doubled his performing input, which in the end was what he had really wanted. However, it included dressing up in pink tights and a Tu Tu, as well as playing the part of an out of tune Zombie who was partial to alcohol.

Probably a good idea not to tell his parents about this just yet.

CHAPTER FIFTEEN

Having been in Wales for four weeks, it was obvious that Terry and Angie's first day off back in Scotland should be at Greenock, and visit Terry's parents. However, with their first week working in Reds completed, they decided that this next day off, would be just for them.

So, the obvious place to go would be where they had spent their very first date. There was no desire to get breakfast at the staff canteen. Much as they loved being in the camp, they could not wait to get into the town.

Once they were clear of the main gate, they could finally walk up the hill toward the bus stop holding hands without reprisals. Ten minutes later, the bus arrived. They were the only passengers, but decided to go to the most private space, to the front seats on the top deck.

As the bus headed along the road into the town centre, they were starting to feel less like Ayr Redcoats, now simply Terry and Angie. 'I have so been looking forward to this day off,' said Terry. Angie rested her head on Terry's shoulder. 'We get the chance to be us,' replied Angie.

'We could have any early lunch, any suggestions where?'

Angie smiled, as she knew the answer that Terry wanted to hear. 'Erm! How about Helen's Place.'

'What a great idea!',

'Helen's Place,' was a restaurant in the town just off the High

Street. Their setting was the perfect place for their first date and it became their favourite eating-place during their days' off.

They had not been back to the restaurant since their emotionally charged final day at the end of last season, which ended with Angie returning to her Gran's house just outside Falkirk and Terry going back to the family home in Greenock. This was one of their favourite places outside the camp. They were excited to be back.

They had turned off the High Street down the dark lane leading to the restaurant where the only sign of life was light coming through the artistic looking glass double doors halfway down. It was exactly as they remembered it. 'I have missed this place,' said Angie.

Terry held open the door as Angie walked in first, noticing straightaway the glass tower, still displaying their tempting range of desserts. Going into the main restaurant, the only change to the décor was a few new pictures hanging up on the walls. At the far end was still the set of double doors leading to the kitchen.

Terry led Angie to the more secluded end of the restaurant, pulling out a chair at the first available table. 'Would Madam care to take a seat?'

Angie smile: 'Why thank you kind sir.' As Angie sat down, so did Terry. 'And what would Madam like to eat, may I recommend Macaroni and Cheese, I hear that it is awfully good.'

'I think that sounds a wonderful idea. Pray tell me, who informed you that I like Macaroni Cheese?'

'Terry smirked: 'Eh - I believe that was most certainly you my dear.'

Angie giggled, 'You remembered.'

'How could I forget something like that.'

'And I would say you would be partial to the "House" Chicken Vol Au Vents?'

'Don't forget the chips, must not forget the chips.'

'Oh of course, how could I forget the chips'?

Not having to think about their daily detail, the romance was back in their lives. The only thing that would stop them holding hands, and take their eyes off each other, was when their food and drink arrived. Terry kissed the top of Angie's hand before letting it go to enable them to eat. Terry picked up his glass first, it was important to mark this special occasion.

'The food looks as good as ever,' said Terry. 'I wonder if the coke is still the same standard'

'This is our time, our place.' He raised his glass. 'This was where we had our first date.' He raised his glass saying softly. 'Here's to us.'

Angie smiled as she chinked her glass against his. 'Yes to us.'

It was a beautiful summer's day, so once they finished their meal, they continued with their walk hand in hand, down towards the beach, where they could take in the picturesque scenery that Ayr had to offer. There was not much activity along the road except the odd businesses and cafes setting up in anticipation of the arriving holidaymakers.

As well as the business brought in from the camp, Ayr was a popular seaside destination in its own right, as well as a town packed with cultural history. Even though it was a Sunday, it was certainly not going to be a day of rest for the local tradesmen. Terry and Angie, taking advantage of the early peace and quiet, headed down to the shore, down the concrete stairs on to the beach, sitting on a ledge in front of the wall looking out to the sea.

'We always need to make the most of our days off, and what a better place than here,' said Terry. He turned to Angie, 'being with you, well it just couldn't be more perfect.'

Angie smirked, leaned over, and kissed Terry tenderly. 'We can't do that at the camp either.'

'I know something else we cannot do at the camp. Something I have not done in a while.'

Angie looked puzzled. 'And what is that?'

Terry reached out his hand and gently caressed her face. I am such a lucky man to have you in my life. I love you so much.'

Angie looked at Terry and beamed. 'I love you too, Terry.' They held each other tightly and kissed deeply. There was no reason to worry about any onlookers as they we cordoned off from the rest of the town.

Terry placed his arm around Angie's shoulder as she snuggled up beside him looking out to sea. 'I could stay here all day,' he said.

'So could I,' replied Angie who then suddenly sat up straight, turned and faced him, clasping on to his hand. 'But we have to put this heavenly moment on pause till later.' Terry sat up. 'Oh really? To do what exactly?'

Angie smiled. 'A small matter of getting you fitted out with a pair of pink tights?' 'Oh good God, I forgot about that.' Terry groaned.

Angie giggled as she stood up and tried to pull Terry on to his feet. 'Come on, up you get. Let's get it over and done with.'

Terry could find no justifiable reason not, to get it over and done with. 'Anything you say Boss.'

They dusted the grains of sand from their clothes before climbing back on to the main road. Off they headed back towards the High Street and the endless number of shops. Terry had been down this road many times, but he had no idea where to go. Thankfully, he was in the hands of an "expert."

Of all the places to choose from, they stopped outside the biggest store in the town, where the open doors showed evidence of some retail activity. 'If we are going to find pink tights, we will find them in here,' said Angie.

Angie started to look around for the women's department. Terry could say nothing, as the feeling of embarrassment continued to grow. This became worse when, Angie, staring at various departmental signs, came across the part of the shop they had been looking for, on the other side of the Menswear Department. There it was, the sign, the stuff of Terry's nightmares,' Lingerie', but it had to be done, he had to enter that scary place.

Terry was doing everything he could to hold on to his composure as Angie led him through the various half-dressed mannequins, focussing on the tights display at the other end of the store.

What did not help, was that Angie occasionally stopped to check out an item of interest, or Terry having to remove the Bras and Pants sets that managed to jump off the displays to snag on to the sleeves of his jacket, with embarrassing frequency.

They finally reached the counter; Angie started inspecting the packets of tights on display across the front of the counter, there were numerous, makes, sizes and colours. She appeared to be scrutinising the whole stock of the tights on display, and was now starting to catch the attention of a member of staff.

'Are you looking for something in particular Madam.'
'Eh Yes,' said Angie. 'I am looking for pink tights, the cheapest end. I need a very large size.'
The sales assistant looked puzzled: 'A large size?' She was looking at Angie's slender build. 'I would not have you down for a large size; I would say you were a size eight?'
Angie replied without hesitation, 'They're not for me. They're actually for him.'
The Assistant, with a barely hidden expression of shock, looked at Terry, whose cheeks by now were glowing hot enough to fry a

burger. 'Don't ask,' he said.

'Don't worry, I won't,' said the Sales Assistant, whose shocked look had now manifested into a quiet smirk. 'I think I have it figured out. Would you perchance work at Butlins?'

'Yep, we are Redcoats,' said Angie.

'I thought that. We have sold a few of these this week in that size.'

'Have any other guys been in here?' asked Terry.

The sales assistant was now sympathetic to Terry's plight: 'They have all been ladies as far as I know. 'I think you are the first Gentleman I've had the pleasure to serve. You had to be a Redcoat.'

'Brilliant!'

Terry guessed that some of his fellow ballet dancers had persuaded some of their female colleagues to purchase tights whenever they were in town. The member of staff knew exactly the kind of tights that Terry was after and quickly placed the large packet inside a carrier bag, which she handed to Terry. 'Thank you,' he said.

The Sales Assistant grinned: 'Thank you for your custom. Do call again.'

'I hope not. These tights have to last me seventeen weeks.'

'No Gentleman has ever said that to me before.' She laughed.

Terry was in no mood for any more shopping. Angie held on to the carrier bag as they left the shop and headed down to the shore to continue the stroll they started earlier. They reached the wall running alongside the beach, when the weather took a sudden turn for the worse.

The blue sky turned a dark shade of grey which meant a signal to dive to the nearest shelter as the heavens were about to open. Sitting on the bench under the shelter, Terry placed his arm around Angie's shoulder looking out to sea, which, was now slowly being covered by the descending rainfall.

'I think we have been in this situation before,' said Terry. Angie giggled as she rested her head on his shoulder. 'It may be a bit cloudy, but it is still a great view.'

'I am certainly not complaining,' replied Terry, leaning over kissing Angie on the forehead.

For a moment, he had temporarily forgotten about the carrier bag, still wrapped around his wrist. It soon came back to him when he held up the contents. Angie started to giggle.

'You're getting a great laugh out of this, aren't you?' he said.

'I am rather,' she said.

'I know couples should do things together, but I never expected anything like this.'

'You have to admit it was funny.'

Terry smirked. 'I suppose it was. I reckon I will remember this moment many years to come.'

'Once the rain stops, shall we get back to the camp?'

'Yeh OK. Go to the Stuart tonight?'

'Yes but back to your chalet first of all', replied Angie.

Terry smiled. He knew that Nick was working today and he saw it as an opportunity for some quality time back at his biller. They would have the place to themselves, something they had not been able to do since they returned to Ayr from Wales. Moreover, a night dancing at the Stuart, the perfect way to end the day. Angie was reading his mind. 'Yes, we can certainly do that. But I want to see you in those tights first.'

Terry squirmed as Angie held out the carrier bag containing the dreaded pink tights. 'Come on!' said Angie, 'it is just you and me. You will be wearing them for the Redcoat show. At least I can show you how to put them on right.'

As before, Terry could not come up with a quick enough answer in his defence, probably because deep down he knew that he had to do it sometime. It would take about ten minutes behind closed doors. A small price to pay for some private time with Angie behind closed doors. The rain soon stopped; Terry took a deep breath. 'Shall we go then?'

Conscious of being caught in another downpour, Terry grabbed on to Angie's hand helping her back on to her feet. They hotfooted it back to the bus terminus, and thirty minutes later, they were back at the camp. They were not in their Reds, but they knew that they still had to behave in an appropriate manner in case they ran into any campers.

As it was a Sunday, the bus would only go as far as the top of the hill. They walked down the road towards the main entrance, looking to take the quickest road back to the staff chalet lines, so they headed along past the Outdoor Swimming Pool, through the car park down towards the staff chalet lines.

Minutes later, Terry opened the door of his chalet and as expected, Nick was working. They both walked in and he closed the door. 'Alone at Last.'

It was early evening, but Angie stepped over and drew the curtains. She turned on the lights, throwing the bag with the tights on the bed. 'Right then – Get em off.'

She proceeded to open the packet and pulled out a large pair of thin pink tights. Terry squirmed as he proceeded to undo his belt. 'Now you know I wouldn't do this for anyone else.'
'I am glad to hear it,' replied Angie. 'Come on now, the quicker it's done, the quicker we can relax for the rest of the night.'

Terry sat down on the edge of the bed taking off his trousers and his socks. Angie proceeded to roll up each of the legs of the tights before handing them carefully over to Terry. 'Take your time and put the toes in first,' said Angie. 'Slowly unravel them up your legs before pulling them up. We don't want to tear them.'

175

'Heaven forbid!'

Terry took great care in putting on the tights. 'God my legs are itchy.' Angie sniggered. 'Stop whining and pull them up.' Terry pulled the tights three quarters of the way up his legs and slowly stood up before completely hitching them up above his waist. Terry carefully inspected every part of his legs, checking for and tears and snags on his new attire.

'Angie could not wipe the broad grin from her face. 'You are definitely loving this,' he said.

'I am,' said Angie. 'You have smashing legs.'

'Thank You,' replied Terry. 'I think they have survived their test, time to take them off.'

'No! Take Your Time!'

Angie stepped back admiring Terry in attire that she had never seen him before. He may be wearing them for laughs, but she liked it a naughty kind of way; however Terry was desperate to get them off and get his trousers back on.

Terry almost jumped out of his lovely pink tights when the chalet door flew open, Nick had returned from the dining hall to freshen up before heading over to the Empire Theatre. The last thing he expected to see was his chalet mate dressed in women's clothing. The door was wide open as Nick stood there with a broad grin on his face as he inspected Terry's new attire.

'Have I come at an inappropriate moment,' he said.

'Funny Boy,' Terry replied. 'Sorting out part of my Redcoat Show costume.'

'There was me thinking that you were searching for your feminine side. Don't let me stop you he sniggered!'

'That's right, laugh! Wait until I see you in your gear.'

'You shall have to wait till the night itself,' Nick replied. 'I don't have time to go shopping for tights.'

'Well it's just as well that we already got you a pair.' Terry reached into the bag and pulled out another packet of tights, which was part of the double pack that he had purchased.

He was originally going to keep this spare box in case the pair he had on got ripped, but he decided to forego his spare pair in favour of his chalet mate, not out of generosity, but to wipe the smirk from his face.

'Thanks for that mate.'

'You owe me a pair of tights, said Terry.

'I cannot believe we are having this conversation,' said Nick, who had no option but to accept Terry's offer. 'I will forego trying them on if it's all the same.'

Terry temporarily forgot his moment of embarrassment as he watched Nick blush slightly, but even he knew that Terry had done him a favour not having to go into the shops on his own during his day off. Like Terry, he was determined to look after his nylons, and carefully placed them in the back of his bottom drawer.

Terry carefully removed his tights, placed them back in the box, put them in his suitcase, quickly putting his trousers back on. 'I thank you for your generosity,' said Nick.

Terry smiled. 'The pleasure's all mine mate.'

As Nick was back on duty soon, Terry suggested to Angie that this would be a good time to go for a stroll. He pulled on his jacket and opened the door. 'We'll leave you to it.'

'Enjoy the rest of your day off guys.'

Terry grabbed on to Angie's hand as they walked down the chalet lines toward the Amusement Park, alongside the sports fields, before heading up to the Stuart Ballroom. Not the privacy he had originally hoped for, but a romantic stroll along the back end of the camp was a decent plan B.

The day visitors had gone home, so there would not be much chance of running into the campers, he was happy to risk just holding hands.

'I've not had a chance to ask you, but how are things with you and Gwendoline,' he said.

'She takes a bit of getting used to,' but she is, nice. We get on fine. You don't seem to have any problems with Nick.'

'Yep, he is a good lad. As soon as he heard about us, he offered to be somewhere else or returning from work if you every wanted to stop over.'

'That would be lovely,' she sighed. 'But I feel guilty leaving Gwendoline by herself. We often talk a lot at night, I think she's a bit lonely.'

'So are you saying that she needs a man in her life.'

'I have no idea, we haven't talked about that. She just wants to be around people.'

'I think she tries too hard.'

CHAPTER SIXTEEN

For Terry, being a second-year Redcoat had its advantages, he would not be working in the Amusement Park for one thing. It was not the most popular detail of a first year Redcoat's life, but it did have its moments.

Whenever it rained, a Red would get to go on the fairground rides with the children, that part was fun. However, aside from those occasional breaks, it would be nothing more standing against the wall pushing a couple of buttons, red for stop green for go, not exactly mind blowing.

Occasionally you may have to tell an over exuberant child to stay in their seats as the ride moved around. Apart from the swanning duties at the dining hall, that was the main part of the day.

When he'd been a first year Red, he'd known, that when he was on "A.P. duty", the *real* fun was going on at the other side of the camp, the kind of activities that he had loved watching as young holidaymaker, the competitions in the venues, and outdoor crowd pleasers like, "It's a Knockout" and the iconic Donkey Derby.

Now Terry would be more involved as a second season Red, and he was looking forward to it immensely. As his working day started to become busier, he would experience another side to working in Red and Whites that he had only scratched the surface of during his first season, and that was doing the evening competitions in the Stuart Ballroom.

Redcoats were there to make a Camper's holiday special, so whatever events were being staged, they were expected to do anything and everything, regardless of any potential physical harm that may come their way. They were often labelled as "indestructible", because whatever happened, they always came up smiling.

One morning in the Stuart, Terry was Redcoat I/C at a popular contest amongst junior campers, "The Picture of Health," a competition in swimwear for boys and girls aged 12 to 13 years. As the contest was catering for youngsters, taking the honours of Compere would be resident children's entertainer, "Uncle Jamie".

Jamie Barker, aged 55, spent the most of his working life working on the Railways as a Guardsman, making use of his spare time working on his true passion of Magic. It was by pure accident he started to receive invites to entertain at children's parties. It was when he was made redundant, he started to find his true calling, when he was offered the position as a resident children's entertainer at Butlins Ayr.

Whilst very popular with the children, Jamie would often use the opportunity to push the boundaries with his Magic, testing them out during his shows, and, whichever female Redcoat that was on duty that night would be very nervous redcoat indeed.

Performing magic for the children was a requirement for all "Uncles" and Redcoats were always on hand to encourage the young "Eager Beavers" to get involved. One evening in the Empire Theatre during a performance, Jamie required the services of a young boy to help him with a "special trick." Redcoat Annie, a first-year Redcoat from Carlisle was on duty, standing smiling and laughing from the side of the stage. When he asked for volunteers, Annie, full of enthusiasm, marched off the stage to find a willing young assistant.

Annie escorted a 10-year-old boy, called Charlie on to the stage towards Jamie. 'Welcome young man. Are you ready to help Uncle Jamie with a special trick.'

'Yes,' said the young boy.

'Right, I am going to bring out a piece of equipment and I need you to stand at the side and make sure that everything I do is correct. Is that OK?' Charlie eagerly agreed. Annie, behind the smile was starting to become curious. She had been one of the regular "Aunties" at the junior shows and was familiar with all of Jamie's routines, but not this one.

Her pulse started to race when Jamie walked off stage, and pulled out a large wooden structure covered with sackcloth. Annie was rooted to the spot. It looked terrifyingly familiar. What was he going to do with that?'

Jamie pulled off the cloth to reveal what resembled a Guillotine, a device used centuries earlier in France for public executions. It came with the standard requirements, a wooden block to put your head in, and right above was a wooden panel with a silver blade at the top. The young boy was impressed. Annie was anything but.

'Now first,' Jamie immediately assured the young boy, 'I don't want you to lie down there. You are going to stand at the side and watch what happens and make sure that I do this right. We will need someone else to lie down here.' Jamie smiled as he turned to Annie. 'I think we should ask Auntie Annie to help us. What do you think boys and girls?'

"YESSSSSS!' screamed the young audience. They were not quite sure what they were going to see, but they knew that it was going to be something more exciting than some of the small scale tricks associated with kiddie's magic shows. Annie stood routed to the spot; she had worked out what he was going to do. She knew that he was a skilled magician, but the prospect of doing something like that terrified her.

Jamie walked over towards Annie, grabbing her by the hand, leading her over to his contraption. 'Jamie, I hope you know what you are doing,' she whispered.

Jamie laughed as he announced to the rest of the audience: "she has asked me if I know what am doing.'

There was the sound of laughter amongst the young audience. There were also some Parents in the auditorium with their children who were now watching with interest. Apart from Jamie and the rest of the Redcoats on duty, they were the ones who knew what was going to happen next. They were delighted that it was not one of them.

Ever nerve in Annie's body was starting to shake as Jamie guided Annie to the bench directly behind the "Guillotine", getting her to lie down. He gently placed her head on the wooden block before fastening it securely in place. Her eyes were open wide as all Annie could see was the shiny metal blade directly above her head. 'OH MY GOD!' she whispered.

"We are going to play a game boys and girls. This is the gadget they used in France many years ago, to chop people's heads off. This is a trick to let you see what it was like.' He turned to his young volunteer; 'As they used to chop people's heads off, they used to have a soldier at the side, playing the drums, so I want you to be our drummer.' Jamie went to the side of his prop to bring out a soldier's hat at toy drum.

'Now we are going to pretend that this is France, 100 of years ago, you play the drums and we will bring down the blade and see if we can chop Auntie Annie's head. Annie was desperately trying to hold back the tears, of fear, repeatedly saying in her head. 'It's just a trick! It's just a trick!'

For added effect, Jamie placed a basket directly under Annie's head and started a countdown with the young audience. 'OK BOYS AND GIRLS! COUNT ALONG WITH UNCLE JAMIE. THREE! TWO! ONE!' Jamie pulled a leaver as the blade came crashing down towards Annie, whose eyes were now tightly shut, as she could not look at that blade any longer. The children cheered, whereas the adults in the audience held their breath. Seconds after the blade came down it appeared to go through Annie's neck.

Jamie immediately winched the blade back up to the top and lifted the top of the wooden stocks holding Annie in place. 'Boys and Girls, as you can see, Auntie Annie has not had her head chopped off. Let's hear it for Auntie Annie!' There was a collective roar of approval around the auditorium as he helped Annie up. She temporarily held onto a chair until she stopped shaking 'And please keep that applause going for our young helper, Charlie.'

Jamie took the boy by the hand and led him off the stage towards another Redcoat Auntie who was on duty, and made sure that he returned to his seat. Annie, her shaking now under control, took the opportunity to walk off stage left, to a quiet and secluded part of the theatre and for the next two minutes uttered some non-Redcoat language.

Terry's working relationship with Uncle Jamie would be restricted to the morning competitions. The one thing that he remembered from the last year was that the MC's liked to get Redcoats "involved". Jamie was no different. Terry knew that he had to be ready just in case "Uncle Jamie" had a moment of inspiration, and for the Redcoats, that would be something either embarrassing, or, some pain would most likely be involved.

Like all other competitions, the Redcoats regular routine was to arrange the contestants in an organised fashion, hand out their numbers, and bring them out in front of the judges in groups so they could be interviewed by the Compere.

Two Redcoats would "dress the stage"; standing at opposite corners, in line with the contestants. Then one of them would take a turn in leading the groups around the ballroom floor in the customary parade before they were interviewed in front of the judges.

That day, Terry led a group around the floor to the sound of hand clapping, encouraging the campers to join in. The venue was not exactly busy, but those who were there, more than played their part, and made as much noise as possible.

Terry had completed his lap of the floor, taking his group of young female contestants back in front of the stage. As he resumed his place "Stage Right," Jamie stepped forward to interview the contestants. 'Ah right, Judges, let me talk to our first contestant. Step forward a wee bit. Can you tell Uncle Jamie your name?'

'I'm Susan.'

'Hello Susan, and where are you from?'

'I'm from Glasgow.' This resulted with a loud cheer from a small group near one of the concrete pillars at the edge of the dance floor. 'Would that be your family by any chance,' asked Jamie.

'Aye! Ma Mum, Dad and brother.' Jamie waved toward them. 'Hello Susan's family!' he said.

'Now this is about finding out who is a picture of health. How do you keep healthy and fit?'

'I like to do Judo.'

'Judo? Martial Arts! That is excellent. Have you got a black belt?'

Susan giggled. 'Nooooo. Just a yellow belt?'

'Still impressive. I bet you are good. Can you do one of those Judo throws?'

'Oh Aye.' she replied. Terry leaned back behind the contestant's line, looking across towards his Redcoat pal Bill. They both had a smile on their faces, a smile of fear, because they had an idea what was coming next.

Jamie smirked: 'Do you think you could throw Redcoat Terry?' Susan looked over her shoulder, looking Terry up and down. 'Oh Aye!' she said.

'Come on Terry, get your coat off,' said Jamie. Terry slowly took off his Jacket, looking directly across at Jamie. It was not difficult for him to figure out what was going on in Terry's mind. Bill was standing at the other end, trying to hold in his laughter.

Terry stayed in character, stepping forward as the unwilling volunteer. The watching holidaymakers and judges sat up in their seats as they waited to see how he would deal with this situation.

Terry carefully placed his jacket at the side of the stage. 'Bill keep an eye on my jacket mate,' said Terry. Bill smiled giving Terry an OK signal. Terry nervously walked forward towards the young lady. This was her moment to shine. Terry knew that as a 12-year-old girl, she would not have the power to dislodge him, so it was down to him to make her look good.

'Right Susan, this is Redcoat Terry. Show us how it is done,' said Jamie.

Terry stood alongside Susan, who grabbed on to his arm with one hand, hanging on to his shirt with the other. Terry looked anxious as he could feel her trying to pull him across; instinctively he threw himself forward rolling over on to his back, hitting the floor hard, making one of the Judges jump out of her seat as his leg cashed against her table.

Terry knew nothing about stunt work and his improvised fall caused him pain in his lower back. The shocked look on his face earned Susan a round of applause from the appreciative audience. Susan, on the other hand, stood there looking at Terry, still lying spread eagled on the floor, with more than a shocked look on her face, she was still wondering how she had managed to throw him so well.

Jamie could not stop laughing as Terry lay there on the floor mouthing the word "help". 'Bill! I think Terry needs some assistance,' Jamie said. Bill stepped forward and carefully pulled Terry back on to his feet, brushing the dust from his shirt, before handing his is Redcoat Blazer back. 'Falling down in the line of duty sir?'

'Remind me not to do that again,' sighed Terry.

Bill smiled. 'Somehow, I don't think I'll need to remind you,' he whispered.

'Round of applause please for Susan from Glasgow,' said Jamie. 'And keep that applause going for our Judo volunteer, Redcoat Terry.'

Terry willingly accepted the accolade as he took his bow; not bending too far forward, in case people could see that his back was hurt from his acrobatics.

Then there was the Donkey Derby, along with the Knobbly Knees contest, often associated with Butlins Holiday Camps just as much as the Redcoats themselves were. This was a major event in the Holiday programme, and it was run on the Sports Field. It was a day at the races, where the adults would get to bet on the "runners and riders," the donkeys were the runners, and the riders would be their own children.

Every week the management would pray to the "Weather Gods" to deliver a rain free afternoon, and on most occasions, the Gods complied. However, it was always company policy to have a Plan B. Entertainment at Butlins; they did not stop because of inclement weather.

Every day Radio Butlins would promote the upcoming Donkey Derby, encouraging people to buy tickets, encourage their children to register as Jockeys, Mums and Dads to become owners of the donkeys for that week, or just turn up to join in the fun.

The message would often end with: "In the event of inclement weather, the event would then be held in the Stuart Ballroom.'

'They are going to have a hell of a job getting those Donkey's up that escalator,' said one camper.

Staying in the theme of a big "day at the races", money would change hands with the on-site "bookies," with the results being displayed on the Totaliser Board beside the MC who would be on this occasion be Redcoat Roddy, assisted by Deke, despite regular complaints to the Management for assistance from a female Redcoat.

There would be eight donkeys per race, six races complete with a Tote open for betting. Under the persistence of Ron De Vere, there was the occasion during the previous season, when a camper came away with a Donkey Derby Jackpot of £1000. Therefore, under the right conditions, there was serious money to be made. There was never any suggestion that history would repeat itself. If there was enough money to cover a winning guest's drinks bill that night, then they would be more than happy.

Like the regular competitions, Redcoats would be stationed at certain points around the circuit, looking after the Jockeys and the designated owners. A couple would always be positioned at the starting line, to make sure that the animals would be moving in the right direction and at a decent speed. The others, around the course, would be making sure the spectators cheered on the competitors, as well as providing organised mayhem in between races.

Deke would often come down from his platform and encourage campers to test his skill catching an egg in his hands.

The contents usually though, came down over his head. The Redcoats would also march up and down the sides the barrier, winding the crowd up, whilst making sure that their white plimsolls would stay clear of the brown deposits left by the donkeys during the race. A worthwhile skill that Redcoats had to master rather quickly.

Terry's participation in the Redcoat on field entertainment, would see him, along with his former chalet mate Bill, giving a small group of spectators a rock and roll master class, a demonstration of their Jive routine from last season's Redcoat Show, which went down well with the punters. However, the biggest applause would be at the end, when a camper sneaked up behind Bill pulling down his trousers. 'Cover those legs up Bill,' boomed Roddy. 'People have just had their dinner.'

Eight Races later, the Donkey Derby was finished, there were no injuries to report amongst the Jockeys, or their trusty steeds, who managed to canter in the direction they were supposed to. Roddy announced that apart from the certificate and rosettes given out on the day, there would be a special prize for the most successful Jockey and Owner at the official prize giving in the Stuart Ballroom at the end of the week.

'Ladies and Gentleman, Boy and Girls, let's hear it for all of our Jockeys, our owners, and all of the people involved in another brilliant afternoon.' Applause and cheers rained throughout the assembled crowd. However, there was still one more race to complete.

'We are going to have one more race,' said Roddy. 'We are looking for looking for some adult volunteers, some big strapping lads and some passengers for a piggy back race extraordinaire.

A couple of large gentleman, feeling the effects of an afternoon drinking session, stepped forward, taking off their tops demonstrating their masculinity, trying to pick up two of the

Donkeys to put on their backs. 'Pit them doon you two!' shouted Roddy. 'We are looking for some ladies to be carried around the course. Redcoats, go search from some lady volunteers for the Macho Brothers here!'

Two Redcoat sprinted across to the end of the field after discovering two star contestants from the Ladies "Cheeky Charming and Chubby Competition,' much to the delight of the crowd and to the shock of the two gentlemen who reckoned that they would be more successful lifting the Donkeys.

The official line regarding guest's participation was that Redcoats were there to encourage them to get involved. Redcoats usually used that as a license to get amongst the crowd and to find and drag their own "volunteers", who would often need a bit of "persuasion". They would initially put up a struggle but once in full view of the crowd, they soon realised that they would create greater embarrassment by walking back to where they had been.

'We don't have enough volunteers,' said Roddy. 'If we can't get enough men, and any of you ladies out there would like to be carried around by some hunky Redcoats, then come on to the field.'

As soon as Roddy mentioned the word "Hunk," that was Deke's cue, resplendent in his School Boy's outfit to run into the crowd to grab the lightest female that he could find. He ended up with a 45-year-old Mother of two, who was egged on by her children. She reluctantly tried to climb on his back, but Deke's 20 stone frame, meant that he could not squat down high enough for her to climb on board.

Terry quickly found a solution to the problem grabbing a large stool at the side of the platform, and along with Bill helped the woman on to the stool so she could get on board. 'We need one more couple,' said Roddy. Terry then got the fright of his life when a grandMother grabbed him by the arm. 'Come on son.' It was an offer that Terry could not refuse.

During his dancing days, Terry was known for his prowess when it came to lifting ladies on the dance floor, but this was the first time he had had to run with one on his back, and a sixty-five year old grandMother at that. He was not sure if his body could take the strain. He turned his back toward the woman, setting himself in the prone position. 'Come on then,' he said.

The lady took a few steps back before taking a short run and jump on to Terry's back who caught her at the first attempt. 'Comfy? 'asked Terry,

'Aye no bad,' she replied. 'You are all skin and bones son. Do they no feed you here?'

Terry laughed despite having a grandMother on his back. His eyes opened wide as she slapped her hand down hard on to his backside. 'Gee up then sonny boy!' She laughed.

It was the only signal Terry needed. He marched straight forward to the starting line. The donkeys had been taken away back to their Pens, but they had left plenty of "deposits" around the field to remember them by.

The starting line-up was Terry, Deke along with the two eager macho male volunteers, complete with their Jockeys. Roddy brought them under starters orders.

'Good luck Gentleman,' he said, 'and I think you are going to need it.'

'Hawd on,' shouted Deke. 'Do we get danger money for this.'

'On our wages? How can I put this,' replied Roddy. 'NAW! AUDIENCE! COUNT ME DOWN!'

'THREE! TWO! ONE!'

The runners immediately took off. The race was on! The sound of cheers and laughter roared amongst the crowd, with Roddy providing the on-field commentary.

'AND THEY ARE OFF. A PERFECT START BY THE RUNNERS AND RIDERS! THE MACHO BROTHERS TAKE AN EARLY LEAD COMING AROUND THE FIRST BEND. HOWEVER, IT APPEARS TO BE ONE BENDER TOO MANY AS BOTH FALL CRASHING TO THE DECK LEAVING A BATTLE BETWEEN THE REDCOATS. TERRY FOLLOWED BY DEKE. COME ON FOLKS WHO DO YOU WANT TO WIN !!!!'

Redcoat Pride was at stake! The crowd roared as both men thundered along the back straight towards the second last bend. In a normal race, Terry would have a clear edge over Deke in terms of years and overall fitness. However, this was no normal race.

Both men were grabbing on to whatever part of their jockey they could hang on to as they came round the final bend. Deke resorted to Redcoat gamesmanship, trying to barge Terry off the track, but his dancing training appeared to be paying dividends, as it was going to take more than Deke to knock him over.

As they were approaching the finishing line, Terry tried to repay the compliment by using what bulk he had charging into Deke, but he forgot to notice one of the donkey's deposits just in front of him, completely losing his footing, crashing into Deke with both men falling over the line.

The crowd roared their approval, with both men lying flat out on the grass, with their jockeys beside them laughing their heads off. Terry then remembered that this was not just a Redcoat race, he had a camper on his back and both had hit the ground hard. Terry immediately sat up and attended to his passenger.

'How are you doing? You OK! Sorry about the hitting the deck at the end.'
The lady was still laughing as Terry helped her to sit up. 'Don't worry about that son. That was Fun.'

Terry stood up as he helped the lady back on to her feet. 'Did we win?'

CHAPTER SEVENTEEN

Having survived the opening weeks of the summer season, Terry had now felt settled back into his life as a Butlins Redcoat, more than he did twelve months earlier. This was a different version of the young man compared to the one that first pulled on the Red and White uniform in 1982.

He was no longer the nervous insecure individual, and even better, he had returned with the young lady that he fell in love with, and they were working together.

If there was a down side, last year, Angie would arrange the spare time in between her shifts to be with Terry, finishing up in his chalet at the end of the evening. Now, apart from their day off, any time together could only be when their working schedule would allow.

When their relationship had started to become more serious, Angie started to spend the night with Terry. This had scared him to begin with, but now he could think of nothing better than having her wake up beside him every morning. They knew though, that after living like a couple during the Kids Venture Weeks at Pwhelli, that they would not have the same level of comfort when they returned to Ayr, but just being together whenever possible was the important thing.

During the opening weeks of the 1983 season and working with a new team, it was obvious to everyone that he and Angie were very much a couple. Terry was relieved when he found out that he had a very accommodating chalet mate in the shape of Nick. He had no objections to Angie staying overnight in their chalet, and he had offered to make himself scarce if they ever wanted some intimate time together.

Like Terry, Angie had a developed a strong friendship with her chalet mate, Gwendoline, regarded by many as an unusual character, with her strange posh accents and her over made up appearance. She never had the heart to bring up the subject of spending the nights with Terry.

Angie, felt that even though they were friends, Gwendoline was lonely, judging by the late night chats that they always had at the end of their shift.

It was the middle of week four of the 1983 season; it was on the hottest day of the year. Having helped the Pentathlete Coach during one of his testing sessions, Terry decided to take some respite from the intense summer heat back at his chalet ahead of lunchtime Swanning.

Once back at base, Terry took off his jacket, shirt and tie, dumping it on the bed; he headed over to the wash hand basin, turned on the tap and proceeded to splash his torso with cold water, providing much needed relief. 'AHHHH! I so needed that,' he said.

When his body went back to something like normal temperature, he grabbed his towel, rubbing his body vigorously to get his circulation going before putting on a clean shirt. He had about forty-five minutes before lunch, so he made good use of the time sitting down on his bed to whiten his evening shoes.

He had still not quite got used to the idea, that a few weeks since coming back from Wales, Angie was still living in different accommodation to him. Sitting in the cool surroundings of his chalet, he left the door wide open letting some light into the room, secretly hoping Angie would pass by his door in between details. It was not long before someone did appear at the open-door way, but it was not Angie.

'Gooood Morrrrning Terry.'

'Ah Hi there Gwendoline,' said Terry. 'Thought you were working today. How's things?'

Gwendoline hesitated. 'Ohhh fine,' she said. 'I have been on "Office" today. I am back in Reds this afternoon on AP. Just going to get changed.'

Instead of heading back to her Chalet, Gwendoline looked over both shoulders, making sure that no one else was around. 'Can I possibly have a word with you Terry?'

Terry was puzzled but he could see something was troubling her. 'Eh sure! Come into the office.' Gwendoline carefully walked in slowly closing the door behind her. She sat down on Nick's bed, facing Terry; something was definitely troubling her. 'Eh! I need some advice.'

Whenever a first year Redcoat asked for advice, it would usually have something to do with work. Judging by the look on Gwendolyn's face however, Terry had a hunch that this was something else.

He was flattered that she appeared to be putting her trust him, but thought she should be talking to Angie because of those late night chats they have. 'What's up? You and Angie had a fall out or something.'

'Nothing like that,' she said. 'I need to ask you about Nick.'

'You have had an argument with Nick?'

Gwendoline was starting to get frustrated. 'I am not having any arguments with anybody. I need your help?' she took a deep breath trying to calm herself. 'It is about Nick though.' Terry still could not work out what the problem was. 'How I can get him to notice me.'

'Notice you?' Terry then finally figured out where this was leading. 'You got the hots for Nick!'

'More than that,' she said. 'I think I am falling for him. Has he ever mentioned me? Has he said anything at all?'

Terry did recall a few conversations he had had with Nick, where he would often refer to Gwendoline as "nice, but a bit weird.' Not exactly the foundation for playing cupid.

'I just don't know what it is,' she continued. 'I think about him all the time and I get nervous when he is near me.' Terry could not believe what he was hearing. He did not want to shatter her hopes, but she was obviously looking for some direction. He personally could not see them as a couple, but he suddenly remembered a piece of advice that he'd picked up last season.

'Honestly, I don't know how he feels,' said Terry, trying to look as convincing as possible. Putting his shoes and bottle of whitener to one side, leaning forward talking to her softly. 'I remember when I first came here; I learned that to get anywhere in the job, you must be yourself. Don't try to be something you are not. If you think Nick is not noticing you, maybe you are trying too hard.'

'Trying too hard?'

'I think you are trying to be a character that is not you. Like your accent for a start.'

'What is wronnnggg with way I talk? What is wrong in speaking properrrlllly '

'Nothing,' he replied. 'When I hear you talk to people, every now and again, you would occasionally slip in a word that I would expect to hear from someone like my Dad. He also came from Port Glasgow.'

Gwendoline took a deep breath; it was starting to dawn on her that he maybe had a point. 'Is it that bad?'

Gwendoline changed her accent and tone. Now instead of using a forced imitation of a resident of the Home Counties, she was began using a gentle accent that was more in keeping with the West Coast of Scotland. 'That sounds better,' said Terry. 'Why did you try using a silly posh accent anyway?'

'I wanted to work in London and someone told me that I needed to change the way I talked if I wanted to succeed down there. I went all posh and I got a job with a Doctor as a Nanny.'

'How long did that last for.'

'A couple of months. They got rid of me for some reason. I think it might have had something to do with those ratbag weans of theirs.'

Terry smiled. 'Now that sounds like someone from Port Glasgow talking.'

Gwendoline laughed, 'I just wanted to be different. Someone that would be interesting.'

'Well you are. You would not be working here if you did not have something special.'

Gwendoline smiled 'Thanks Terry.

She was now speaking in her normal dialect, and was starting to feel like a huge weight had been lifted from her shoulders. 'You think this will make a difference in getting Nick to take an interest.'

'Honestly? I cannot answer that,' replied Terry. 'I cannot speak for him. He could do. If he did, he would at least be interested in you. Not a version of you.'

Gwendoline, slowly nodded. 'I'll give it a go.'

'If nothing happens between you two, then it wasn't meant to be. There will be somebody out there for you. I am sure of it. If it is him, then excellent. You could do a lot worse."

Gwendoline stood up and opened the door. 'Thanks again Terry.'

'No worries. So, is it Gwen now, instead of Gwendoline?'

'I think it always was. I am away to change into my Reds now.'

'See you later.'

Terry felt rather pleased with himself and he went back to sorting out his shoes. It was only a matter of minutes before the door opened again. This time it was Angie, smiling at him. 'Someone had an easy day then.'

'I have been rather busy if you must know. Been on Pentathlete and I have been having a very interesting conversation with your chalet mate.'

Angie quickly sat down on the bed opposite. 'Oh yes? Tell me!'

'Terry smiled. 'I am afraid I can't tell you.'

Angie opened her eyes in surprise. 'Eh since when did we start keeping secrets from each other? Come on tell me!'

Terry smiled. 'I'm sorry Angie, it wouldn't be right.'

Angie got up, walked over looking closely into Terry's face. 'Tell me! Or I will remove your Custard Cream rations.'

'I love it when you are in a dominant mood.'

There was a glint in Angie's eyes. She smiled. 'Do you now! You are still not going to tell me though.'

'Like I said. I can't. It wouldn't be right.'

Angie was none the wiser. 'I will leave her to tell you when she is ready,' continued Terry, 'if things go the way I think they will, then everything might become clear pretty quick.'

'Well, it's almost lunchtime. Get your tie and Jacket on,' said Angie. 'By the way, where is Nick?'

'I just remembered,' replied Terry, 'he was "Hunting the Pirate" this morning. Oh Dear!'

Right on cue, Nick arrived, not in his Redcoat Uniform, but was wearing an official Butlins tracksuit, completely soaked from the top of his head, all the way to his toes, and he'd left a watery trail all the way down the chalet line and was now dripping all over the chalet floor.   He stopped, looking at Terry all stern face. Terry and Angie, looked at Nick, trying to hold back the laughter. 'Ahwright Nick.'

'Aw right Terry.'

'You look wet.' Nick continued to keep a straight face.

'Just slightly Terry.'

Tears were staring to appear at the corner of Angie's eyes, she did not know how long she could contain herself.   Terry continued to question his chalet mate. 'So what happened,' he asked.

'We were "Hunting the Pirate" and the little sweethearts pushed me in the pool. That is what happened.'

Angie could not hold back any more as both burst into hysterical laughter. 'That's right. Laugh you rotten lot.' Terry regained some of his composure, placing his hand onto his Chalet Mate. 'It goes with the job pal.   At least you can swim.'

Nick stepped back outside, started to remove some of his soaked garments before stepping back into the chalet to dry off. Just then, a female Redcoat appeared from the top of the stairs. Nick forgot about his sodden clothes as he watched her slowly walk down the stairs, his expression stunned. Had they recruited a new member of staff, he certainly was not aware of it. The look on his face suggested that he had found the girl of his dreams.

Nick was mesmerised by this woman's long blonde hair, her perfect figure and her natural beauty, enhanced with the slightest touch of make-up. He was even more shocked as she appeared to know them all. 'Awright Guys.'

Her eyes were drawn in the direction of Nick, still dripping wet from his exploits by the pool earlier.   'Well! If it isn't Mr Darcy! The wet look suits you. I'll see you guys at Swanning.' Everyone watched as this "new Redcoat" walked up towards the end of Staff Chalet Lines before disappearing on to the main road of the camp.

'See you later Gwen,' said Terry.

Nick and Angie looked stunned. 'Gwen!'

Terry feeling rather smug finished off fastening his tie, then putting on his Red Blazer. 'Yeh Gwen! Your chalet mate Angie my love. '

'Who is Mr Darcy?' enquired Nick

'The good-looking hero from a Jane Austen novel. Pride and Prejudice, 'said Angie. 'I remember reading it at school. Somewhere in the story he got a soaking as well.'

Nick now thought getting soaked had its merits. 'Really?' He could not get the vision of loveliness out of his head. Gwendoline, and her new look. Who'd have thought it.

Terry placed his hand on Angie's shoulder gesturing to her that it would be a good time for them to head to Swanning. He decided that the time was right to give Angie the whole story, because she knew that she would be interrogating Gwen about her "makeover" the moment they reached the dining hall.

'Let Nick get himself sorted, we can head up to the dining hall. Shall we?'

'Eh Yeh – OK' As they walked up the chalet lines themselves, the cold water started to remind Nick that now would be a good time to get changed and that should be as soon as possible.'

It only took them five minutes to reach the stairs leading to the dining hall where there was the usual crowd of guests waiting to get in for their lunch. Right amongst the crowd was Gwen, who had given a wave to her chalet mate. By then, Terry had given a full account of their earlier conversation. He told her it was in confidence and she should wait until Gwen said something.

Angie left Terry to mingle with the holidaymakers and she went over towards Gwen, who immediately headed in to the dining hall with some other Reds after seeing an open door. Terry was not in any hurry just yet. He let the ladies have a private chat, whilst he kept himself occupied, staying outside with the holidaymakers. Besides, he was on the lookout for Nick to arrive.

Minutes later, an out of breath Nick came bounding down the stairs. Terry looked at his watch. "Awright Sir. And what time do you call this.'

'I am not late,' replied Nick.

'You would never have guessed by the speed you came down those stairs.'

Nick looked around, he appeared to be looking for somebody. 'I think that it should be a good time to hit our stations and open the doors.'

'That's exactly what I was thinking,' said Nick, noticing Angie and Gwen on the opposite of side of the wooden doorframes. 'It won't be long now,' said Nick to the guests as they went into dining hall.

Terry took his place in front of one of the wooden partitions facing one of the set of double doors. Nick walked over to join Gwen and Angie. Angie took this as a sign for her to leave the two together.

Nick and Gwen stood talking, waiting for the signal to open the doors. Angie walked over towards Terry with a broad smile on her face. 'Well?' said Terry.

'She told me everything,' said Angie. 'That was a really nice thing you did for her.'

Terry went back into smug mode. 'Yes I thought so.'

Angie lent forward and whispered in his ear. 'You are lovely'

Terry smiled. 'Eh yes!'

'Have I told you that I love you.'

'Not since yesterday when I brought you a bar of your favourite chocolate after AP yesterday.' He leant back towards her ear. 'I love you too,' he whispered

'All we can do now is wait and see how things progress.' The doors then flew open; it was time for the guests to come in for their lunch. 'RIGHT PEOPLE IN YOU COME! THE LAST ONE IN DOES THE DISHES!'

Terry and Angie smiled as the holidaymakers continued to come into the dining hall, but he would occasionally glance to his side to see Nick and Gwen starting to have fun together with the guests.

She had wanted Nick to notice her, looks as if he had now, the real Gwen at last.

Later that evening, all the Reds were in the Stuart Ballroom, dancing to the sounds of "Caledonia". At the end of the night, Nick had joined all the male Redcoats on to the stage to pack away the disco equipment along with the group's instruments into the back room behind the stage.

Terry helped Nick carry the Disco Consul down the stairs. 'So what are you up to on your day off tomorrow? 'asked Terry

'Well I am going to spend the day in Ayr,' said Nick

'Doing anything special?'

'Yeh I have got a date.'

'Ah excellent! Anyone we know?' Nick smiled as he gently tapped the side of his nose. He was not saying a word.

Terry smirked. 'Well have fun. Moreover, be good. If you can't be good, be careful. And if you can't be careful...'

'I know, get a pram,' said Nick. 'Let me guess. You heard it at Late Night Cabaret.'

'Yep-Late Night Cabaret

It had come to the end of another long day, which as usual finished in the Stuart. Having finished striking the stage, Terry and Angie walked along the main road of the camp back towards the staff chalet lines. They reached the bottom of the stairs, leading up to Angie's chalet. 'Well it won't be long till our day off,' said Terry. He held on to Angie's hands. 'If there is one thing I don't like about this job, is having to say good night to you at the bottom of these stairs.'

Angie leaned forward gently kissing Terry. 'You understand why I can't come down?'

Terry sighed. 'Yeh! I understand, but that doesn't make it any easier.'

'I'll make it up to you on our next day off.'

Terry smiled, not knowing exactly what she actually meant. However, it did sound good.

'I look forward to that,' he said. 'Look, I will let you get your beauty sleep.' Terry leant forward and kissed Angie 'Goodnight.'

Angie walked up the stairs towards her chalet line. She gave a final wave before finally closing the doors. Terry sighed as he turned towards his own front door. As he opened it, there was no sign of Nick. Terry began to undress, ready for his bed.

He hung up his Jacket on the rail before slowly taking off his tie. Stepping over to the sink, he proceeded to brush his teeth, but was stopped half way through, following a knock at the door. 'Don't tell me Nick lost his keys.

He walked over the door, ready to give his chalet mate a piece of his mind for being careless. He opened the door to see Angie standing there. She looked deep into his eyes, smiling.

'Hey Mr Redcoat! Room for one more?'

CHAPTER EIGHTEEN

The morning light shone through the curtains onto Terry's face, slowly waking him up from what had been a perfect night's sleep. He was certainly not in the mood to get up.

He turned his head to one side and looked at Angie, sleeping beside him. It was something they had been hoping for, ever since returning from Wales to Ayr. It had taken longer than they hoped, but they were grateful that it finally had happened, even if it was by accident. Nick was now unofficially living with Gwen upstairs, and Angie was downstairs with Terry. Life could not be any better.

Two weeks on, they had worked out a system to avoid any problems with security checks. Nick and Angie's personal belongings would remain in their official accommodations, so they would be ready to temporarily move back in at a moment's notice.

In terms of everybody's personal life, everything was settled, but as they were moving into the peak of the 1983 season, Terry was starting to think about what it was he wanted out of the actual job this year. Last season he was "Terry the Dancer," and even though he was still actively involved on the dancefloor of the Stuart Ballroom, he wasn't as busy, when it came to using the microphone.

Last year, he was thrown in at the deep end, fronting the disco during the opening night of the season, and he even got to compere the mid-week disco dancing competition. It scared the life out of him to begin with, but by the end of the summer, he wanted more. Thanks to the change in management and the recruitment of personnel, those opportunities had virtually disappeared. This time it would be no more than occasionally fronting the Bingo.

During a conversation with Deke on the train back to Ayr from Wales, Deke suggested that he should look at trying other things besides dancing. Though he may have agreed with Deke in principal, doing it was a different matter. He was not regarded as Children's Uncle Material, as his pale complexion, and dark hair and eyes, seemed to be a bit off putting with the younger campers. He did not scare them, but they felt more at home with other members of staff.

Dressing up in a Tu Tu and doing a ballet routine in the Redcoat show, or standing in front of a coffin during the Old-Time Music Hall, certainly did not help his case, even though it did get many laughs.

What had made the biggest impression on Terry last season, had been the Redcoat Characters he had worked with, and how big an impact they'd made with the holidaymakers. Mainly those who dressed up in apparel away from their traditional Redcoat Uniforms, whether it was on the stage or on the complex interacting with guests. That idea became obvious with Deke, dressing up in a schoolboy's uniform.

Maybe that was the answer, he would try to find his own character, but maybe not as extreme.

Terry was a lot more confident and funny in the way he interacted with guests, however he was never extrovert enough to hold attention on his own. He was not a solo comic. He knew that the bosses were happy with the way he carried out his job, but personally, he felt that as he was back, he wanted to do more.

As a young boy, he had been a fan of TV and Radio comedy. His favourite pastime would be to sit in his room listening to the radio recordings of old music hall comics, and the manic antics of the "Goon Show." He would sometimes try to mimic some of the characters as he listened, in the quiet of his own room, he did a decent job of it.

Acting the fool did not come easy. Nevertheless, he knew that he had to do something. One day, coming out of the Stuart Ballroom, he walked along the road, hoping for some inspiration. As he passed one of the souvenir shops, something told him to look inside.

A few feet on entering the shop, he stopped at a counter packed with a selection of small toys and joke novelties. There was nothing different here to any other toyshops. He was looking just for the sake of looking, but his attention was drawn towards a small packet lying on the counter, containing a packet of large plastic ears.

Terry had a flashback to when he was still at school, he used to get a kick out of Saturday Morning television programmes, like "Swap Shop" and his favourite; "TISWAS" – "Today is Saturday, Watch and Smile." He did more than smile. It was one of the funniest programmes on the box.

One of his favourite memories a few years before, was seeing a young impressionist, sticking on a pair of plastic ears, impersonating Prince Charles. Back in those days, all impressionists were doing him. It was not a difficult voice to master. If they did not have the decent material, then the ears would get the laughs, and laughter was an important weapon for any Redcoat.

He stared at the packet. Normally he would chuck them back with the rest of the "merchandise", but something told him to buy them. Sticking them in his blazer pocket, Terry marched along the road towards the staff chalet lines whilst not forgetting the golden rule for all Redcoats, smiling and saying hello to passers-by.

There was half an hour before he needed to think about lunchtime Swanning. The sensible thing to do, was to get back to his chalet and dispose of his new acquisition. It would not be good walking about the camp, with your pockets full. They were never designed to hold things anyway.

Back at the chalet, he took out the package and threw it down on the bed. For a brief second, he stood there looking at a set of plastic ears, wondering if he had wasted his money. 'Ah bugger it,' he said, grabbing the package ripping it open, picking up the ears, carefully hooking them on to his own.

He stared at this strange vision in the mirror, immaculately dressed in his Red and White Uniform, sporting a set of oversized ears. 'Right, I certainly look the part – a right idiot! Now what!' he said. Continuing to stare at this strange reflection in the mirror, he was starting to think again about the comedian on Saturday Morning TV with his oversized ears, walking about with one hand behind his back speaking in a Royal fashion, like the Prince of Wales.

'How did he do it,' thought Terry.

He remembered that it all started with him putting his mouth in an awkward shape. 'Ehhhhhhhh,' went Terry. Terry stopped for a second. 'Hold on, that was not bad,' he thought. Terry adjusted the shape of his mouth, bringing his hands together in a connecting gesture, whilst speaking in a deeper than normal tone. 'Ehhhhhhhh, Good Evennning. What a pleasure it is for you to have me here.'

'Is there something you would like to tell me.'

Terry sharply turned round to realise that he had forgotten to close his chalet door. Standing there was Angie, back from another morning at the Amusement Park. Unknown to Terry, she had been watching him from the doorway for the last five minutes. 'Seriously though. What are you doing.'

'Just a bit of experimenting,' said Terry.

'What for.'

'I don't know. Trying to do something the punters might like. What do you think. Ehhhhhhhh It is an absolute pleasure . I am delighted abite it.' Angie started to laugh. 'It is nothing like the Queen.'

Terry laughed. 'Funny! You know who I was trying to do. What do you think.'

'I think it is hilarious,' she said. 'Save it for later. We don't want to put them off their lunch.'

Terry pulled the ears off and placed them in the drawer. He felt that he was on to something, and he wanted to keep the idea to himself for now. He seemed to have cracked it with the voice, how could he make it funny with the campers as opposed to annoying them. The beauty of this idea was that he could switch into it at a moment's notice. It was too early to start it yet.

That night Terry was heading back to the dining hall with Angie, this time with his "ears" in his pocket. He was about to reach the top of the stairs when he stopped, making sure that he was out of the view of the assembled campers. 'I think that this would be a good time to get changed.' He quickly put on his plastic ears. 'Eh. Do you know what you are doing?' she said. Terry put his hand up against his large ear. 'Pardon?' Angie giggled. 'I shall leave you to it.'

As he walked on ahead of Terry, he took a deep breath and in his best Royal voice. 'One's gotta do, what one's gotta do.' Hand behind his back, Terry carefully walked down the concrete stairs, giving the "Royal Wave.' However, it took one child to notice the Redcoat with the funny ears to give their parent a dig in the ribs. It was not long before a number of adults had sussed out what Terry was trying to do and were soon joining in on the gag.

Terry walked amongst them, staying in character, occasionally getting a curtsy from a couple of the Mums, as well as laughter from some of the Dads. Terry had started something, it was important to stay in character. Shaking hands with passers-by, interrogating them Royal Style. "Eh good evening. How are you. Are you enjoying your holiday.'
'Evening your Royal Highness, where is your Butler?'
'It's is Night Orf.'

The campers loved it as Terry continued to walk amongst them, he certainly attracted the attention of babes in arms, who constantly tried to pull off his ears. Terry usually stopped them by reaching out and shaking their hand. 'One is delighted to make your acquaintance,' he would say.

Angie made sure that she stayed as far out of the way, watching from the distance as Terry continued with his act. Normally Redcoats would be amongst the campers, just talking to them, making sure that they would be relaxed whilst waiting for the doors to open. Thanks to Terry, they were being entertained as well.

Terry was no longer worried about what people would think, they were enjoying themselves and so was he. So much so that he did not notice that all of the other Redcoats had gone into the dining hall, taking their places at the various partitions ready to finally let them in. Terry's former Chalet Mate Bill, who was I/C at the Dining hall that evening came back outside, tapped Terry on the shoulder, and bowed.

'Excuse me your Highness. But your presence is required in the Hall.'

Terry continued to stay in character. 'Ah thank you my good fellow. Kindly lead the way.'

Bill was now joining in the fun as well. 'Excuse me your Royal Highness, who is this Gentleman. Is he your Batman.'

'No he is Robin,' replied Terry. This got a few sniggers; however he could hear a few guys muttering 'Ouch that was so corny.' However, Terry did not care as he and Bill walked over to one of the open doors.

'Whatever you are doing, it appears to be working,' said Bill. As he reached the door, Bill indicated that it was time to let the punters in. 'Would Sir like to do the honours.' Terry smirked and stepped away from the door standing on a large stone at the bottom of the concrete wall.

'Ehhhhhhhh My Lords! Ladies and Gentleman. I would like to welcome you all to tonight's State Dinner. It gives me enormous pleasure to declare the dining hall, officially open.' This resulted in cheers amongst the masses as the Redcoats simultaneously opened the doors.

As they started to walk into the dining room and take their seats, Terry was about to remove his ears, but Bill stopped him. 'Not yet Charlie Boy. Royal duties are not finished yet.'

The campers continued to walk in smiling and Terry continued to greet them in the style of Prince Charles. Once they had taken their seats, he decided that they had been treated to enough of a "Royal Fanfare" for now. His upper-class test run was a success.

After the meal, Terry was on duty in the Gaiety for the weekly Lucky Dip show, a popular break from the usual variety productions, hosted by Resident Compere Jackie Cooper, where selected holidaymakers would compete in several hilarious games and antics for prizes. Like the midweek Talent Contests, they would only be performing for one house.

A couple of female Redcoats would assist him, whilst the others would attend to normal "theatre duties" stationed at various exits and entrances around the venue. This was a favourite detail for Terry, because of the different characters taking part. Every show was different. As he was I/C for that show, he always made sure that he had the best view in the house, watching from the door half way up.

After the show, it was obligatory for the Reds to perform the necessary "fire check", making sure that when all the guests had left, all the seats would be placed upright before they could let the people in for the second house - and there were a lot of seats.

When the group had finished, Terry, in his capacity as I/C took a brief trip backstage to let the Theatre's Stage Manager know that the Fire Check had been completed, before heading up to the Stuart Ballroom.

When he went backstage, he saw the Stage Manager, Alex talking to Jackie Cooper. He kept forgetting that the Stage Door had a strong spring, which would result in it closing behind him, creating a hefty thump, alerting the other men of a presence in the room.

'If my ears did not deceive me, I would detect that would be young Terry here to inform me that the fire check is complete and they are about to vacate the premises. '

'I never had you down as Psychic,' said Terry.

'No,' said Alex. 'You are the only one that forgets to close the bloody stage door quietly.'

Sorry about that,' said Terry.

'If it happens again, I will send you my laundry bill.'

'We're finished and I am heading up to the Stuart.'

'You can go out through the Fire Exit,' ordered Alex. 'That door is already opened.'

Terry smiled. 'Ok Boss.' As he headed towards the back exit,

Jackie Cooper stopped him. 'Before you go up to the Stuart Terry. Can you spare five minutes.'

'Sure.'

Terry followed Jackie back to his Dressing Room as he continued to pack away some of his stuff before heading home. 'I came out of the Ents Office tonight and I saw something interesting,' he said. 'I saw this Redcoat walking amongst the guests, doing an impression of Prince Charles.'

'Ah,' replied Terry, preparing himself for the ridicule.

'And rather good it was too.'

'Really?'

'Yep. So much so it has given me an idea.'

Jackie went to explain that the next night was the weekly talent contest final, and was looking at a way of providing breaks in the programme. After seeing Terry doing his Royalty bit, he thought it would be a great idea to come on doing a stand-up routine as HRH himself. Whilst he did not automatically dismiss the idea, he told Jackie he would not know where to start.

'Don't worry about that,' he insisted. 'All you are talking about is about a three-minute routine. I have written down about half a dozen gags.' Terry scanned the hand written note, a lot of the topical gags seemed vaguely familiar, talking about being a father for the first time, talking about "his little Willy," along with comments about keep falling off his horse.

'You just end it with something like, a performer is as good as his audience, therefore one has been absolutely marvellous etc. Trust me,' he said. 'Do those gags in the way you did at the dining hall and you will go down a storm. I will speak to the Boss and make sure that you are detailed here every week. What do you think?'

Ever since he'd first become a Redcoat, Terry had wanted to gain stage experience, but he didn't have the confidence to develop an act of his own. However, here was a man who had lived and breathed show business all his life, and he was offering to give him that opportunity.

Terry took a deep breath. 'If the Boss says it is OK, then fine by me.'

'Excellent!' said Jackie. He told Terry to hang on to the piece of paper and learn the gags.

As he was on detail doing Bingo at the Conti Bar tomorrow afternoon, he suggested Terry nipped over to the Gaiety and have a quick run through the routine itself.

Later that night, Terry was back in the Chalet with Angie. They lay there in bed, snuggled up to each other. 'So, tell me again. What does Jackie want you to do tomorrow?' she asked.

'Well after doing my HRH bit at the dining hall, he wants me to do a guest spot between the Talent Show acts tomorrow night, doing a stand-up routine as Prince Charles.'

'How do you feel about it?'

Terry hesitated. 'I don't know really. Part of me is excited. I am also terrified as well?'

Angie turned on her side looking towards Terry. 'You terrified about going in front of an audience? You do that every day here.'

'Terrified of failing. I have never experienced anything like that before. I don't know if I could cope with it.'

Angie started to stroke his head, kissing him gently on the cheek. 'You are not going to fail. People loved what you did today. Jackie would not suggest it, if you were not going to be any good. He knows his stuff. She turned her face towards her. 'You are going to be brilliant.'

Terry smiled, pulling her towards him, in a long passionate embrace. 'What would I do without you? I'm such a lucky guy.' 'I know you are she sniggered,' then she looked deep into his eyes.

'If anyone's lucky, it's me.   Not only do I have a gorgeous boyfriend who loves me as much as I love him. He is also mega talented, a great dancer, can sing, and is now a great impressionist.'

'Thank you,' said Terry. 'It is a shame you are not with me back stage tomorrow.'

'Just remember when you go on stage tomorrow. Close your eyes for a brief second and you'll find me inside your head, telling you I love you, and I am so proud of you. I want you to knock em dead.'

Having a vote of confidence from Angie, meant so much to him. Having someone like Jackie helping as well, was enough to convince Terry that he might just pull this off after all. It didn't take him long to memorise the jokes. He'd gained some experience in line learning, when he took part in several school performances. That was the easy part. Having previously just larked about, now he had to step up to the mark, and do it on stage for real. This was very different. He needed to feel as a comfortable as possible, and get into the character.

To get him used to the idea, Terry would sometimes walk along the camp road going into "HRH" mode interacting with as many passers-by as he could – and the campers loved it. He was now starting to believe in his character, which was a big help, if he was going to do a full routine.

After Bingo, he headed over to the back stage door of the Gaiety Theatre, where Jackie was waiting. During the next ten minutes, Terry was given a crash course in the art of stagecraft. He was not going to tell him how to act as Prince Charles, but he made sure that he was comfortable on how to walk on to the stage properly, being able to maintain eye contact with the audience as well as some tips on one of the most important aspects of comedy – timing.

He was used to taking instructions during his dancing days, but this was well out of his comfort zone. He was a bag of nerves. It felt as though he was back in charge of the Stuart Ballroom during the opening night of last season. Just thinking about it, was tying his stomach into knots. Jackie continued to reassure him.

'There will be an audience, wanting to be entertained tonight, and you're the guy that's going to do it. You will get laughs, I promise you. If they go on laughing, wait until they finish. There is no point in telling a joke if no one hears you. The more you do it, the more you will recognise when to pause and how to deliver. Do not rush it, and you'll be fine. Let me sort out the time.'

Terry gave a less than reassuring smile, but he fully appreciated Jackie's help, and he was determined to repay his faith in him. 'Listen there is nothing wrong about having nerves. All performers get them. Make sure you enjoy it, because once you do the first one, you will want to do more and more.'

Those last words did ring true with Terry. Whenever he performed, he loved hearing the sound of the applause at the end, it was the greatest feeling ever. Normally he would be part of a group or, dancing with a partner. Now he hoped that he could earn that applause in his own right. He'd always wanted to perform and now he was being handed that opportunity. 'Thanks again Jackie.'

Jackie explained that he had cleared it with the Boss. Terry would be working backstage with the contestants, and he needed to be at the theatre at least thirty minutes before the start of the show.

At Swanning, Terry went in to "Redcoat mode", laughing and joking with the guests as they came in for their evening meals. He was in no mood for food that night, but he had to make the effort, as he was sitting along with his table family. Angie began to head over to her next detail, but she stopped beside Terry first and she bent over and whispered 'good luck' in his ear, resulting in a smile from Terry, who mouthed the words 'Thank You.'

He managed to finish his tea before leaving the table to head over to the Gaiety. The door was open and there was no one around. There was still a bit of time before the show started, so Terry decided to seek sanctuary, deciding that the Gents toilets would be the best place for him to remember his lines, and more importantly, calm his nerves.

Forty minutes later, he heard activity around the side of the doors. He realised that he could not commandeer the toilet facilities any longer. He needed to get back to work. As he walked along the back stage corridors, he could see that the contestants were starting to arrive. He could not do any more with his act. He knew the routine. It was in the hands of the Theatre Gods now. He just prayed they were listening tonight.

The talent night had finally begun. For the next hour, they were treated to six singers, some of them in tune, some not, along with a wanabee disco dancer. Not exactly, the top echelon of show business, but the audience appeared to enjoy it. This was a holiday camp audience. It was interval time, the time for the judges to choose their winner. It was in this interval that there would be a guest performance. Terrys' moment had come.

Terry was worried he was going to be overcome by nausea as he stood at the side of stage. He wanted to enjoy the experience, but his body was defying him. He closed his eyes, and Angie's voice came running through his head. 'I love you, I am so proud of you. You have wanted this for ages. Go knock em dead.'

Terry opened his eyes, and banished his nerves. He was now desperate to get on the stage, but he had to wait for Jackie's introduction. Must not forget to put on the ears.

'Ladies and Gentlemen, whenever we do these shows at Butlins, we always like to give Redcoats a chance to do a guest spot, singing, maybe a little bit of dancing, but one of the most difficult things in show business, is the talent to make people laugh. We have a young man working here as one of our Redcoats, and tonight he is going to entertain you and make you laugh. And he is also going to learn the most difficult thing in comedy – timing. So that is what you are going to be used for, but I have a feeling that you are going to enjoy this, please give a warm Butlins welcome to the very funny and very talented, Terry!'

The duo in the orchestra pit burst into a short royal anthem as Terry strode on with his hand behind his waist waving to the crowd. He had never done this act in front of a crowd, but they had an idea what was coming.

Maintaining the Royal pose in front of the microphone, Terry looked intently into the eyes of the first four rows, took a deep breath determined not to show any deviation in his voice. 'Good evening, I would like to say what an absolute pleasure it is for you to have me here. 'He had not cracked any jokes yet, but the voice was good enough to match the ears. The audience immediately laughed and burst into applause.'

Remembering the comments about timing, Terry kept the moment going with a Prince Charles mannerism, consistently joining his hands together 'Ehhhhhhh You are incredibly kind. If you could save it till the end, one has a rather weak finish.'

The laughter grew stronger as he could see Jackie standing at the side of the stage, with a broad grin giving the thumbs up. Terry was now more than a GD Redcoat, he was now also a Redcoat Entertainer

CHAPTER NINETEEN

There was more than one Gaiety Theatre in Ayr. In the town, there was an iconic Variety Theatre, which played host to some legendary show business characters. The other was right in the heart of Butlins Ayr camp, and one of the many popular venues on site.

The Gaiety at Butlins had so much going for it. Every night, hundreds of campers would pour in through the doors, to take in the various theatrical productions shows like, the "Resident Review Company,' Sunday Star Time" headlined by a well-known face from the TV, the midweek "Lucky Dip" game show, the "Butlins Talent Trail" and not forgetting the "World Famous Redcoat Show.'

For Terry, this theatre was the perfect place to help him develop as a performer. It would also teach him how to cope with whatever curveballs that got thrown his way, curve balls like, faulty equipment, members of the audience, or even more challenging, Mother Nature.

Terry's "HRH" guest spot in the Talent show had become a hit with the guests, and he was developing a reputation as a man of many talents. He still had his supporting roles in Redcoat shows, alongside his own solo spot, together he was learning all aspects of stagecraft, working on his own or as part of a team.

Whilst performing as Prince Charles was a lot of fun, after a few weeks, he was starting to feel moments of frustration. He had a desire to do other things in his act, whilst not entirely ditching Charlie, after all, he was the reason he got the spot in the first place, he wanted a little bit less of HRH and more of 'Terry'.

He had developed a taste for mimicry. He was doing impressions of other people as well as Royalty, and he was including more of his own jokes that he had heard from visiting artists from the previous week, as well as ones picked up from campers.

His confidence on stage became more evident during the Old-Time Music Hall, where he was playing the part of the Zombie, Rigor Mortis, standing straight faced in front of a coffin, walking out to the front of the stage and back again every week. It was there he was getting the feel of how to work an audience.

Whilst he continued to stick to the original script, his subtle pieces of improvisation throughout the show were noticed by the audiences, and made them warm to his character even more. This included the battles between "Rigor and "Mr Chairman".

With his character having to keep a straight face all night, "Mr Chairman" would sometimes see how far he could push him to make him crack, whereas Rigor AKA Terry would respond by accidentally standing on his foot whenever he passed by. When it came to being made to drink Lager, he would sometime spit the dregs back at him.

Embarrassment was no longer an issue. He got what he wanted in being able to test himself with his various roles during the week, but the Redcoat show at the Gaiety was always his favourite, even though his appearances were brief.

He did not mind dressing up in silly costumes any more, as long as it was necessary for the performance and for the laughs. In fact, he was now starting to take dressing up in Tu Tus very seriously indeed.

As he was developing his talent for mimicry, his performance as Fagin was starting to become more authentic, in the voice at least, he still had not quite mastered the art of coming through the through the curtain at the back on stage, on cue.

As a venue, the Gaiety, had everything, it provided great atmosphere, a perfect place to stage a theatrical production. However, the building did have one major flaw, during the 1983 season, and it would become evident during one of the stormiest days of the year.

It was usual for Redcoat shows not to go according to plan. On this particular evening, it was during the Ballet Routine. Because of the manic nature of the sketch, it was always a major talking point. However, this performance would be remembered by both the audience and performers for a long time to come.

As before, the act would open with two male Redcoats trying to perform the Ballet of Swan Lake in the proper manner, when constantly being interrupted by apprentice Swans along with an oversize Ballerina in the shape of Deke. The sketch would conclude with a Keystone Cop chase around the theatre, ending with the ensemble assembling for a final pose before jete-ing off stage left.

The first house audience loved every minute of the show, outside though Mother Nature was doing her worst. They had been lucky with the weather since the start of the season, but this evening the rain was thundering down.

Unknown to the performers, some rain had already seeped through a narrow gap in the roof of auditorium prior to the start of the show, resulting in a sodden carpet, right across the central pathway. The audience were not bothered too much as the seats were still dry.

Aside from watching their feet as they moved to their seat, there was nothing much that they could do. The message did get through to the stage crew; however, they were more focused on protecting the stuff behind the stage curtain. There was never any intention of cancelling the show, and the stage crew made sure that there were no hidden dangers for the performers.

The show was going ahead as planned and on time. After a hassle free opening section, it was soon time for the Ballet. As in previous weeks, the curtains opened to show Redcoat Gavin as "Rudolph Neerenuff", striking a typical male ballerina pose. Cue the hysterical laughter from the audience.

As the routine progressed, the sound of laughter increased, building up to the "big chase" when the lead dancers went in pursuit of Ballerina Deke around the theatre. Cutting across the middle horizontal aisle, Deke stepped on a piece of soaked carpet and not surprisingly, hit the ground heavily.

The audience, thinking that this was part of the act, were shrieking with laughter. Terry quickly realised that as this was supposed to be a group chasing Deke, they had to create the illusion that this was part of the chase, so he decided to throw himself on to the floor. Thankfully, the others picked up on the idea, and did the same.

The move allowed Deke some time to get back on to his feet and continue running down the side aisle and on to the stage with the rest of the group, taking their thunderous applause from the audience, which continued as they danced off stage. The sketch once again was a roaring success and they now had time to attend to their battered and bruised limbs.

It was after they took their final bow at the end of their "Oliver" singalong, they could discuss their near miss earlier. They still had another show to do. Once Terry had got out of his Fagin outfit, the adrenaline was starting to ease off and he was now starting to limp.

'I think I came down on my ankle, 'said Terry. 'I don't want to do that again. '

'Did someone leave the window open?' said Deke sitting down

rubbing the back of his calf.

'We don't have windows Ya Muppet! There must have been water coming through the roof. Can we make sure that we don't run on that wet patch in the second house?'

'Instead of going stage left and clockwise,' said Deke. 'We cut across the front of the stage, going in the opposite direction, running back on to where we started. The whole carpet cannot be wet.'

'Well we have to do something,' said Terry. 'Anti-Clockwise it is. You lead the way as usual.'

'You know me Terry Boy, I always like to be out front.'

'Well if we go down again, this time we will land on something a lot softer – namely you!'

The queue for the second house was starting to build up outside. It was not too long before the on-duty Redcoats, opened the doors to let them the new audience enter.

Backstage, the cast were dressed in their Reds, ready for the Opening Number, with some of the male members walking off their injuries from the earlier performance. Terry had a much better way of shaking off his first house mishap; he was standing in a quiet end of the backstage corridor with Angie, holding on to each other. When Angie had heard about Terry's fall, she spent most of the spare time making sure he was OK.

'Overture and Beginners Ladies and Gentlemen,' announced Alex, the Stage Manager. This was theatrical code for 'get your backsides on stage, we are about to start the show.' Terry and Angie finally released their grip of each other taking their respective places at either side of the stage.

Stage Manager, Alex began his announcement. 'Good Evening Ladies and Gentlemen and welcome to the Gaiety Theatre. May we respectively remind you in accordance with our fire regulations'; smoking is not permitted in the theatre.' The lights went down over the auditorium, the orchestra started the Overture. As the curtain came up, the Redcoats marched on to the stage, the atmosphere was electric, and the second house was well underway.

Word had obviously spread about the "Ballet," which became obvious when Jackie announced it, resulting in cheers amongst the audience. They were not surprised backstage, as there was never a Redcoat show where this routine did not go down a storm. Unknown to the performers, there was an even bigger storm going outside as the weather had taken a real turn for the worse. Therefore, the water continued dripping on to the carpet in the centre aisle.

The audience was in hysterics as the Ballet reached the final chase around the theatre. As before, Deke ran down the stairs along with the rest of the Ballet ensemble, doing what he said, running across the front of the stage, heading in the agreed opposite direction to that in the first house.

Coming around the final bend, the group headed across the centre aisle at full speed, where Deke, well ahead of the rest slipped on the carpet again, which was even more sodden than before. Instead of hitting the ground hard, his speed and heavy bulk meant that his momentum carried him across the carpet heading toward the middle exit door.

Standing there was first year Redcoat Karen, terrified of this Man Mountain coming towards her at speed. She instinctively relied on her Redcoat training, opening the exit door, where Deke shot through, and bounced down the three stairs on to the main reception floor.

The audience were now once again in hysterics, still thinking this was part of the routine. The band continued to play. 'Ohhh shittttttt!' thought Terry.

He could see the partially opened door and Deke recovering

from his "daredevil slide" he was getting back on his feet, and looked virtually unscathed. Terry signalled to the remainder of the group to go out there with him. When they went out of sight, Terry and Bill helped Deke regain his focus.

'Go Deke, run down the aisle on to the stage, we will follow you,' said Bill.

'Aye,' said Deke. They could not hang about too long. Orchestra Leader, Ted Harkins was looking around the auditorium. They couldn't play for much longer.

Seconds later, Deke came sprinting out of the door, followed by the rest of the Ballerinas, running down the side of the theatre sprinting on to the stage. The band kicked in to the final chord as they took their bow, dancing off the side of the stage. Now in the wings, they were putting their hands on their knees, with gasps of relief; Compere Jackie and the Stage Manager on the opposite side of the stage, saw what was going on and could not do anything about it.

Instead of letting them get back to the dressing room, Jackie brought them back on for a well-deserved second bow, which they took, to a roaring ovation.

The second show was a resounding success. At the end, Entertainment Manager, Simon Barker, assembled the full cast back on to the stage for a quick briefing about the evening's events. He knew that he could have had a disaster on his hands and were fortunate that there were no serious injuries.

'First off all, I need to apologies to all of you,' particularly all of you Gentleman in the Ballet. It should not have happened. Disaster was avoided thanks to Karen remembering her Redcoat Training, and some quick thinking by you guys.'

Terry was standing close to Angie as Barker delivered his speech. He was angry about the position everyone was placed in. He knew that things could have been a lot worse, but the management should never have placed them in this situation. However, his anger softened as Barker said that he would be having words with construction to avoid such a thing from happening again.

'In the meantime, when you are all at the Stuart Ballroom later, I have had words with the Bar Manager to make sure there is a drink there for you all,' he said. 'I will keep you posted of any developments. Thank you all once again. Do you have any questions?' Deke immediately put up his hand.

'Just one Boss. Who is going to pay for a new set of tights?'

CHAPTER TWENTY

Working as a Butlins Redcoat meant at least a ninety-hour week. Those who worked the full season certainly did not do it for the money. It was anything but easy; but it was still the ultimate in Job satisfaction. However, when it came to the end of the working day, Terry was always happy to get back to his chalet. However, he would always make an exception when it came to working at the Midnight Cabaret.

Whilst the entertainment programme during the week was free, Midnight Cabaret was always an all ticket affair; considering it featured a top TV or Theatre act, it had to be, and it was always a sell-out.

For Redcoats on duty, it was the easiest working detail of them all. Instead of standing on duty, at the Midnight Cabaret they would have really good seats. Once the guests had been seated, the Reds would take their designated table and enjoy the show, just like guests.

The normal duties for Redcoats at Midnight Cabaret, would be mainly directing the guests to their respective seats. There was no need for them to stay in their uniform, but they were still on duty. Therefore, it was imperative that they were dressed appropriately. For a couple of female Reds, there was still a uniform involved.

It was well into the peak period of the 1983 season at Butlins Ayr, and this was one of the busiest ever nights at Midnight Cabaret. Terry had made quick work in helping to clear the stage in the Stuart Ballroom, and quickly nipped back to his chalet to get changed into his "evening civvies".

Angie had gone on ahead as her duties that night were different from the other Redcoats; they were tied with the event's sponsors. She and fellow first year Redcoat Suzie from Middlesbrough had been designated as the "John Player" girls for that evening.

Terry was not able to wipe the smirk on his face as he came through the main double doors of the Stuart Ballroom, veering to the left and into the Beachcomber Bar, he knew what to expect once he went into the venue.

Walking through the dark entrance, he came to the short footbridge that crossed the artificial stream, where both Angie and Suzie were standing holding containers full of cigarettes. They were wearing long black dresses with sponsor's branded gold sash, draped across their shoulder.

Terry had never seen Angie in a long gown before. She had never worn one, especially a piece of clothing that was designed for a woman at least five inches taller. Thankfully, Angie had improvised, hooking the middle of the skirt over a black belt across her waist. She smiled as she saw Terry. 'Would you like some cigarettes sir, courtesy of tonight's sponsors.'

'Mmm tempting,' he replied. 'But I am afraid I don't have any bad habits.'

Suzie sniggered. 'Of course you don't.'

'Absolutely nothing,' insisted Terry. He turned to Angie. 'Come on help me out here.'

Angie thought for a moment. 'Not being able to shave properly?'

'Well apart from that. I am good boy?'

Angie sighed. 'Yeh!'

'Thank you for that,' said Terry. 'I will leave you ladies to it. I will attend to my other duties.'

Before he left he stopped and leaned into Angie's ear. 'You look absolutely gorgeous,' he whispered.

Angie smiled and mouthed the words 'thank you' before turning back and continuing to hand out cigarettes to the guests as they continued to come in.

Terry took a couple of steps away from the "John Player" ladies, joining up with the other on duty Reds occasionally checking to make sure he had brought his seat plan. He only needed it for the guests, he knew that the Redcoats would always have the same seats, at the back end, next to the Bar.

It took at least thirty minutes for the guest to take their seats and get the first set of drinks in. It was then not long before Resident Compere Jackie Cooper jumped on to the Beachcomber stage to introduce the musicians who would start the evening off.

After one number, he returned to introduce tonight's star act, Scottish Theatre and TV icons, the Alexander Brothers, who came on to a tumultuous reception from the packed Beachcomber audience. This was the "Glasgow Trades Holiday" week, so it was going to be a brilliant evening.

Terry bought himself and Angie a drink each and he sat down at his table along with the rest of the Redcoats. It was not long before Angie joined him. Seeing the Alexander Brothers on stage immediately brought back happy memories of when he used to watch them at the Greenock Town Hall and at the Cragburn Pavillion.

However, five minutes in, Angie, along with several other female Redcoats, became very interested in the tall broad shouldered figure standing at the bar. "Hey Ladies, the Navy is in tonight.' said Angie. Standing at six-foot-tall, probably somewhere in his early thirties, was a fellow dressed in a white dress naval uniform complete with what appeared to be the insignia of a ship's Captain.

'Corrrrrr!' 'Check this guy out!' exclaimed some of the female Reds, who suddenly had no interest in what was going on the stage. The male Redcoats sat trying to look unimpressed, watching their female colleagues, sit up to attention, feasting their eyes on the Officer at the Bar.

Angie wasn't saying much, she was sitting back wide-eyed, with a broad grin on her face. 'I think you may have some competition Terry son,' said Deke. Terry smiled, but was anything but convincing as he looked across at Angie, still smiling broadly, occasionally looking across at Terry, knowing that he was watching her every move.

What they did not know was that the Naval Officer was Simon Jackson, a special guest of his brother, Assistant Entertainments Manager Roderick Jackson. Midnight Cabaret had never been so interesting; certainly, as far as the women were concerned.

They were never going to get anywhere with him, but that did not stop them sitting there with impure thoughts running through all of their minds. There was never a photographer around when you wanted one. He could have generated a lot of business taking pictures.

Deke was enjoying winding up Terry; he was relentless as he continued to alternate his gaze between Angie and the latest "attraction to the camp.'

Angie would occasionally reach out and squeeze Terry's hand to reassure him. 'Have you ever thought about joining the Navy,' she enquired. Terry sniggered as he leant forward towards her. 'Not a chance!' he whispered.

'Ahhhhhh,' said Angie disapprovingly.

Terry remembered the last time he saw that look, was at the Cinema, and with Angie's birthday coming up soon, it did give him a moment of inspiration, and he hatched a plan.

It was the end of the week and the morning of Angie's birthday. She woke up slowly turning on to her side expecting to find Terry lying beside her. When she saw that he wasn't there, she immediately sat up to see him sitting at the edge of the bed with a single Red Rose in one hand and a carefully wrapped parcel in the other. 'Morning gorgeous. Happy Birthday.' Angie beamed. 'AWWWW Thank you,' she said.

Terry leaned over kissing Angie tenderly as he handed her the Red Rose. It was not a real one, but the sentiment was more than appreciated. She completed the illusion by sniffing the flower, Terry then handed over the large present, which she excitedly started to rip off the wrapping paper. 'You wrapped this up,' asked Angie. Terry nodded furiously. 'I am impressed.'

Angie let out a mild shriek as she saw that the present was a Radio Cassette Recorder. 'Aww this great,' she said. She threw her arms around Terry.

'Thank you so much.'

'I am glad you like it.'

Angie loved her music. 'We must get some mood music for later,' she said.

'One step ahead of you,' he replied as he pulled out a cassette tape containing tracks that he had made earlier, a play list with several romantic songs.

Angie carefully scrutinised the list of tracks. She beamed when she was drawn towards two of them; "You Light up My Life," by Debbie Boone, bringing back memories of that "waltz" at the Cragburn Pavilion, "Up Where We Belong," by Joe Cocker and Jennifer Warnes, from Angie's favourite movie "Officer and a Gentleman." 'Full marks for your choice of music,' she said.

'That last track has nothing to do with the "Petty Officer" at Midnight Cabaret the other night.'

'Now now!' she said. 'He was many things, but he was not Richard Gere.' She reached over and grabbed Terry's hand. 'I have told you before. I don't need a Hollywood Hunk, when I have you.'

Terry smiled as he lent forward to kiss Angie's hand. 'Once again an excellent answer.'

'And I mean every word,' she replied. 'I love having you in my life.'

'I love you, birthday girl,' said Terry.

'And I love you Terry. Thank you for my gift. '

'We'll do some more celebrating in the Stuart tonight.'

'We'll be working,' replied Angie. 'We can have our own party afterwards.' Angie could not help noticing a bit of a glint in Terry's eyes. 'You got something else planned?'

Terry smirked. 'That's for me to know and you to find out.'

He placed his hands on to Angie's face as he pulled her towards him kissing her again. 'Shall we get ready for breakfast?'

Angie sighed: 'I would love for us to stay here all day, but needs must I suppose.'

Terry stood up and reached out his hand. 'Yes. Needs must. Come on! You will need to get ready. You have stuff up in your chalet. Nick will be coming down here soon.'

'You trying to get rid of me,' questioned Angie.

'Not at all,' he insisted. 'The last thing I want is for you to get the sack on your birthday.' Terry pulled the covers away, and pulled Angie towards him. He locked her in a long loving embrace. 'Have a great birthday.'

Angie looked lovingly into his eyes. 'It is already. Thank you for this.'

Angie placed her birthday gifts into Terry's suitcase for safekeeping. She pulled on her clothes before heading back to her chalet to get ready for the start of the new day, as had been her regular routine after unofficially moving in with Terry, and Nick with Gwen. She opened the door of the chalet, blowing Terry a kiss as she headed back upstairs. 'See you later.'

Terry waited until Angie had closed the door before getting ready for work himself. He stood over at the wash hand basin carefully washing his face and torso before starting to shave. For once, he managed to complete the process without any mishaps to his face.

Terry was getting dressed as the chalet door opened and Nick appeared. 'Morning Squire,' said Nick.

'Morning young sir. How are you this morning?'

'Tired! But I feel terrific!'

'Anything else is too much information,' laughed Terry.

Nick had not been with Gwen for long, but Terry could see the difference in his chalet mate, he had moved from an inexperienced teenager to a young man, in love for the first time. Twelve months earlier, that had been him.

Terry knew that things were going well with Nick and Gwen, as it had been several weeks since they set up their "chalet sharing" arrangements. Moreover, whenever he was back in his normal accommodation, all he could ever talk about was Gwen.

'What was Angie like when you gave her the card from the two of you,' asked Terry.

'I would say a bit shocked. She didn't think anyone knew about her birthday.'

'Well…'

'You've got some other stuff planned, haven't you?' enquired Nick

Terry said nothing. His smile said it all.

Both men were now ready for breakfast. Nick was standing in front of the mirror, sorting his tie. 'Gwen said that you are doing something in the Stuart tonight?' There was the sound of

footsteps approaching the door as Terry let out a discreet cough.
'Yep. Schtum!'

The chalet door flew open with Gwen and Angie standing there in their uniforms. 'You guys ready?' said Gwen.

'Absolutely,' said Nick. 'Shall we?'

Both men stepped out on to the main path of the chalet lines, heading on to the main road. Nick and Gwen walking on in front with Terry and Angie following on behind.

'I got a lovely card from Nick and Gwen,' said Angie.

'Excellent,' replied Terry

'You knew about it?'

'Of course.'

'Oh, smiled Angie, 'have you told anyone else?'

Terry retained his innocent look. 'Just those two.'

'So, everyone knows then?' Terry smiled and said nothing as they were now on the main road.

It was just a regular working day at the camp. Following Breakfast Swanning, Angie, Nick and Gwen were back on Amusement Park duty, with Terry working on early morning competitions in the Stuart, before heading over to the Regency Ballroom to play records for the early morning Sequence Dancing; a passion for Terry's parents, something he hated. Thankfully, he just had to play records and let them get on with it.

When they had gathered for the evening meal, Angie was nervous about what other surprises Terry had up his sleeves. The guests came through the dining hall without any fuss. Angie was told there were no birthday parades planned so, she headed over to her allocated table; her face then went as red as her blazer when she heard Deke's voice boom in the distance. 'EVERYBODY CLAP!'

It was a regular feature of Redcoat's duties at the dining hall;

guests would leave a birthday cake or a bottle of champagne with the manager. The Redcoats would then parade around the dining hall towards the guest in question, getting them to stand on the chair for everyone to see, so the 1000 strong Diners would join in the chorus of "Happy Birthday."

Angie watched as Deke headed up a large group of Reds, and did a full lap of the dining hall, where the Diners joined in as normal. Angie's heart was racing as they moved closer to her table. When it was becoming clear that this birthday parade was not for a guest, but for a Redcoat, the volume of the clapping and cheering grew louder.

'Right Missus Woman, stand up.' Deke, took Angie by the hand helping her on to her chair. 'RIGHT LADIES AND GENTS. OUR LOVELY REDCOAT ANGIE IS CELEBRATING HER BIRTHDAY TODAY. IT IS NOT NICE TO TELL A LADIES AGE, SO I WON'T. SHE IS 30!' The Diners immediately started to laugh as she slapped Deke on the top of his head. 'CORRECTION – SHE IS SWEET 19. AFTER THREE! THREE!'

Angie fanned her face trying to stop her face getting any redder whilst grinning widely as the crowd burst in a chorus of "Happy Birthday". This was followed by roaring three cheers. Deke handed her a small birthday cake with a single candle, which he lit up and she blew out, resulting in even more cheers from the dinners.

As Angie sat down, Deke planted a kiss on her cheek. 'Thanks' guys,' said Angie.

'You can thank your "Old Man",' he replied. 'He set it up.' As the group went to their respective tables, Angie realised that Terry was missing from the group. She knew that he was going to be at the Theatre for the evening Redcoat Show, she was starting to wonder what else was he up to.'

Normality had been restored to the dining table as the waiters and waitresses were starting to dish out the meals, Angie was carefully dividing her "birthday cake" amongst her fellow diners. Forty minutes later, Angie was heading over to the Theatre herself for the show.

There was still no sign of Terry, but as Angie walked through the open Stage Door, she walked down the narrow corridor at the back of the Stage, past the opened door of the Men's dressing room. She finally found Terry sitting in the corner, eating some sandwiches and a drinking a cup of tea. 'That is meant to be you eating healthy?' asked Angie.

'I am allowed the odd exception,' replied Terry. 'Did you like the cake?'

'Yes. Thank you for that. Sorry I could not save you a piece.'

Terry laughed: 'That is OK. We have another one back at the chalet.'

'Why were you not at Swanning?'

'It is Ok. I cleared it with the Bosses. I had to speak to Jackie about my act, go over a few points for next week. Plus, I had some other stuff to sort out.'

'I never thought I would ever say this,' said Angie. 'But I don't believe you.'

Terry smirked. 'Ouch! That Hurt! Angie. '

'Are you going to tell me what you are up to?'

Terry put down his tea, stood up and gave Angie a hug. 'It's still your Birthday. All will come good. Trust me.' Angie was not convinced, but she was not going to argue. 'Okay,' she said.

It was not long before the rest of the cast arrived to get ready for the two performances of the Redcoat Show, which thankfully went incident and error free. Later that evening all of the Redcoats had gathered in the Stuart Ballroom for the end of week Au Revoir.

As in previous weeks, all of the Redcoats were on the dance floor, getting into the end of week party mood with the guests, building up to the end of week Au Revoir. As usual, the Redcoats assembled at either side of the stage. However, Angie was looking around for Terry, who was nowhere to be seen.

Jackie Cooper jumped on to the stage, talking over the microphone to join the rest of the Redcoats, who were at the side of the stage, ready to be introduced one by one on to the ballroom floor. Angie was getting worried. Still no sign of Terry.

Jackie continued to bring on each of the Redcoats on to the floor, with Roddy the last one to be announced, he then signalled the Redcoat DJ to get back on to the stage. He leaped back on the platform and returned to the disco unit, whilst Simon Barker came on to the stage to make his regular speech with the Redcoats standing around the edge of the ballroom.

The Entertainments Manager then passed the microphone back to his Compere, who was expected to make his closing speech before the band kicked off the final number of the night. However, Jackie had a slight change to his running order.

'Now Ladies and Gentlemen, on behalf of all the Redcoats, we all hope you enjoyed your holiday here at Butlinland Ayr. At this point before our fabulous band joins the Redcoats in a final song, we have something special for you.'

Angie was starting to panic. There appeared to be something major happening and Terry was not there. She soon had a real reason to panic. 'Some of you may know that one of our Redcoats, Angie, is celebrating her birthday today.' The Stuart Ballroom collectively burst into a round of applause. 'We won't be asking you to sing Happy Birthday. We have something even better.'

Angie maintained a wide grin, but she was shaking inside. She then yelped when Roddy started up the disco unit one more time; the instrumental version of "Up Where We Belong," the lead song from "An Officer and a Gentleman," Angie's favourite movie. The Reds standing around the room were all puzzled, looking to Angie for an answer. She was now shaking.

However, as Roddy slowly pushed up the volume controls, Angie let out a loud shriek as a figure appeared from behind the partition at the back of the stage, dressed in white navy uniform, wearing dark sun glasses, carrying a bunch of flowers. The majority of the Reds thought that it was the Navy Guy at the Midnight Cabaret from earlier in the week.

The figure started to move his body in time to the music, occasionally breaking into short pirouettes. Coming down the stairs at the front of the stage, he started to move in Angie's direction; she was now starting to cry, with joy as the "Naval Officer" standing in front of her, smiled before removing his glasses. It was Terry, wearing a custom-built uniform courtesy of the Entertainments Department who helped him put it together.

Terry had been laying on surprises for Angie all day; this was his ultimate present, a re-enactment of her favourite film, the final scene in particular. The only difference was that this "Officer and a Gentleman" presented her with flowers and in keeping with the spirit of the movie, Terry swept her off her feet, carrying her on to the stage, to the back of the partition, out of the view of the Stuart audience who were now roaring in appreciation.

Terry gently placed Angie back on the ground, taking her hand and leading her into the back-dressing room. He knew that with the band set to play one more song, he did not have long before they would start clearing the stage.

Angie was still crying tears of joy as she wrapped her arms around Terry before kissing him passionately. She had never had anyone go to so much effort for her on her birthday. 'You are crazy,' she said.

'I would not do this for anyone else,' he replied. 'Did you enjoy your birthday.'

'It was the best ever.'

'I am so pleased. Do I suit the uniform?'

Angie smiled: 'Who needs Richard Gere.'

CHAPTER TWENTY ONE

Terry stood at the side of his bed, staring at a poster on his chalet wall. It reminded him how far his life had come during the last twelve months; this was a special print of a billboard advert four years earlier he had made with the Scotland Latin American Formation Team.

A copy of this picture had been given to all of the participants in the dance team, as a token of gratitude from the advertisers, after what had been an eventful photoshoot. For Terry this picture helped get him the job as a Redcoat in 1982. As he looked at the picture, he felt nothing but pride.

When he put in a copy of that pic along with the job application form, it caught the attention of the then Entertainments Manager, Ron De Vere, who invited him for an interview. Not only did he get the job, but also it helped him to close the door on his childhood and open another into adult life.

The job changed him as a person, but it also changed his life, as it led him to Angie. He started to learn about relationships as well as about true friendships, strong friendships with staff members within his team, as well as those from other departments. By the end of that first year, they were more than friends; they were family.

However, like all families, there were the "black sheep" members, who were more interested in looking after their own interests as opposed to thinking of others. Under the tenure of De Vere, they were found out during the opening weeks of the season, and promptly given the sack or, "sent up the hill". The 1983 season was no different.

Under the new management, a number of people had already been "sent up the hill." There were a few others with the same attitude as those who had already been sacked, but with a different approach, they were the more difficult to catch out. They would usually put on a false image in front of the bosses, but once out of sight, were determined to make the most of the unofficial benefits a job like this brought.

Reg Marshall was a first year Redcoat, and, after a few weeks, it was clear to those working on the ground that Reg was not interested in the job, and that Reg didn't want to be part of a team.

With his athletic build, he did not look out of place as a Lifeguard and thrived on being an attraction to many of the female guests. Standing at over six foot tall, with a strong muscular physique; as far as he was concerned, he had it all and was not afraid to tell those who were willing to listen. Many of the staff were just fed up with him.

Whilst he would do his job at the side of the pool, Reg carved a less that favorable reputation for himself when, he used to report his fellow Lifeguards to the Entertainments Manager for the most trivial of reasons and made him a very unpopular member of the team. He did not care. He was only after one thing.

Away from the pool, his main objective was to see what campers he could bed with that week, especially the winners of the "Lovely Legs Competition in the evening." He used the military as his chat up conversation. It would consist of him bragging about his top-secret military training, and he became in his own words 'a natural killer. 'It was all in his own mind too, in fact, his "military experience" had never gone any further than a few weeks of basic training in the regular army. He had been kicked out after only three weeks.

The management could not find any real evidence to sack him, there had never been any complaints made. He was good in covering his tracks, but they could see that he had anything but a friendly relationship with his colleagues.

'I can get a woman every night', he regularly boasted to the male campers. Even if that was true, he never got anywhere with the female Redcoats, who made their feelings more than clear whenever he "tried it on," but despite the constant knock backs, he was never one for giving up.

Terry never had any problems with Reg; maybe because he spent most of his day at the pool, they would never work together. Terry knew that Reg was not popular guy, that alone was a good enough reason for Terry to keep his distance. He was certain that Reg would not last the full season and that the managers would eventually find a reason for rectifying their mistake in hiring him.

That morning, after spending five minutes looking at his prized picture, he decided to sort out some of his clothes for the evening. He had a few minutes to spare before the lunchtime swanning. With Angie once again on Amusement Park duties, Terry would always leave his door open to let her know that he was in.

Sitting on the edge of the bed, whitening his evening shoes, Terry could hear conversation going on outside his door. It sounded very much like Reg, on his day off, trying it on with another female staff member. Terry would not be too concerned as he was waiting for the girl in question to end by saying "sod off Reg!' However, on this occasion, Reg was sounding more aggressive.

'You want a real man,' he said. 'No, you don't! I am not letting you past until you tell me that you are going to dump that pussy you call a boyfriend and spend the night with me.' He had his arm placed against the window blocking his victim's path. He lent close into her face. 'You know you want to.'

Terry knew that he did not come close to matching the physical capabilities of Reg, so he wasn't planning to get involved. However, when he heard the female voice starting to crack under the emotion saying 'Sod off Reg! Let me past,' Terry threw down his shoes and dived outside the door. He was furious to see him blocking Angie's path. 'She said let her past Reg.'

Reg turned round and smiled as he saw Terry standing there. That was enough of a distraction for him to grab Angie's hand and made sure that she was standing directly behind him. He tried to get her into the chalet, but she was not for going inside. She continued to stand behind Terry squeezing on to his hand.

'Well if it isn't your Knight in Shining Armour,' Reg sneered. 'You've gone too far this time,' said Terry. 'You do not come anywhere near Angie, Ok!'

Reg's eyes widened as he stared directly into Terry's face. 'And who is going to stop me? You?'

Dealing with confrontations, was Terry's biggest nightmare, but he was determined not to show it. He took a sharp intake of breath. 'Yeh! If I have to.'

Reg laughed loudly. 'You honestly think a Runt like you, could take on me, a natural killer? I could take you out just like that.' Reg clicked his fingers directly into Terry's face. Terry did not move.

He did not even blink. He could feel Angie's hand squeezing his. It gave him the courage he needed.

'You probably could,' said Terry stepping forward towards Reg., 'but it is the only way you will ever get close to Angie. Terry took one-step towards him. 'But I tell you this, whatever happens to me, I know that I will damage at least one part of you. What is it going to be?'

Reg 's eyes narrowed. He had never been challenged like this before. Moreover, the fact that he was being confronted by someone obviously physically inferior to him; he regarded that as an insult. He stepped up the intimidation even more. 'I would be happy to end your existence on this earth Terry,' he sneered. 'Look around! There are no witnesses. I could take you both out and no one would be any the wiser.'

'What were you saying about witnesses.' said one voice. 'Reg looked behind him to see Bill appearing from behind his chalet door; he had also taken a break before lunch. 'Look up here you Muppet!' Reg looked above to see Deke and Roddy standing on the upper level looking down below.

'Get the message! You lay so much as a finger on our friends and you will have to deal with the rest of us.'

Reg looked around, still smiling. He knew that despite his physical prowess, he could not take on so many at the one time. He gently tapped Terry on the cheeks who continued to look directly at him, brushing his hand away. 'Will see you around Terry,' he said

'I am not going anywhere,' Terry replied.

Terry turned and watched as a smiling Reg walked up the staff chalet lines on to the main road of the camp, eventually disappearing from view. Still holding on to Angie's hand, Terry turned in the direction of Bill, Deke and Roddy, mouthing the words 'Thank You,' before going back into the chalet with Angie.

There was still ten minutes before they were back on duty. Terry closed the door behind him, sitting Angie, down on the bed, passing over a handkerchief, dabbing the tears forming at the corner of her eyes. 'Are you OK?'

'Yes.' She leant over and kissed Terry on the cheek. 'Thank you for being my Knight in shining armour.' Terry smiled kissing Angie's hand. 'I am your humble servant my Lady.' Every muscle in his body was tense and every nerve was shaking, but Angie needed his strength, so he smiled and oozed confidence, false though it was.

They may have seen the last of Reg, but Angie was still worried what might happen next time. 'He won't try anything here,' said Terry. 'If he thinks he can do something without witnesses at a holiday camp, he is more than a menace. He is an idiot.' Angie was starting to feel more relaxed. Terry stood up. 'Come on deep breath, time for lunch.'

Despite his assurances, Terry was certain that he had not heard the last of Reg. After lunch, Angie was back to the Amusement Park and Terry felt that he needed some time back at his chalet to get his head together and to put away the stuff he was working on earlier prior to the interruption by Reg.

He realised that he could bump into Reg again and was starting to think the worst; as he neared his chalet he could see the door was wide open. He definitely remembered locking it. Terry cautiously walked in; just case someone was behind the door. The chalet was empty; maybe he hadn't closed the door properly after all.

However, Terry's heart sank as he saw all of the contents of his case scattered across the bed and on the floor. On the wall, his prized picture of the Formation Team advert had been badly defaced with felt tip pen, with several circles around Terrys face. This was the only official copy of the advert that he had, there was no way on Gods earth of him getting another. He was devastated.

'THE BASTARD!' muttered Terry through gritted teeth. It

could only be one person.   He was I/C at the Bingo at the
Continental Bar and needed to collect microphones out of Radio
Butlins, so he could not hang about.   However, the job was the
last thing on his mind.

The lock on his door was still intact - just, so he was able to
lock his chalet. Terry was raging, but he took great care in
closing the door. It was not as secure as he wanted, but he was at
least able to stop it from flying open. He knew that he would
have to report it, but he was more interested in finding the
person that did it.   He knew there was only one suspect.   He
was never going to win in a physical standoff, but the way he was
feeling now, he could quite easily throttle him!

Terry "power walked" in the direction of the main road,
unaware that his friend and Redcoat Lifeguard Jonty was walking
towards him having finished his morning shift at the outdoor
pool.   Whatever anger he felt, he was going to have to lose it as
he was going to be amongst the guests.

'Hey Terry, where are you off to, 'said Jonty.
'Hoping to bump into one of your fellow life guards,' replied
Terry, who was not in the mood for chatting. However, Jonty
appeared to have an idea what was going on. He put his hands
on Terry's shoulders, stopping his progress.
'Right! You have to calm doon pal! You are not going to do any
good searching for Reg.'

Terry was not prepared to listen. 'Being a lazy arse is one
thing, but scaring Angie and destroying my stuff?   He is not
going to get away with it. Can you get oot the road, please Jonty.'
Jonty did not release his grip from Terry's shoulders. 'Don't get
yourself sent up the hill cause of him. HE IS NOT GOING TO
GET AWAY WITH IT,' he insisted.   He tried to reassure him.
'Trust me.   It is being dealt with.'
'You know something I don't?'

Jonty said nothing. All he wanted was to try calm Terry down, because once he was on the main road, he was back on duty, albeit unofficially. Jonty was not going to let him progress any further until he promised he was not going to do anything stupid. Terry could not argue with Jonty and he finally relented.

He promised him that he would not do anything stupid, but deep down he was still furious. He knew Angie was not aware of what was happening and she would not thank him for losing control, after showing much strength earlier.

There was no point in walking up towards the pool as Reg was on his day off, so taking in what Jonty had said, he was now starting to think about his next detail, going up to the Entertainments Office to pick up the microphones for the Bingo. Once past the main Reception doors, he turned the corner, jumping up the stairs towards the Ents Office.

He was walking along the narrow corridor towards the Radio Butlins room at the far end, when he was interrupted by a voice calling his name from the Office next door.

'Terry! Have you got a minute?' The voice from behind the wall was Entertainments Manager, Simon Barker.

'Eh Yeh Boss,' he replied. He had a hunch about what was going to be said.

'I heard there was an incident at the Staff Chalet lines

'What about,' replied Terry, trying to look as if butter wouldn't melt.

Barker twitched as his moustache: 'I think you know fine well! What happened between you and Reg.'

'He was harassing Angie.'

'I heard it was a bit more than that.'

Terry knew he could not hide anything from the Squadron Leader. 'It verged on the aggressive and it upset her. I wasn't having that. Words were had! Thankfully it came to a head.'

'Yes! That was what I heard,' said Barker.

'Who told you.'

'One of your friends. I heard that he came back and ransacked your chalet when you were at the dining hall.'

Terry knew that it was Reg, but he had no real evidence. 'So, it was him.'

'Yes,' replied the Boss. 'Now I don't want you to get involved.'

'It will be difficult not to, 'replied Terry

'It has been dealt with!' insisted Barker. 'Mr Marshall is no longer an employee of Butlins'

'He has been sent up the hill?' Said a shocked Terry.

'Yes, he has.' Barker placed his pen down on the desk, joined his hands together as he leaned forward looking directly at Terry. 'So, forget about what happened and get back to your detail. The Accommodation Office are sorting out your door and putting on a fresh lock. Jonty is down there now to make sure it is sorted and will drop off a set of keys at the office.'

Terry felt a great sense of relief as he realised he did not have to have any further stand offs with Reg. He also learnt a lesson in trusting the management when it comes to dealing with problems within the work place. 'Ok! Thanks Boss!'

Terry knew that he now desperately needed to be over at the Conti. 'Will pick up the keys after Bingo. I need to get the mics and get to work.'

'The microphones are already over there,' said Barker. 'Get yourself over there now.'

'Ok Boss, straight away! '

Terry shifted back out of the door, headed down the stairs on to the back road of the camp. Walking past the Outdoor Pool, he was soon at the Conti Bar, which was filling up with guests ready for an afternoon of Bingo.

When Terry arrived, Redcoats, Shirley and Steve were already there. Barker had sent word with AEM Roderick that Terry was going to be late, so the Reds had made sure that everything was set up ahead of Terry's appearance.

Two hours later, the Bingo had finished without a hitch. As IC at the Bingo, Terry made sure that he had gathered the microphones and leads to take them back up to the Ents Office. When he walked along the corridor towards the Radio Butlins room, Barker was nowhere to be seen, but was surprised to see Jonty talking to Barker's Secretary, Beverly having dropped off Terry's new chalet keys.

'How are you doing now buddy,' he said.

'I am doing well, 'said Terry. 'Listen, thanks for earlier.'

'Don't mention it; we're on the same team. So, you heard that Mr Marshall is no longer on site.'

'Did you tell him about what happened at the chalet?'

'Not me. Reg had many things going for him, but he was not the brightest penny in the pile. When he kicked in your door, he forgot about the security guy in his chalet across from you. Once he came out, he was taken to his, get his stuff and escorted off the camp.'

'That is good to know.'

Jonty smiled. 'He may be a "natural killer" but in the end he was no match for the security guys.'

CHAPTER TWENTY TWO

It had been one of the most eventful weeks of the 1983 season, now Terry and Angie, were ready for their routine day off in Ayr. They did not fancy heading up the hill to take the bus in to town. It was a beautiful summer's morning, a perfect day for a walk along the beach.

They had settled well in their job as Redcoats; however, with a few weeks to go, a moment was approaching that they could not avoid. They needed to start thinking about when their stint in the Red and Whites finally ended. The best way to do that was to get as far away from the camp as possible and head into town.

Having come through a challenging time during the winter months, they could not have been happier working at Butlins. They were sharing more experiences as a couple, helping each other through any challenges that faced them during their working life, and also personally.

Because they were living on site, they had no financial responsibilities, and they had been putting some of their wages aside on a regular basis in a post office account. They could see their bank balance slowly increasing, but there was not enough to set up home just yet, that was their ultimate aim.

With the season entering its final weeks, going back to alternate journeys between Greenock and Falkirk in a few weeks' time was now looking like a real possibility. They had shown that they could cope with it, despite it being anything but easy. If only, there was another way that did not involve constant travelling.

Their day off always started the same way, with Terry attending morning Mass at the Empire Theatre. Angie was not of the same religious persuasion, but she would always be there by his side during service. It was an important part of his life and she wanted to share that with him.

Once Mass had finished, they walked down the chalet lines towards the beach. Crossing the Sports Field, and going through the main beach gate, they walked down to the shoreline. When they were clear of the camp, Terry grabbed Angie's hand walking down the pathway down towards the sand. They both turned and looked back up the path back from where they had come.

'I remember the first time we did this, I said that it looked like another world on the other side of that fence,' said Terry. He turned towards Angie. 'It still looks much more attractive here.' Angie smiled as she wrapped her arms around Terry in a loving embrace. 'I am so happy we met,' she smiled.

The sun was shining, the sea was calm, and so there was no rush in covering those four and half miles into to town. Slowly walking along the shore, they would occasionally stop to test their abilities skimming stones, failing miserably, but they had plenty of fun trying.

There had been no mention of the "Reg" incident since it happened earlier in the week, but walking along the beach, Terry felt that it was something they had to discuss. 'How are you feeling now after what happened the other day,' he said.

'I try to put it to the back of my mind,' she said. 'It was scary. What scared me the most was what he might have done to you.'

Terry knew that he would have never been able to stand up to Reg physically, but he was more than a match, mentally. Then with the added support of his friends, there was no contest. Reg knew that. When he smashed down Terry's door, it was his way of getting him back on a one to one situation, even though it had been a desperate move.

'We'll never know,' Terry replied. 'We were all just ignoring him, treating him as a nuisance, but It wasn't till I saw him harassing you, I realised he was more than that. In the end, I did not care what happened to me. All I thought about was protecting you.'

Angie held on to Terry tight as they continued their walk along the beach. 'One thing I did learn was how safe I feel when I am with you.' Terry stopped and faced Angie, stroking his hands across her face; he leant forward kissing her gently. 'All I want is to be there for you and look after you.'

Angie heard what happened to Reg, when she came back from the Amusement Park and was shocked when she saw what had happened to Terry's chalet. She was as devastated as he was. However, she was far from happy with Terry when she found out that he wanted to spend the rest of the day looking for him.

Angie was thankful that there was someone there to stop him, even more so, that it had been Jonty. 'I understand why you did it,' she said. 'But you hate confrontations; that is not you. You could have lost your job. Just promise me you won't even think about doing that again. If there is a problem, we deal with it together.'

Terry smiled. He knew she was right. 'I Promise!'

The sun continued to shine on what was a perfect day. They walked along the shoreline occasionally looking back, admiring the Isle of Arran in the distance. Soon, they were within reach of the town and the road running alongside the shore. The Amusement Arcades, shops and Ice Cream Parlours were open for business.

Coming up the path from the beach, led them straight to the

Putting and Crazy Golf Course. This was an opportunity too good to resist. Terry smiled. 'Fancy a rematch?'

Angie laughed. 'Are ready for another thrashing?'

'Thrashing? You were lucky last time?'

'Eleven holes to seven. I would say that was more than luck.'

Terry took a deep intake of breath. 'It will be a different result today. Unless of course, you're scared of the challenge.'

'Hah! Put your money where your mouth is Mister,' replied Angie. 'Whoever loses, has to buy the ice cream.'

'You fair lady – are on!'

Both Terry and Angie loved Putting and Crazy Golf. It was always a favourite childhood activity during family seaside trips. They had not played it at all during this season, so a rematch from last year was long overdue.

The course was exactly as they remembered it, 18 individual colourful mini courses pointing in different directions, complete with the various sculptures, slides and of course, windmills. Ever since his dancing days, Terry had developed a competitive streak. Having lost last time, he was determined to grab the bragging rights on this occasion. The rematch was still played in fun; however, he was taking as much time as possible with every shot. Thirty minutes later, they were both at the ice cream van across the street.

'Would Madam care for her usual Double Nougats?'

Angie could hardly speak through laughter. 'Yes please.'

'I cannot believe you beat me again,' he said.

'It might have something to do with the fact that I am a far better player than you. Have I damaged your male ego.'

'Nah, that happened when I was told to wear tights every week in the Redcoat show.' Terry handed over her ice cream then kissed her on the cheek. 'My moment will come one day,' he insisted.

Angie smiled. 'Keep practising,'

There was no let up on the summer heat, so Terry and Angie got into the shade to finish their ice cream, they sat under one of the covered seats looking out directly out to sea. Angie snuggled up close to Terry, watching the holidaymakers enjoying themselves on the sand with Heads of Ayr clearly visible in the distance.

When they finished, they were both happy to remain on their bench for the next hour, before heading to the High Street for Angie's regular shopping therapy fix. She would very rarely buy anything; just looking at the merchandise was enough.

They briefly interrupted their trip into the shops for a drink at "Rabbies," the favourite bar for all Butlins Ayr Staff. There was no sign of any familiar faces from the camp that day, so they stayed for just the one before heading back along the road to their favourite restaurant, "Helen's Place."

The restaurant was not in the most elegant part of the town, down a dark lane just off the main street, but once inside it was just as good as any of the eating places around, with the perfect relaxing setting and the more than decent selection of food. Both Terry and Angie, had their usual Chicken Vol au Vents and Chips and Macaronic Cheese. The flavour of the food was so good; it more than disguised the taste of the slightly flat soft drinks. Terry raised his glass. 'Here's to us.'

Angie chinked her glass against Terry's. 'Yes, to us, and always will be. I wonder what the next chapter is going to bring?'
'Well we can only hope it won't be back at Butlins,' said Terry. 'Don't get me wrong, I have loved everything about this season and I have got so much out of it.'
'So have I,' said Angie. 'It has boosted my confidence, we have been living and working together, which has been fantastic. We can't rely on this all of the time, but at the moment it's the only work we have.'

Terry knew that there was no guarantee when it came to working for Butlins. The first season had done a lot for him personally and this season, it had opened doors for him as a performer, being recognised for other things, for being more than just a dancer. He hoped that this would lead to other opportunities. However, they would soon be in the real world, there would be no opportunities for would be performers.

Terry was determined that this was going to be their last season, but it would be wrong to rule out both of them returning for the 1984 season. That of course may not be down to them, even if they wanted to.

It was still the best job in the world, but working at Butlins was not going to give them the security they craved. This was vital for a couple wanting to plan for their future; this was their aim since the end of last season.

Having finished their meal, they decided to embark on one last journey along the beach before taking at taxi back to the camp. Walking slowly hand in hand, they were back at the wall along the edge of the shore. It certainly felt a lot cooler than earlier in the day, mainly due to the tide having come in, the waves were crashing gently at the base of the concrete structure.

Terry stood there with his arm around Angie's waist, looking back out to sea, in the direction of Heads of Ayr. It had been a great day, but they were not in the mood to return to base just yet. 'When we get back to camp, I want a photo of us standing in front of the Isle of Arran sunset,' said Angie. 'We have never had a decent picture done of us yet.'

'I would love that,' said Terry.

Angie rested her head on Terry's shoulders as he continued to look out to sea. Working at Butlins Ayr had been an inspiration to him. He altered his gaze towards the direction of the camp hoping for a "eureka" moment; a solution other than them coming back for another season.

Aware of the long silence, Angie raised her head, looking towards Terry. 'You OK? 'A penny for your thoughts.'

'I was just thinking about the end of the season,' he said. 'We are going have to start sometime.'

'We've still got a few weeks to go,' said Angie.

'I know that. I am thinking about what happens after.'

'We enjoy the rest of the season, and then we deal with it.'

Terry knew that she was right. He remembered giving her the same kind of advice at the end of last season. This situation though, was different. 'Are you ready for the journeys between Greenock and Falkirk? 'Asked Terry.

'I know it's not ideal, 'replied Angie, 'but we managed last time and we can do it again."

'We would do a better job if we lived under the same roof. '

'We don't have enough money to get a flat,' replied Angie.

Terry was not really thinking about putting down money for flat. It would not go down too well with his folks for a start; he came from a strict Catholic upbringing. He made a point of keeping their living arrangements at the camp a secret from his parents, because he knew what their reaction would be. They never talked about it, because they did not think he would tell them much anyway. They could see how happy he was and his parents thought the world of Angie.

It was the first time that their son had had a Girlfriend and they made every effort in making her part of the family, but whenever she came to stay, they made sure that there were boundaries. It was the same whenever Terry stayed at Angie's Grans.

They had their own ideas of how couple's relationships developed. This was something new to Terry, but he was learning very quickly. He had never discussed it with his Dad much. Mainly because he was starting to have his own ideas.

As far as his parents were concerned, they were still teenagers. With the now annual spell working at Butlins, and the journey back and forward, his folks were looking at this as more of a personal adventure, as opposed to a long-term serious relationship. If they were both serious, they would be settled in one place, working in the same town.

What his parents forgot, was that there was no chance of that happening due to them spending all that time travelling back and forwards, just so they could be together. Terry therefore had to let them know how determined they were about each other.

'We have to do something different,' said Terry. 'I found it really difficult saying good bye to you at the train station at the end of last season. I do not want to do that again.'

'Even if I have to kip on the couch every night, it would be worth it; just being together every day. We would have a better chance looking for work for a start. I need to let everyone know how serious I am.' Angie faced Terry, holding on to both hands and smiled.

'And how are you going to do that.'

Terry looked deep into Angie's eyes. 'Will you marry me?'

CHAPTER TWENTY THREE

'Married?' Yes, she was madly in love with Terry and he was with her. However, she didn't think they would be discussing something like this so soon. 'Eh. Don't you think we're a bit young? We don't exactly have enough money to support ourselves.'

'I am not talking about eloping,' said Terry. Angie sighed, as wonderfully romantic as it sounded, they were living in the real world, and she had to be realistic. Terry explained that he wanted them to become engaged, but to take their time when it came to naming the day. It would send a clear message about their future.

'I know we've only been together for just over a year,' he said, 'but I know that nothing would make me prouder than to walk down the aisle with you as my wife someday. It may take a few years, but I know what I want out of life.' Terry held her hands tightly. 'My life is with you, you are my whole life.'

Angie smiled as she wrapped her arms around Terry. She was not saying much, but she was not voicing any objections either. This was encouraging. 'So are you saying that if we got engaged, your mum and Dad would let me stay at your house.'

'I won't expect them to be doing cartwheels,' said Terry, 'but I'm sure they would accept it. You would pay rent like the rest of us.'

'What if they object,' asked Angie, still trying to get used to his idea. 'I don't want to cause major fall out with your family.'

'That won't happen,' said Terry. 'We get engaged. We are not getting married yet, but it will happen when we are ready. If it means I have to get lodgings in Falkirk, then I'll do that.

I am certain that my mum would rather keep an eye on us. If we live with them, the one thing I know is that both of them will help us.'

Angie thought for a second. She certainly was not going to forget today in a hurry, it hadn't been the most romantic of proposals; however, she liked the idea of being engaged. There was a time when Terry could not say if he loved her or not. Now, he couldn't have made it any clearer.

She smiled; Terry was starting to get nervous. 'Would you keep me in the style that I am accustomed to?' said Angie.

'Certainly not,' said Terry.

Angie put her finger to her mouth. 'Mmmmm I don't know.'

Terry could sense a wind up. 'Come on! It's so right! We will have a brilliant future together.'

Angie smiled the smile that had mesmerised Terry twelve months earlier. 'Please tell me that is a yes.'

'OF COURSE IT'S A YES!' yelled Angie, she threw her arms around Terry kissing him passionately, not caring if anyone was watching. She looked lovingly at Terry. She could see tears in his eyes, but he had a massive grin on his face. 'You make me so happy,' he said. 'I love you so much.'

'I love you too! I need to ask you one thing though.'

'Oh yes? What's that then?'

'Do I get a ring?'

Terry smiled. 'But of course. How about we pay a visit to the Jewellers on Saturday.'

'One problem with that,' Angie pointed out. 'We are working at the Station that day.'

'True,' replied Terry. 'but we are allowed a lunch break, and Ratners the Jewellers is a few hundred yards from the Station. I'll let the Boss know. As long as we don't stray too far, he aint going to mind.

'You have it all planned, don't you?'

It was now early evening; Terry and Angie were keen to get back to the camp before sunset, which was not that far away, so they grabbed the first cab they could find. They wanted to mark what had become a momentous day with a "Sunset over Arran" picture at the top of the Fire Escape stairs in the Stuart Ballroom.

It took twenty minutes for the taxi to stop just outside the gates at the camp. They hotfooted back to their respective chalets to make sure that their uniforms were ready for the next working day. Once that was done, it took them a few minutes to get to the Stuart which was starting to fill up with guests getting ready for the evening's entertainment.

At the far side of the ballroom was the Portrait Stall, where guests would get charcoal pictures done by the resident artists. The stall was right next to the Fire Exit, so, thankfully was one of the Camp Photographers, who stood perched against the Fire Door, sorting out his camera, with the expectation of another busy evening. "Sunset" pictures were immensely popular with the campers. It was a perfect summer night and the sunset over Arran had never looked more striking. 'We would like to be your first customers this evening, Colin,' said Terry.

The Photographer had become friends with both Terry and Angie during the season, having already taken many pictures with them on duty with the guests. He opened the doors for them to take their place at the top of the stairs, 'Ok folks, and smile for the camera.'

Normally the pictures would end up on a display board the next day, for those who wished to purchase a copy. Terry was looking to get his order in early. 'This picture is going in a frame. Can we get a decent sized copy please?' He was tempted to tell him the reason why, though Colin knew how "loved up" he and Angie were.

Picture now sorted, they headed over to the bar and ordered a bottle of the "house special", some Shloer Apple Juice. Terry carefully poured out the contents in to two glasses. He picked up one of them. 'Here's to the future.'

Angie chinked her glass against his and smiled. 'Yes! To the future. When are you going to tell your Parents then?'

'I think we should keep things secret until we get the ring on Saturday.

'Can I tell Gwen?'

'Of course, tell Gwen, and I'll tell Nick, but will make sure that they don't say anything till Saturday.'

The following morning Terry was getting ready for the start of new working day, Angie had gone back to her own chalet, to get changed. Nick was at the mirror shaving, whilst Terry was just behind him adjusting his tie. 'I have to tell you something,' said Terry.

'Let me guess, you are going to be a Daddy?'

Terry laughed rather nervously. 'Eh No. I asked Angie to marry me last night.'

'What?' Nick certainly did not expect to hear that. It made him cut his chin shaving. He soaked some paper hankies trying desperately to stem the flow of blood. 'I take it she said yes?' he said.

Terry realised that he was maybe the cause of Nick's bloody face. He grabbed some more paper hankies and passed them over to his chalet mate. 'She certainly did.'

'That is brilliant news mate. Can I put my name down for the Best Man.' Terry immediately started to giggle.

'What's funny.'

'Nothing,' said Terry. 'You don't have to worry about that just

yet. We need to look for regular work, and get settled before naming the day. When we do, I will certainly bear you in mind.'
'Cheers Mate. I am so happy for you two. Angie is lovely.'
'Thanks Pal. I could not be happier. One thing though, you cannot say anything until Saturday. We will be getting the ring when we are on at the Station.'
'My lips are sealed. Can I tell Gwen?'
No need to, Angie is telling her now. Remember. Schtum till Saturday!'

Terry could hear Angie and Gwen coming down the stairs, as was their normal routine. Both of the men came out of the chalet, with Terry closing the door behind them. 'Morning Gwen,' said Terry.'
'Morning Terry,' replied Gwen, who had a smile on her face. Angie had obviously told her the news. She leant forward whispering in his ear. 'Congratulations.' No other members of staff were around, so she quickly gave him a peck on the cheek. Nick did the same with Angie. 'Thank you.' Terry replied.

It was now time for breakfast swanning. Terry and Angie, had an added spring in their step, and of course, no one knew why. He knew that this was going to be a fun week, but he could not wait for it to end.

Saturday finally came; it felt like the fastest week of the season for Terry and Angie. They were ready for another working day, saying goodbye to the guests and the friends they made during the week at the Ayr Train Station.

They had never been so keen to get to there, not because it was one of their favourite details, but because they could not wait until it was lunchtime. Today they would be doing more than going for their usual lunchtime bacon buttie.

The campers were slow to turn up at the station to begin with. However, it soon chimed 12pm and time for their lunch break.

Instead of heading to the café across the street, Terry and Angie went further down the road to Ratners, a popular jewellery shop in the town.

The shop assistant was startled to see a couple of Butlins Redcoats walking into her store. She immediately wondered if the management had set up a promo event and had not told her about it, but she soon realised that they were a young recently engaged couple looking for a ring.

Terry had £80 in his wallet, which were more than adequate funds for a decent ring. He wanted to give Angie the best one possible. What he did not expect was her choice; she chose one for just a quarter of the price. It led to a long debate that Terry was never going to win.

For Angie, the look was more important than the price, which did not necessarily mean the more expensive option. Whatever happens during the rest of their life, Terry was given notice that his new fiancé was very careful when it came to handling money. She was proud and happy with her choice, so was Terry, even though he was puzzled at the same time.

When they got back to the Station, the platforms had become a lot busier, with campers ready to head home. Terry had the ring in his pocket. He could have easily waited till he got back to the chalet, but he did not want to chance losing it. The passengers were unaware of what was going on as Terry pulled out the small package, lifting Angie's hand, placing the ring on her finger. 'There you go,' said Terry.
'Hold on,' replied Angie. 'If you are going to do it, I'd like it done properly.'

He knew straight off what Angie wanted him to do. Terry took a deep breath, he stepped on to the platform bench, and he addressed the waiting passengers. 'Ladies and Gentlemen, especially those of you who have been on holiday at Butlins.

Something is going to happen on this platform now that I think you may be interested in.'

The holiday crowd, who knew both Terry and Angie from the camp, watched bewildered. What was he going to announce? Was this just Redcoats larking about? Terry jumped off the bench walking towards Angie. The station staff were not too enamoured about their schedule being interrupted, but they looked on with curiosity all the same.

Terry shouted for the passengers to stand back and give him space as he pulled the ring out of his pocket again. There was a collective gasp amongst the onlookers as Terry took Angie's hand, and stepped back, then he went down on bended knee. 'Angie, you are the love of my life. I cannot think of anything more wonderful than spending the rest of my life with you. Will you marry me?'

Angie beamed: 'Nothing would make me happier. Yes!'

The onlookers burst into a round of applause as Terry got up placing the ring on Angie's finger, wrapping their arms around each other. For the next few minutes a number of the guests came up to both of them, shaking their hands, wishing them well, with one guest handing them a box of chocolates. 'Our first engagement present, thank you,' said Angie.

They were both buzzing with excitement, with Angie constantly inspecting the ring on her finger, occasionally smiling at Terry, who was bursting with pride. Just over a year ago, he never thought he would find a girlfriend, and now here he was committing himself to a young woman that had changed his life.

They returned to camp floating on cloud nine, neither of them quite believing what they had done, but both ecstatically happy. They went to their separate chalets to freshen up for the evening swanning, Terry found Nick getting changed out of his Pipers gear. 'Can we say it is official now,' he said.

'Yep! I even got down in bended knee in the middle of the train station.'

Nick sniggered, but was also impressed. 'You old romantic fool you.'

'Less of the Old,' said Terry.

It was a normal evening swanning, as the Redcoats welcomed the guests into the dining hall. Angie and Terry were still on a high from the earlier events of the day, Angie and Terry's tables were fairly close to each other, when they headed to their allocated seats, they were oblivious to their fellow Reds assembling at the other end. They then realised that the parades had not finished, when they heard Nick shouting at the top of his voice: 'EVERBODY CLAP!'

The audience started clapping, thinking that there was still one more birthday parade, but the group dispersed into two sections, with Nick leading his to Terry's table and Gwen leading hers towards Angie. 'Come on son, on yer feet!' said Nick. Both groups made sure that Terry and Angie were on their chairs.

LADIES AND GENTLEMEN CAN WE HAVE YOUR ATTENTION PLEASE. WE HAVE A SPECIAL ANNOUNCEMENT! TODAY, AT AYR STATION, OUR FRIEND, AND REDCOAT TERRY PROPOSED TO THE LOVE OF HIS LIFE – THE LOVELY REDCOAT ANGIE.' The audience let out a collective "AHHHHHHHH". Terry and Angie's face started to glow with embarrassment but beamed with pride when Gwen finished off the announcement 'AND, SHE SAID YES!'

The diners roared with delight bursting into a round of applause, followed by three resounding cheers. As Terry and Angie sat down there were a lot of shaking hands and pecks on the cheek. They eventually sat back down at their table, blowing a kiss in each other's direction.

After lunch, Terry was back in the ballroom, and Angie, was detailed for the first house at the Theatre, for the Resident Revue Show, before she would join Terry, along with the other Reds at the Stuart for the rest of the evening.

Terry had a little a bit of time on his hands, so he thought that this was as a good moment to call his folks and deliver his special news. He had plenty of coins, because he had a hunch, that this may be a long telephone call. He was feeling nervous, but he had made a commitment to himself and his new fiancé, and he was not going to let her down.

It took a while before someone finally got round to answering the phone; it was Terrys Dad, Charlie. 'Helloooo!'

'Hi Dad! How's things?'

'Terry? Aye we are doing fine son. Any problems at the Camp.'

Terry took a deep breath. 'No. Quite the opposite.'

'I am intrigued,' said Charlie.

'Angie and I are engaged.'

'Engaged?' The moment he said those words, he could hear his mum, Mary, shouting in the background.

'HE IS WHIT?'

She could be heard marching over to the receiver, jostling with Charlie for the phone, before positioning it in the best way possible so they could both hear. 'Right explain yourself,' said Mary.

'We are engaged.'

'I hope you have not got her into trouble.'

'No Mum, certainly not, I just don't want to be apart from her any more. '

'You are only 19. You can't even support yourselves.'

'We are not naming a day yet, we'll get married when we are ready. If it takes a few years, then so be it, but we will be getting married some time.'

For a few seconds, there was no response from either Charlie or Mary, before Terry's Dad came out with the main question. 'You said you don't want to be apart. You plan to move into a flat?' Terry could hear his Mother mumble in the background 'No he is not!'

'Haud On!' said Charlie.

'No, either Angie comes here and signs on, and we both look for work, or I get digs in Falkirk.'

Both Charlie and Mary realised then that Terry was determined. They would never entertain the idea of them living as a couple. This was why he never wanted to discuss their living arrangements at camp 'Like I said, I don't want to be apart from her any more,' said Terry. 'We waste too much time travelling back and forward. We work on this together, at either Falkirk or Greenock. That is the best chance of getting work.'

Mary was anything but keen on the idea of her son getting engaged, he did not have a good track record when it came to making sensible decisions, and this was in a different league. However, they realised he was serious.

He was prepared to move to Falkirk, to find work, if he did that, she would worry constantly that he was doing things right.' 'Forget Falkirk. When you finish the season and if it is all right with her Gran, then she can sleep in your room and you can kip on the couch.'

'Are you Ok with that?' asked Terry.

Both parents answered in unison: 'YES!'

'I want to keep an eye on you and make sure you two do things right.'

'Excellent,' said Terry. 'I told Angie you would say that.'

Terry could hear his Dad sniggering as it dawned on him, that they had been played beautifully like a vintage fiddle...

'You have really got it planned haven't you.'

'Of course I have, by the way,' added Terry, trying to drop a hint. 'I have never been happier.'

'Oh yes,' said Charlie. 'Congratulations to the two of you.' His Mother did not say anything. He surmised she was still in shock. 'Thanks Dad.' Terry put the phone down feeling smug. He was starting to feel in control. 'I got one congratulations, so that's a start,' he said.

Terry could not wait to let Angie know that their accommodation had been sorted, but she was busy at the Gaiety Theatre. He vaulted up the stairs, feeling more energised than he had ever been in his life. He was more than ready for another opening night at the Stuart.

An hour later, the ballroom was packed with campers, all revelling in the party atmosphere, dancing to the sounds of resident band, Caledonia. Angie appeared midway through the bands second set, having finished her duty at the theatre. The band had one more song to play before they handed back to Roddy.

'We are going to slow things down before we hand back to Redcoat Roddy,' said Bandleader Chic Wilson. 'This is something that we don't normally do, but this is a special request, it's for two of your Redcoats, Terry and Angie, who got engaged today. Redcoats don't normally dance together whilst on duty, but tonight it's a special occasion, and we will make an exception to that rule, for at least the first 30 seconds.'

Angie glanced across to Terry smiling, trying to maintain the look of innocence. 'Ladies and Gentleman, let's hear for our newly engaged couple as they take to the floor'

Terry and Angie walked cautiously toward each other. Tears were starting to appear at the corners of her eyes when the band announced the song, not just any song, but a song very special to their hearts.

'Made famous by Debbie Boone, You Light up My life,' announced Chic. Angie wrapped her arms around Terry as they slowly moved around to the sound of the music with some of the couples dancing around the edge of the floor, giving them as much space as they could in the centre.

'You had something to do with this?' asked Angie.

'He just said that he was going to play a song for us. I did not know he would do this. Did I pick right? Angie still dancing with Terry smiled. 'Excellent choice, Fiancé.'

CHAPTER TWENTY FOUR

'Ladies and Gentlemen, for the final time this season. Please show your appreciation for your 1983 Butlin Ayr Redcoats !!!!!'

It was the final act of the 1983 season at Butlins Ayr, and the Entertainment Staff were taking their final bow in front of thousands of campers in a packed Stuart Ballroom. There was always a fantastic atmosphere in there, on the final evening of the week, however, nothing, could top what was the final evening of the final week of the season.

Amongst the guests, were returning campers from earlier in the season, not forgetting those other regulars who would only come at the end of the year. They looked on these final seven days as the most memorable part of the summer.

For the Redcoats, Au Revoir nights were always special, not just because of the electric atmosphere, but it gave them a chance to say farewell to those holidaymakers who had become their friends. The holidaymakers in turn, wanted show their appreciation, not just to the Redcoats, but also to all of the staff that had made their holiday so memorable. Of course, there was also the added bonus of having a great party.

This particular night was certain to be the most poignant as well as very exciting. For some of the Redcoats it would be their last hurrah. After a long and enjoyable season, this would be their final night with colleagues, who had become more than friends, they were a family. They did not know whether they would ever meet up again. So, after seventeen fantastic weeks, everyone was determined to go out on a high.

Terry and Angie were certainly in a party mood. They were celebrating their first season together as Redcoats, but they were also celebrating the start of the next chapter in their lives, after becoming engaged a few weeks earlier.

It had been eventful final meeting at Empire Theatre earlier in the day, and Simon Barker and Hugh Chappell, had thanked everyone for contributing to a very successful first season, for what was a brand-new department. In fact, it had been a major success for all of the departments around the camp.

'We have had some major highs,' said Barker, 'and there have been times, some of you lot have seriously wound me up, but you should all be proud of yourselves. You have all worked incredibly hard, but we still have one more day to go. We keep that professionalism until the very end. You do not switch off until you return to the staff chalet lines at midnight.'

Earlier in the week, the Staff had been asked about their intentions for coming back to work the 1984 season without committing themselves. Not just for the benefit of the management but also as an indicator for the rest of the team. Sometimes this would be a deciding factor for returning Reds.

The Assistant Entertainment Managers proceeded to hand out slips of paper that had been prepared earlier in the week, which included details of who might fancy come back next year along with contact details for those who wanted to stay in touch. Both Terry and Angie were not thinking that far ahead, though they were thinking about their future.

The last two years had been so special for both of them. The place had changed them as people and it had changed their lives. During the off-season, they were trying to find stability away from camp, but they never ruled out a return if there was nothing else available. So never, say never as far as next year was concerned.

They would have no complaints if they returned to the camp in 1984 as holidaymakers, and if they did return as holidaymakers then, it would be because they were in regular work and possibly married. However, they had marked themselves both as returning next season. They could always change their mind if their personal circumstances changed.

However, in the Stuart Ballroom that evening, both were feeling emotional, as they, along with the other Redcoats had taken their final bow in front of the thousands of holidaymakers. This was a Butlins family and it was a close family, they were proud to be part of it.

At the end of the final "Au Revoir", the party continued until the early hours; a few people were reluctant to return to their chalets because the moment they finally walked down those stairs on to the main road, the season was would be officially, over.

Terry and Angie could not wait any longer. Terry whipped open his bow tie as they headed towards the exit. Before they started to go down the stairs, Terry was stopped by his good friend and former chalet mate from the first season, Bill Watson.

'Need to say our goodbyes here mate,' he said. 'I've got a very early start in the morning. It looks like my new Agent is starting to earn her money.'

'I'm intrigued,' said Terry. 'What's happening.'

'I have a meeting in London with some hotel people about doing some residential work in a place in Spain.'

'And it is not washing the dishes?' laughed Terry

'Not quite!' said Bill 'Compering and Cabaret slots.'

'Wow that's brilliant news,' said Angie. 'You make sure that you stay in touch. You've got our address.'

'Absolutely,' replied Bill. 'I certainly don't want to miss your wedding when that happens. You still got my application for the post of Best Man.'

'Terry smiled: 'It's there with all the others. Listen mate, keep in touch and I know you will knock them dead out there.' Bill hugged both Angie and Terry.

'You are two special people, you look after each other. '

They left Bill to bid a fond farewell to the rest of his colleagues and they went down the stairs to the main road. They got as far as the shops, when Terry, grabbing on to Angie's hands, took one last look around the camp, before finally looking back at the lit up Stuart building. The programme had officially finished, but there were still some party animals not ready for their beds yet.

'I do feel sad that it's finally over, said Angie, 'but we have something bigger to think about now.'

Terry wrapped his arm around Angie. 'I have so much to thank this place for. It changed me as person.' He then turned to face Angie. 'It also brought you to me.'

Angie smiled. 'You know how to say the sweetest things. I love you Terry Mc Fadden.'

'I love you too Angie.' The both looked up towards the Stuart one last time. 'I think we have seen enough. Let's go back to the chalet.'

Earlier in the day, Angie had already packed her stuff and had moved her clothes down to Terry's chalet. Nick had done the same, moving his clothes up to Gwen's. He and Gwen had also been making their own plans for after the season.

The following morning, the campers had gone and the staff were ready to start their journeys home. Terry and Angie were amongst the first at the store for it opening, to hand in their uniforms, which they did, very reluctantly. They wanted to take them home with them, but at least they had managed to hold on to their name badges.

When they returned to their chalet to pick up their cases, they saw both Gwen and Nick standing outside the front door. 'Ah good, you haven't gone yet,' he said.

'You been waiting for us,' asked Terry.

'Yep. We are ready to make a move,' said Gwen. Nick is going to stay with me and my parents for a week before we move into our new flat in Liverpool.'

'That's great news,' said Angie. 'Make sure that you send Terry your new address, I will be living with him and his parents.'

'Things are really moving for you two.'

'And you two as well,' said Terry.

'I have you to thank for that,' said Gwen, who hugged her chalet mate before wrapping her arms around Terry. 'Thank You for everything.'

Terry smiled. 'You are so good together. Look after each other.'

Nick also hugged Terry and Angie, before he reached out to grab Gwen's hand 'Shall We?' he said. 'Bye Guys. Will definitely be in touch.'

'Make sure you do,' said Angie.

As they watched their chalet mates walk into the distance, there was now an eerie silence as they stood in the chalet lines. The last time it was this quiet was at the start of the season. This was the beginning of the next episode in their lives.

The bus journey into town was a contrast to the one they made last year. Back then, there had been a lot of sadness. They had gone to "Helen's Place" for one last time, planning their next move before heading home on separate trains.

This time their destination was the same. They had taken a bold move in becoming engaged, but it reinforced their commitment to each other and today, the mood at their now favourite eating-place, was one of excitement.

'How do your family feel about you staying at Greenock,' asked Terry.

'I would say the same as yours. They could not understand why to begin with, but they are behind us 100%'

'Support from both of sets are such a help,' said Terry. Whilst waiting for their food to be served, he picked up his glass of coke. 'Here is to our next chapter.' Angie raised her glass, chinking it against his.

'I cannot wait,' she said.

When they had finished their meal, they went along the High Street, briefly stopping at the favourite pub for all Butlins staff, "Rabbies", which looked as if it was having one of its busier days. They had promised to show their faces for one final drink with their Butlins family before heading home.

They looked inside, but could not see any familiar faces, so they decided to pass on that final drink, grab their case at the station and get their train to Glasgow. They could have got off a few stops earlier to get their connection to

Greenock, but they were more interested in having a day out.

The train arrived at Glasgow Central, with the train to Greenock a few platforms along, but there was no rush. They opted to dump their cases in Left Luggage, before heading over to the City's George Square picking up some ice creams along the way. Sitting down on a bench, they just sat there looking at the passers-by.

'How do you feel about staying in Greenock,' asked Terry.

'I'm excited and a bit nervous, but definitely more excited.' said Angie. 'This is a big step for us. By the way, I never asked you, what made you decide you wanted to get engaged?'

'When you moved back in with me, that's when I realised that I don't want to be apart from you anymore.'

Angie rested her head on Terry's shoulder. 'Well that is not going to happen,' she said. 'We are a team. Nothing can separate us.'

Terry picked up Angie's hand looking at the gold ring on her finger. 'I knew that, before I put that on your finger.'

'It will never come off,' said Angie, 'but I don't need a ring to tell people how much I love you. '

Terry smiled 'I look forward to the day I put the gold band on your finger and complete the set,' he said.

Angie smiled, pulling Terry towards him kissing him tenderly. They were in the middle of Glasgow on one of the busiest days of the week, but they did not care. 'It is going to be brilliant,' said Terry. 'We will have some challenges along the way, but that is what couples do. As you told me, together we can achieve anything.'

'So, we are sitting here, as a couple, we have a decision to make,' said Angie. 'Do we sit here all day or do we go somewhere. '

'Let's go somewhere, where do you fancy going?'

'I hear they have some good art galleries in Glasgow.'

'Art Galleries?' Asked a shocked Terry.

During the next two hours, Terry was going to discover a cultured side to his new fiancé that he never knew existed. Terry did not realise that there were so many museums and galleries in the city, they walked, rode buses and checked out numerous places.

Reading, History and Art had been Angie's favourite subjects at school. She loved learning, and for the rest of the afternoon tried everything to broaden Terry's knowledge as they toured around the most cultured parts of the city. However, even when Angie tried to explain the meaning of the various paintings and exhibits, he was still none the wiser.

'You are not very cultured, are you? 'Said Angie.

'I happen to be very cultured,' he said. 'I once starred in the school production of the Desert Song.'

' What about Opera?'

' Preferred listening to me Dad's Glenn Miller records.   I liked watching Mario Lanza Films, would that do.'

It's a start, I suppose,' Angie laughed.

'You'll be suggesting going to watch some Shakespeare next.'

Angie grinned: 'What a good idea.'

'We'll be living in Greenock, and it's not exactly known for performances of the Bard!'

Angie smiled. 'I'll find somewhere. We have plenty of time. You know I like a challenge.'

'Well it'll make a change from "An Officer and a Gentleman. I'll tell you what, if I come with you to all of those things, this means you are coming with me to Greenock Morton's first game of the new season. You might even enjoy it'

Angie smirked. It was a small price to pay. 'OK. Agreed.'

It was now getting close to the early evening, and it was time for both of them to starting thinking about completing their journey to Greenock. Terry knew that his Mother would more than likely have their tea ready, and he'd never hear the end of it if they were late. He had gone to a lot of trouble in arranging for Angie to live at the house, he certainly had no intention of getting things off to a bad start.'

It would not be long before their train to Greenock left. They grabbed their cases out of the Left Luggage and marched up to the platform. Having had an enjoyable afternoon, they were starting to get excited about getting back on the train again.

Thirty minutes later, the train trundled alongside the platform at Balloch Station, located at the bottom of a steep hill, and the McFadden residence was located at the very top. Terry grabbed Angie's case as well as his own, before helping her off the train.

They walked along the platform and went through the barrier. They then paused at the bottom of the hill, looking up the steep incline.

'Well this is where the next chapter begins.' Terry smiled as he grabbed Angie's hands, 'Shall We?'

Angie beamed. 'Absolutely!'

ABOUT THE AUTHOR

Frank McGroarty, born in Greenock 1963, married with two children. Worked as a Butlins Redcoats at Ayr for three seasons during the early 1980's. Went on to become a freelance journalist for 15 years before moving to online publications, radio broadcasting and now book writing and publishing.

Studied Creative Writing as part of a Batchelor of Arts Degree from the Open University eventually graduating in 2013.

Has taken a brief break from broadcasting to concentrating on his writing with a number of projects planned for 2017, print and online as well as rediscovering his passion for performing on stage

Hobbies include still lying about his age and his ever expanding waistline.

Printed in Great Britain
by Amazon